Something

ANGELA CAMPBELL

Harper*Impulse* an imprint of
HarperCollins*Publishers Ltd*
77–85 Fulham Palace Road
Hammersmith, London W6 8JB

www.harpercollins.co.uk

A Paperback Original 2013

First published in Great Britain in ebook format by HarperImpulse 2013

Cover Images © Shutterstock.com

Angela Campbell asserts the moral right to
be identified as the author of this work

A catalogue record for this book
is available from the British Library

ISBN: 9780007559664

This novel is entirely a work of fiction.
The names, characters and incidents portrayed in it are
the work of the author's imagination. Any resemblance to
actual persons, living or dead, events or localities is
entirely coincidental.

Automatically produced by Atomik ePublisher from Easypress

For my niece, Brittney, who has always made one heck of a ghost-hunting sidekick.

And for my brother, David, who forced me to watch horror films as a child. Thank you both for sharing my love of a good ghost story. This one is for you guys.

Chapter One

She'd only been at the restaurant five minutes and already a freaking ghost had zeroed in on her.

Crap. Crap. Crap.

Alexandra King jerked her gaze away from the tall man in the corner near the bar—the one wearing a double-breasted black coat with a gray vest underneath—and drummed her fingers against the table top as she waited for her waitress to bring her a bowl of she-crab soup and Caesar salad. The white cotton shirt the man wore was too long for his arms and erupted in ruffles at his wrists. His hair curled below a low Derby hat, and he looked as real as any flesh-and-blood man in this place.

Except for the bloody gash at his throat.

She couldn't help it. She risked another glimpse in his direction. Still watching her, the dead man tipped his hat and winked at her.

Pushing out of her chair, Alexandra shoved her way through the small crowd of people gathered for a Wednesday evening outing at the Southend Brewery and Smokehouse in historic Charleston, South Carolina, and headed toward the sign marked Restrooms.

This stylish specter made about the tenth dead person she'd seen since checking into her room at the inn forty minutes ago. Thankfully none had shown more than a passing interest in her... so far.

She glanced over her shoulder to see if this ghost was going to make a pest of himself. He didn't seem to be following. Good.

Derby Hat Guy was behind the bar now, pouring himself a draft, unseen by the bartender shuffling around him. Stifling a chuckle, she ducked her head and pretended to find the floor interesting. She'd learned long ago that if she ignored dead people, nine times out of ten, they would do the same. It was the ones who didn't that gave her headaches as they chipped away at her mental barrier, made her lose sleep, and do stupid stuff like fly hundreds of miles to hunt down a person she didn't know.

A vibration against her right hip distracted her, and she dug her phone out of her pocket. Glancing at the caller ID, a smile tugged at her lips as she saw her newest—and possibly closest—friend's picture on the display. She leaned against the wall outside the ladies room and focused on the call.

"Hey, Hannah. Did you get my text?" She'd sent a quick one as soon as she'd landed to let her friend know she had arrived safely.

"Yep. You made it there okay? No problems with the flight or getting checked into the hotel?"

"The flight was surprisingly easy, and the place you chose for me to stay at is incredible. More like an apartment than a hotel." Much better than the dumps where she usually stayed anyway. It had been her fortune, meeting Hannah Dawson three months ago. Not only was the woman richer than sin but she had a generous heart that extended to her friends and anyone she assessed had a dire need.

In this case, that had included Alexandra on both counts.

"Good. I wish I'd been able to come with you. You're doing me as much of a favor as yourself." Hannah's voice lowered a notch. "Zach is still being stubborn."

Alexandra resisted the urge to roll her eyes. When wasn't Zachary Collins stubborn?

She'd come to appreciate just how pigheaded the man was when she accepted a job working for him at his private security and investigations agency a few months ago.

The steady paycheck was hella nice, and she loved using her gifts as a psychic medium to help people. Already she'd assisted a family in finding their runaway daughter and helped a desperate single mother locate the good-for-nothing ex-husband who owed her thousands in child support.

Dead people could be so full of useful information.

But she and Zach had butted heads more than once—usually over the fact he refused to use their resources to track down his younger brother and make amends for something—what, she had no idea.

None of her business. She got that. She was *fine* with that. She would've stayed fine with it, but Zach's dead mother had taken up residence in Alexandra's new apartment and refused to leave until her two sons had been reunited. Every time Alexandra lowered her guard, oh look, there was Rebecca Collins again, harping on about her sons. Zachary this. Dylan that. Nag, nag, nag.

Stupid ghost was driving her *insane*.

"Yeah, well, tenacity must run in the Collins family," Alexandra told Hannah. "I've been trying for weeks to get his mom to cross over, or at least get the heck outta my apartment. She doesn't listen either."

Hannah snorted. "I'd believe it. Once Zach gets an idea in his head, he doesn't let go."

"Still pestering you to move in with him, huh?"

"Yes." Hannah drew the word out on a long-suffering sigh. "It's not even that I don't want to. It's like I've told you before. I am crazy about the man, but we need to get to know each other better before we both dive into the deep end. Plus, I'd feel better if he patched things up with his brother first. I know it's important to him, even if he won't admit it."

"Hopefully, the lead that Spider got for us will pan out." Alexandra twirled the ends of her long blonde hair between two fingers. Two guys at the bar hadn't even noticed yet that the bar's friendly spirit had switched their drinks while they'd been distracted checking out the female bartender. Oh my. This was a mischievous ole fellow. "If Dylan Collins is in Charleston like Spider thinks, I'll find him."

The young female hacker Zach had hired to bring his security firm into the twenty-first century had become everyone on the team's "little sister." She was wicked smart and had tracked Zach's brother from Baton Rouge, Louisiana, to Charleston, South Carolina, in under ten minutes. Spider would have probably given them a phone number and address if Alexandra hadn't opened her mouth to ask what the heck that weird action figure was on Spider's desk. It looked like a demonic wild boar on steroids, wearing spikes and armor. Creepy.

Alexandra rolled her eyes at the memory. After a lecture about how awesome the Guild Wars online game was, Spider had been offended enough not to offer any more help in the matter.

Annoying little sister, more like it.

So here Alexandra was, voluntarily in one of the most haunted cities in America, surrounded by freaking dead people, with no idea where to start looking for Zach's little brother.

"Is, um, Rebecca with you?" Hannah's question about Zach's mother drew her back to their conversation.

Alexandra sighed. "Haven't seen her since I boarded the plane. She'll pop up. She always does. Hopefully she'll point me in the right direction so I can get this over and done with."

She'd kind of been counting on Zach's mother to manifest and lead her the rest of the way to the mysterious Dylan Collins. The fact it hadn't happened yet was pissing her off. She'd left herself open to communication with Rebecca, which also left her vulnerable to any ghost, spirit or whatever in search of a conduit between dimensions.

If she didn't show soon, Alexandra was flipping her mental Open sign over to Closed.

After promising to check in with Hannah with frequent updates, Alexandra ended the call and washed her hands to give herself an excuse for visiting the ladies room. She was a little hungry and a lot tired after her evening flight.

She hadn't mentioned it to Hannah, but she'd also been uneasy since touching ground in Charleston. The feeling had intensified the closer she'd gotten to her hotel. She'd never seen anything like the spiral gray beams whirling up toward the skyline from what she assumed was the city's historic district. She'd never encountered so many ghosts so quickly in such a small area either. Not even when she'd lived in Germany, where ghosts were *everywhere*. A heavy, sick weight had sunk into her stomach, manifesting in a mild headache as she'd watched the beams wave and shimmer against the setting sun. This city felt…unhealthy.

Or she could be feeling ill because she'd skipped lunch. She hoped that was the reason. Hopefully a decent meal and a good night's sleep would right things.

This place had been highly recommended by the desk clerk at the inn, or she might have opted for junk food out of a machine and called it an early night. She rubbed her eyes and blinked them open again, only to see the man in the Derby hat standing directly behind her, grinning like the Cheshire cat. He lifted a finger and pointed at her in the mirror.

"Ya can see me, can't ya?"

Crap.

A woman came out of the stall behind her, so Alexandra kept her mouth shut and made a quick escape. Maybe if she kept ignoring him —

"I don't mean ya any harm." The Derby Hat Guy followed her back to her table and took the seat opposite her just as the waitress appeared with her food. "I hear the food here is delicious. I know the brew is!" He lifted his mug and chugged back several gulps. The bloody gash at his neck shifted with every swallow. Since the mug gave off a slight orange glow, Alexandra knew it wasn't visible to anyone else. Ghost mug. "Tell me, miss." Reluctantly, she looked his way. "How can a pretty little thing like yer'self see me when no'un else can?"

Alexandra kept her mouth busy, pushing spoonful after spoonful of soup between her lips, avoiding eye contact as best she could. Sometimes she forgot she was in public and launched into a full-fledged conversation with her unseen visitors, but she had no plans of doing so now. Nuh uh. No way. The place wasn't overly crowded, but there were enough people around to notice if she suddenly started talking to The Invisible Man.

But maybe this guy didn't know he was dead. Maybe he needed her help crossing over.

Maybe —

Stop it! Don't engage him. He's not the reason you're here.

As the man rambled about the dress of the men and women around them—"Woo-wee! Ain't ever seen the likes! She's practically wearin' nothin'! Would ya look at that?"—Alexandra finished her salad, quietly amused by his observations. He was a chatty fellow, and if she had spoken, she doubted she could get a word in edgewise. Seeing he wasn't going away, she began to study him as he yakked. She'd guess he was in his late thirties, maybe early forties. Lanky. Not overly handsome, but not a dog either. Kind of reminded her of that guy who'd played the Doctor on that British show Hannah had been making her watch. Oh, what was his name? David Tennant. That was it. Except this guy wasn't the least bit British.

Where was Zachery's mom, Rebecca? She might get on quite well with this character—being that they were both highly obnoxious and all. Perhaps she could hook them up in the afterlife and give the dead woman someone else to nag for a change.

"It must be your lucky night, hon." A woman's voice drew her attention.

Alexandra blinked up at her waitress as the young woman slid a mug of beer in front of her. Did the girl seriously just call her hon?

The redhead nodded over her shoulder. "The hunk at the pool tables bought you a drink." She winked. "Enjoy."

Oh, no. Not only were the dead people around here clamoring for her attention, so was some a-hole on the prowl. She bit back a groan and lifted her gaze to give the man a polite shake of her head, a silent thanks but no thanks and –

Hello, Mr. Delicious.

He was hands-down the most criminally sexy man she'd ever laid eyes on, and for a woman who worked with some serious man candy these days that was saying a lot. He studied her from the billiards area as he chalked up one of the cues. He was the only person over there, playing a solitary game while most people congregated at the bar. A slight smile teased his mouth as she managed to lift the mug and nod. So what if she hated beer? She'd gulp the whole thing in one go if that sex god wanted to watch. He nodded back, gestured to the pool table beside him, and—

Oh, yeah. She was tempted to saunter over there and see what happened. Beyond tempted. She'd never had a one-night stand in her life, but maybe this was as good a time as any.

"Well, I'll be! He sure seems to have struck yer fancy."

Oh, no. She scrunched her brows and shook her head. She had a bad feeling about this.

The ghost wooped. "Oh, but I think he has." He glanced toward the billiards. "And I dare say he has taken quite a fancy to you, miss. Comes in here a lot that one does. Never been able to spook 'em though." Derby Hat Guy abruptly stood and started walking toward the other man, saying, "Let's give 'em a game. Have a bit of fun with the rascal." He rubbed his hands together.

"Wait! Uh," Alexandra jumped to her feet and realized a few seconds later she was practically on top of the pool table when Mr. Delicious said, amused, "Whoa now. I'm guessing you like a good game of pool?"

Among other things.

She bit her lip and tried to ignore the ghost bent over the other end of the table, reaching for two of the balls that had been scattered near a corner pocket. She'd made this poor, delicious man a target of the ghost's tomfoolery. Oh dear. She needed to fix this.

"Pool?" Her eyes widened when Derby Hat Guy picked up the white ball behind Mr. Delicious and moved it clearway across the table. There was no orange glow to it, which meant the ball had actually moved. Had anyone else seen that? This ghost was an old and smart one. Not many could move objects like that. "Yeah. Yeah, I love pool. Game on." Leaning over, she slapped the green felt and flicked her fingers a few times toward the wall, trying to convey the message to Derby Hat Guy to get lost.

Mr. Delicious held out a cue stick to her in offering, distracting her from the ghost past his shoulder. "Great. We'll start a new game. I was getting tired of losing to myself." He looked her up and down where she leaned against the table and seemed to like what he saw. His smoldering blue eyes burned with heat so intense, she felt her insides ignite. He wriggled the cue in his hand. "You know how to use this thing?" His smile was kicked up to full charge on the suggestive meter.

Oh, my, he was flirting, and that was a game best played by two. Accepting the cue from him, Alexandra arched a brow and slowly ran a finger along its length. "I can handle a stick pretty good." She pursed her lips, blew at the chalk on the end, and slowly batted her lashes when she looked at him again. "Besides, what woman doesn't love to bust some balls every now and then?"

He gave an appreciative chuckle. "Alright." He began setting up a new game and she sighed, watching his taut backside move deliciously against his faded jeans as he bent over. Whew. Levis should pay him a royalty. Who looked that good in jeans, besides Calvin Klein models? No one, except this guy. Maybe he *was* a Calvin Klein model. He definitely had the face and body for it.

And maybe she should offer to buy him a drink or something—you know, to apologize for making him a target of the resident ghost.

"Can I get you a beer?"

"Nah. I'm good." His back muscles stretched against his black t-shirt when he rested his elbows on the table, highlighting some serious muscle definition beneath.

"Something else? Whiskey?" She tilted her head at him. Me?

"No thanks." His eyes twinkled with amusement as he straightened and moved closer. "Girls take advantage of me when I drink. I can see I'll need to keep my wits around you."

"Is that so?" She cast a meaningful glance over her shoulder at the beer he'd ordered for her. "Crap. You've obviously found me out. Whatever will I do now?" She sent him a pointed look that she hoped said *I know your game. Trying to take advantage of me, eh?*

He selected a stick from the cue rack and sauntered over to her, not looking the least bit remorseful.

"I was hoping if you drank enough, I'd start looking good enough for you to come talk to me. Since you didn't even take a sip before rushing right over, I'm flattered."

She snorted, but yeah, she was as embarrassed as heck about

the way that must have looked. "Maybe I thought you were someone else."

"Who?"

She said the first name that came to mind. "Robert Pattinson." And then winced.

His eyebrows squeezed together. He looked almost offended. "Really?"

No, not at all, but what was she supposed to say—oh, there was a ghost coming to play with your balls? She shrugged.

"I won't hold that against you." He winked. "And I should probably warn you." He leaned in close, the tantalizing scent of raw masculine energy exciting her nostrils and causing her inner siren to sit up and sing. "The guy I've been playing against tonight is pretty tough. He might not go easy on you."

"You mean, the guy you were playing pool with earlier?" She glanced around, spotted only Derby Hat Guy leaning against the table, drumming his fingers impatiently, sending her a bored look. "Who is he, Casper the friendly pool player?"

He grinned. "He's the guy who sent you the beer—the one who thought to himself, 'I think the most beautiful woman in the world is in this room, and I'd like to talk to her.'"

Oh, mercy, that was both the best and the worst pickup line she'd ever heard. He had a sense of humor as well as being sexy. She liked that.

She tilted her head and feigned concern. "Have you seen a doctor?"

His eyes widened. "For what?"

"Multiple personality disorder. I think you have it." She smiled to let him know she was only teasing. And she gripped the cue tighter to keep from doing something ridiculous like ripping his shirt off. "Here's a hint, Casanova. Guys who talk about themselves in third person tend to come off as a little bit crazy."

He leaned so close his hot breath teased her face as he tried to stifle a laugh. "Good point. And I'm a jackass. I haven't even asked your name."

"Alexandra." She held out her hand. "And who will I be crushing in this game tonight?"

The warmth of his fingers against hers was stimulating. "Name's—"

The sound of wood knocking against wood startled them both, and Alexandra sprang away. Derby Hat Guy had moved to the cue rack and was purposefully knocking the sticks against one another. He stopped when Mr. Delicious turned around to inspect the noise.

"I thought we were gonna have some fun with the rascal!" complained her newest dead friend. "Come on, already. Let's play!"

Ghosts. They could be so annoying.

***

"You know, they claim this place is haunted."

Dylan Collins leaned against his pool cue and watched as his enticing opponent lined up her shot perfectly—and abruptly banged the white ball against the left side when the words left his mouth.

She swore softly and sighed. "You don't say."

He shrugged and moved to take his first shot, regretful he no longer had a good view of her cleavage as she bent over the table. She'd already sunk a number of the balls. The woman knew her way around a billiard table. "I don't believe in that stuff, personally. If that's your thing, Charleston has a ton of ghost tours."

"Hmm." Her concentration seemed off as she frowned slightly, gazing toward the wall. Maybe she was like him and thought the whole Haunted Charleston spiel was just a gimmick to attract tourists.

Change the topic, dumbass. He didn't want to scare her away or make her think he was a paranormal freak when he wasn't.

He couldn't believe his luck in luring a beauty like her over here. He circled the pool table and lined up his cue with the ball.

His favorite way to unwind from a bad day at work was to come to the Southend Brewery for a beer, a game of pool, and a game on one of the TVs above the third-floor bar, but he'd never seen a woman like this one here. Usually the women he attracted at bars were young, more than a little tipsy, and as sexually aggressive as sailors turned loose in a whorehouse.

His partner on the force liked to think of them as cop groupies, although Dylan never advertised the fact he was with the North Charleston PD before he decided to take one home. Besides, Reedus was wrong. Usually in this part of the city they were either co-eds or tourists looking for a little naughty fun before returning home to their mundane lives or boyfriends or husbands or whatever. Didn't matter a bit to them that he wore a badge. They were more interested in what he *didn't* wear.

But this one, there was something different about her.

Older than his usual pick up, definitely. He'd guess early 30s.

Lifting his gaze from the end of his cue and toward the blonde across from him, he drank in the sight of her curvy figure. The ball soared forward and clanged against two others that drifted into the corner pocket. He wouldn't stretch his credibility by saying she was the most beautiful woman he'd ever laid eyes on, but she was close. She had something else too that had caught his attention from across the room before he'd ever glimpsed her pretty face. The way she carried herself. Confident. Classy, even in jeans. Two traits he found sexy as hell, and then to come to learn she was smart *and* funny, too? Hot damn.

Normally he went for petite brunettes, but he wouldn't mind a change of taste sampling this leggy blonde for a night or two. Especially tonight, when he needed to erase thoughts of the case that had been eating him up all day.

Was she willing to help him with that?

Let's find out.

First, he had to sink the rest of these balls to impress her. He took his time finding the right angle—oh yeah, he could nail three in one shot from here—and made a show of leaning over, sliding the stick through his fingers, oh so slowly, and then snapping forward with just enough finesse to hit his target in the right spot. The white ball clanged against the orange No. 5, sending it into a corner pocket, then spiraled toward both the green No. 6 and purple No.4.

The white ball abruptly took a sharp detour to the left, missing his remaining targets completely.

What the-?

Alexandra's eyes and mouth were wide open, probably a match to his own expression. She blinked and shook her head. "That was…a little weird, huh?" Red began spreading from her neck up through her face.

He scratched at the hair on his head. "Yeah, weird."

"You sank the five though. Uh, good job. Still your turn."

"Right." He bent to find his next shot, narrowed his eyes and spotted three balls clumped together near the middle pocket. That might get him at least two scores. He slid the cue forward then jerked it back when the white ball began slowly rolling toward the left.

He straightened and grabbed the white ball, picked it up and felt its weight in his hand. Damn thing felt normal. He glanced at the woman standing on the other side of the table, her hand now covering her mouth and her eyes glistening with amusement.

13

She lowered her hand and placed it on her hip. "Are you trying to cheat?"

"What? No. Hell, no. Didn't you see that? The ball moved—" He bit back a curse and put it where it was before.

He sat his bridge hand on the table, kept his angle smooth, and struck it this time.

Almost every ball on the table rolled out of its way as it bowled forward. It banked off the corner pocket and fell in.

What the—?

He reached a hand out over the table. Had someone turned the air conditioning on full blast? Was there a vent he couldn't see?

He didn't feel anything abnormal.

Instead of the impressed cheer he'd been soliciting, he was rewarded with feminine snickering. "Smooth," Alexandra said, pushing him out of the way. "Let me show you how it's done, hot stuff."

She backed her ass up, spread her legs, set up her shot and sent the white ball sailing. She clinked one into the middle pocket, then three more she hadn't even touched flew into other pockets, one after the other.

"How the hell did you do that?"

She held up her cue and blew the tip. "Guess I'm just better at this than you."

Something weird was going on here, but hell, that was okay. She wore amusement well. It lit up her face and looked damn attractive on her. He leaned closer. "Still your turn."

She moved around him to find her next position. He waited until she had leaned down with her cue arranged to follow. He curved over her, resting his hands on the table edge on each side of her, and breathed in the intoxicating scent of strawberries. Mmm. Nice.

Her back lifted slightly, pressing against his chest. "What do you think you're doing?"

He nuzzled his mouth close to her ear. "Making sure you don't cheat. Got a problem with that?"

Judging by the way she wiggled her backside against him, he didn't think so. "You're in my way."

He eased up, but didn't move away completely. He left his right hand resting on the spot above her belt.

She pulled her elbow back, slowly, and sank two more balls. He thought she did, anyway. He wasn't really paying attention to the table anymore. His mind was distracted by the strip of bare skin his fingers had discovered between her jeans and shirt. Smooth, silky smooth. And hot, so hot to the touch.

She turned her head back to glance at his hand before lifting her gaze to his. "Well go on, then. Keep fondling me. I'm still gonna win despite your little distractions."

"Oh, really?"

"Yep."

And then she sank the eight ball.

Game over.

He liked this woman, liked that she gave him a lil bit of hell. "Where are you staying?"

Straightening, she curled both hands around her cue and considered him. "Why?"

"Cause I'd like to know where I'll be spending the night."

She laughed. "Presumptuous, aren't we?"

"Mmm-hmmm. And cocky too."

"No kidding."

He couldn't resist touching the strip of skin still visible between her belt and shirt. Her breath hitched at the contact, so he knew she wasn't as unaffected as she played. "I live just around the corner. We could be there in less than ten minutes."

She said nothing for so long, he started to think he'd overshot this one. Handing him her cue, she arched a brow. "My hotel sounds closer."

They made it there in eight, and if his steps slowed a little when he realized she was leading him to the Lodge Alley Inn, she either didn't notice or didn't care.

Too weird.

His place was on the next street over.

But he kept his mouth quiet about the irony of her stay and put it to better use, nibbling her earlobe as she struggled to open the door to her room. He liked hearing her breathing quicken and turn raspy as his hands had fun, too, sliding around and beneath the hem of her t-shirt. He trailed his fingers along the silky smooth skin of her stomach as he pressed his front against her backside. He couldn't remember the last time he'd wanted a woman this much.

Pushing inside, she didn't turn on the lights, just pulled him in after her, reaching up to devour his mouth like a woman starved for kisses. Man, she was hot.

She tore away from him. "Bed is upstairs." She toed off her shoes and hurried up the spiral staircase inside the entryway of her room. He was right behind her.

***

Dylan must have fallen asleep because the alarm clock read three o'clock when a sound awoke him from a pleasant dream hours later. Alexandra grumbled and snuggled deeper into the sheets as he maneuvered his way to the end of the bed and found his phone.

Speaking quietly, he answered, "Collins."

"Sorry to interrupt your beauty sleep, but we've got another one," his partner's voice was brisk. "Same calling card as the one last month. Pretty sure we've officially got a serial on our hands."

Dylan swore and glanced at the woman sleeping peacefully behind him. It had been nice while it lasted. Reedus gave him a few details and the address while he tugged on his pants.

Picking up the rest of his clothes, he ended the call and moved quietly to the stairs. He hesitated, glancing back toward the bed. A smile tugged at his lips as he walked over, knelt beside the mattress and just looked at her for a minute.

He leaned and kissed her lips softly, quickly, so as not to disturb her.

"See ya later, beautiful."

And he had every intention of doing so.

Chapter Two

She was alone.

Alexandra wasn't sure if she was relieved or not by that revelation when she opened her eyes, looked around the unfamiliar hotel room and stretched lazily the next morning.

Oh, not because of the guy she'd brought back to her hotel room last night. She'd expected him to be long gone—her first one-night stand. Had she really done that? A painful tug in some of her more underused muscles reassured her she had.

Her confusion was because she had fully expected Rebecca Collins to be sitting in the chair beside the bed, tapping her foot and waiting for Alexandra to wake so she could start complaining about her sons again.

But Alexandra was alone.

No one-night stand. No ghost.

It was so quiet. How freaking weird was this? How long had it been since she'd woken up to this kind of peace? Months, maybe.

She showered and dressed, glancing around often and expecting the dead woman to pop out of the wall and start making her *please-you've-got-to-help-my-son* demands. Nope, nothing. She'd heard someone say at a spiritual conference once that ghosts couldn't travel over water. Was that the case here? She shook her head. Rebecca had followed her from Atlanta to Denver and back again. But not here?

Weird.

It was next to impossible to keep her guard up while she was sleeping, so the first thing Alexandra did each morning before leaving her apartment was close herself from communication with the dead. She hesitated in doing it now. What if Rebecca finally made an appearance? She peeked out the curtains, saw that weird gray aura shooting up, and decided she'd better be safe than sorry until she figured out what the anomaly meant.

Closing her eyes, she took a deep breath. Released it. And another. She envisioned a brick wall.

Only the living can communicate with me. No spirits can pass beyond this barrier.

Over and over, she repeated the mantra until she felt…almost normal. Another deep breath, and she opened her eyes.

Alexandra's stomach rumbled, so she set out in search of food. She found a small café serving breakfast, asked to borrow the phone book, grabbed a newspaper and sat down to make a plan.

She started by checking for Dylan Collins in the phone book, hoping the good, old-fashioned resource would trump her Internet searches. She found only one, called and reached an older-sounding man with a strong Southern accent.

Nope. Not him.

She went down the list of D Collins and knew each time a woman claimed a variation of the name she wasn't getting any closer.

And it sucked that every time she marked off a name from the list, her mind happily somersaulted to an image of Mr. Delicious's handsome face.

Had he ever told her his name?

Heat warmed her face as she realized she hadn't noticed. She couldn't believe she'd slept with a total stranger when she'd needed to be focused on the reason she came here in the first place. But she had.

This would have been a lot easier to do if her mind didn't prefer to think about Mr. Delicious. Oh, yes, he'd rocked her world last night. Was she only one in a long line of women, or was casual sex as new to him as it was her?

She snorted. Who was she kidding? That man had been on the prowl before she'd walked into the room. If she hadn't taken him back to her hotel, no doubt some other lucky woman would have been charmed into doing so. Ridiculous that she felt the hot rush of jealousy blur her vision at that idea. No one that good in bed was a saint, and she had no claim on him anyway. Nor did she want a claim on him. She'd done the long distance thing once, and her marriage hadn't survived it.

Slamming the phone book shut, she sighed, feeling a little depressed by that memory.

She looked up and caught a young woman on the other side of the window staring in at her. Tiny sparks of orange electricity shot off from her body, just like they always did from dead people. Another ghost. Alexandra tensed and tore her eyes away. She'd done the proper meditation to disconnect. She knew she had.

She glanced back and the young woman was gone.

She must have been mistaken. Her shoulders relaxed, but a feeling of unease lingered in her belly.

As she spread cream cheese over her bagel, she glanced at the newspaper. In a side strip on the front page with no photo, a smaller headline immediately grabbed her attention.

Woman found murdered in cemetery.

The sudden image of a cartoon figure dressed in a black robe and holding a scythe overtook her vision. She'd always likened the experience to someone holding up huge flash cards in front of her eyes unexpectedly. Sometimes a word was written for her to see. Sometimes it was a symbol or a photograph. Alexandra braced herself for more, but her gaze saw nothing now but the newspaper article.

Her hand lowered to her abdomen, which rumbled with anxiety. This wasn't good. Her morning disconnect hadn't worked if a ghost—the young woman in the window?—was sending her this information.

She puzzled over the image of a grim reaper that had been relayed to her, but then again, she usually did until she learned more information to give it substance. She felt an immediate urge to turn the page and found herself flipping to the article's reference on page 3 of the Metro section and zeroing in on a different article buried in the middle of the page. *Homicide investigation launched after body found in alley.* Again, the grim reaper cartoon flashed before her.

Were these two murders related?

Yes. She didn't have to read the details of either story. She just knew they were. Did the police realize it?

She flipped back to the first page and skimmed the article as she chewed and then nearly choked on the piece of bread when she read, "Police are seeking information from anyone who saw anything suspicious in the area, according to lead investigator Dylan Collins, Special Investigations Division of the North Charleston Police Department."

Holy crap.

She laughed and glanced around. Looked like one of her problems was going to be easier to solve than she'd thought.

On the other hand, it was a little disconcerting to realize her mental keep-ghosts-away barrier wasn't working.

She looked around but didn't see any more people with sparkly auras. The young woman had been dressed modern. Probably a new ghost. Could be as wary of Alexandra as Alexandra was of her right now, hence the telepathy instead of face-to-face conversation.

Suited her just fine.

Alexandra used the phone book to find the number for the North Charleston Police Department then waited to be connected to Detective Collins. After holding several minutes, a gruff, older-sounding man came on the line.

"Detective Reedus," he barked.

"I was trying to reach Dylan Collins."

"What's the nature of your business?"

Uh, crap. What should she say? The truth? Yeah, she'd give it a shot.

"I'm a friend of his brother's. I'm trying to reach him. It's important."

There was a brief pause. The man grunted. "Detective Collins doesn't have a brother. If you have a crime tip, please call our special hotline." He rattled off a number. "Have a good day." Then the line went dead.

Okay, maybe not so easy after all.

Time for Plan B.

Alexandra scrolled through the contacts in her phone until she spotted a familiar police sergeant's name. He answered after the second ring.

"Sergeant Coronado, got a minute?"

She could hear the smile in his voice when he answered, "For one of my favorite ladies? Always."

She nibbled at her lower lip. "Tell me. Do you know anyone in the bureaus down in Charleston, South Carolina?"

***

"Collins, captain wants to see you in his office." A uniformed officer made the announcement on his way to the water cooler.

22

Reedus banged a crumpled paper ball off of Dylan's shoulder and grinned. "Probably another false confession or maybe the cap just wants to tell you what a great job you're doing. What's your guess?"

"Did the cemetery murder make the news yet?"

Reedus picked up the newspaper on his desk. "Yep."

Dylan groaned and rubbed his eyes. If he had a quarter for every time some whackjob came in, wanting to confess to a crime he obviously knew nothing about but had seen in the news, Dylan could've afforded one of the mansions on Rainbow Row.

"Why don't you take this one?" He glanced hopefully at the older man sitting at the desk across from him.

"Ha!" Reedus leaned back. "You're the lead on this case, not me. Besides, I got a stack of paperwork to finish on another case before lunch."

"I'll do your paperwork."

"You'd trade paperwork for that?" He made a *yeah, right* face and leaned forward.

Well, yes, he would've, but Dylan didn't argue.

Walking toward the captain's office, Dylan rubbed the back of his neck and rolled his head around his shoulders. He was so tense, he was starting to feel stiff and sore. A far cry from how he'd felt last night: relaxed, sated, and in seventh heaven wrapped around the blonde from the bar.

He couldn't remember the last time he'd had so much fun with a woman. Both in and out of bed.

Maybe when he ended his shift, he'd track her down and enjoy another night of mindless sex. Would she be up for that?

Maybe. It wasn't as if he didn't know where to find her to ask.

Alexandra. He loved that name. Loved that she didn't shorten it. She'd been on his mind on and off all morning. How long was she staying in town? For all he knew, she'd already checked out, and that would suck. He itched to lay eyes on a living, breathing woman after spending the morning with the lifeless one at the cemetery. He wanted to hold someone, feel her warmth soak into his skin like medicine, and remind him not everything in this world was bad.

He knocked on the captain's door and entered.

And then froze.

"Collins, get in here," the captain ordered after a minute, his attention half focused on the computer screen in front of him. Dylan stepped inside and closed the door behind him, his eyes not leaving the woman seated in the chair in front of his boss.

Her eyes wide, Alexandra looked about two shades paler than he remembered as she gawked back at him.

"Detective Collins, this is Alexandra King."

Dylan nodded but couldn't manage to push out any words. What was she doing here?

The captain looked at him, leaned back in his seat and tented his fingers. "Miss King is a private investigator from Atlanta. She also happens to be a psychic medium, and she's offered her services to us on this case free of charge."

Private investigator? Psychic medium?

Hell.

The captain held up his hand in a hear-me-out gesture and nodded toward his phone. "Miss King comes highly recommended from some of my friends in the Colorado police bureau. I'd like for you to include her on this case."

"What? Captain, we never—"

"You talking back to me, son?" Captain Lloyd Devereux pushed his chubby body out of the seat. His finger tapped the top of his desk for emphasis as he spoke. "The victim was the niece of a county councilman. How long do you think it's going to be before there's pressure to turn this over to SLED or call in the feds?"

Probably a day at most before someone begged the South Carolina Law Enforcement Division to send a man in to help.

Pushing a hand through his hair, Dylan said nothing, just met the older man's eyes. As the youngest detective in this department, he'd learned not to press his luck. He suspected the captain hadn't liked him since the day Dylan had transferred in from Baton Rouge last year. No idea why. Dylan's cases were always handled professionally, and his conviction rate was higher than anyone else's in the division. He was good at his job. He took pride in that.

"Sir, I mean nothing but respect here, but I don't understand. I've never worked with a psychic before on a case." He glanced at Alexandra then back to his boss. "I'm a little curious why we're even considering this. It's not like this is a cold case we're working."

Devereux relaxed his stance. "I don't want this to become a high profile case, and if that means taking advantage of Miss King's help, so be it. Hear her out. If she can't help, fine. Let me know. But until then, she's consulting. I'm already drawing up the paperwork." He reached for something on his desk. "We don't do it often, but we've listened to what some so-called psychics have had to say before. Here. This is what convinced me to give Miss King a shot."

The captain tossed a yellow steno pad across the desk in front of Dylan. The older man said nothing, just waited for Dylan to glance at what was drawn on the paper. When he did, Dylan swore.

Scribbled on the page was a child-like drawing of a hooded figure holding a scythe. A grim reaper.

"Miss King said she had a vision of that when she read the article in the paper this morning. She thought it was relevant. I haven't confirmed or denied to her that it is."

Dylan took a deep breath and glanced at the woman still staring at him as if Bigfoot had walked into the room in his place.

He picked up the steno pad and gestured with it, focusing on his superior. "Did this get leaked to the press?"

"No." Captain Devereux sighed. "I don't want it to, either. Once she signs the non-disclosure agreement, show her what you need to from the files. Take her to the crime scene and see if she can give you anything. I want these cases solved before any reporters piece together the facts. Understand me?"

"Yes, sir."

Their desk clerk Kathy knocked on the door and said, "I've got that contract ready, sir."

"Miss King, if you go with Kathy, she'll explain everything to you." To Kathy, he said, "Let Detective Collins know as soon as everything is filed. He'll be waiting at his desk."

Dylan glanced at Alexandra as she stood to follow the other woman and wondered who she thought she was fooling. Had he talked in his sleep last night, said something about these cases to tip her off? She still looked shell-shocked. He'd never told her his name. Maybe she hadn't known he was the detective in charge of this case, but maybe she had. Maybe she was a great actress, pretending to be shocked to see him.

His libido wasn't driving anymore. His cop instincts had taken the wheel.

She could be involved. An accomplice. They could be toying with the police.

Maybe she'd come to Charleston to scam them, or had she seen a chance and jumped at it when she read the paper this morning? He couldn't remember seeing her at the bar before last night. He'd have to make inquiries at the inn to find out when she'd checked in. Find out why she was in town. She could have been watching him for days.

The captain instructed Dylan to close the door behind her.

"I know you don't like doing this, but we've got three homicides connected by this." Devereux gestured to the drawing on

26

the notepad. "And we don't have a single lead yet. It's only a matter of time before the press calls us out and starts proclaiming we've got a serial killer in the city. I don't need that kind of grief. Understand me?"

Dylan crossed his arms and nodded over his shoulder. "How do you think she knows about the reaper? You really believe she's psychic?"

"I have no idea, but I'm desperate enough to give her a chance to prove herself. Do me a favor, Collins, and do the same." The captain reached into his desk drawer and pulled out a bottle of pills. "What is Dempsey saying? He confirmed anything yet?"

Dylan shook his head and thought back to his conversation with the coroner. "He said he'd try to have a report to me after lunch, but it depends on when the autopsy is done. Don't worry. I've called, and they know it's a priority."

"Head over there and make sure they hurry. Take King with you."

Dylan clenched his jaw to keep from arguing. "Anything else?"

"Just keep me informed." The captain gestured toward the door, giving him permission to leave, but adding one last comment. "My friend in Denver isn't an easy guy to impress, and he was impressed by her. She might surprise us."

He didn't tell the captain she already had.

Dylan went back to his desk and did a search on Alexandra King. She came up empty on a criminal records background check. Her driver's license had recently changed from Colorado to Georgia. No past bankruptcies. Divorced. Interestingly, she had filed for an order of protection against a man named Kevin Alred a few months before she'd moved from Denver to Atlanta, but the details in the system were slim.

The internet gave him hits on several articles from Colorado, citing her involvement in cold cases, and a few more hits on spiritual conventions at which she'd appeared as a guest.

He added private detective to her name in the search field, but no new results came up. Had she lied about being a private investigator? If so, it would be easy enough to determine. PIs were required to be licensed in most states.

He'd just picked up his phone to call and ask Kathy to peek and tell him what agency Alexandra claimed to work for when Kathy's voice startled him from behind.

"Paperwork is filed. She's all yours, Collins."

***

So he'd been checking her out.

Alexandra wasn't surprised. She'd expected it. Glancing at the computer screen in front of him, she recognized her name in the search field and tried to take note of the results shown before Dylan turned around in his seat.

A sick, worried feeling gripped her stomach and made her feel momentarily nauseous. Had Spider updated the firm's website to include her name and bio yet? She hoped not. At least, not yet.

She wanted to talk to Dylan before he made the connection between her and his brother, feel him out and see how receptive he was to reconciliation first. If there was as much bad blood between the two men as Zach seemed to think, she sensed that type of connection would not be to her advantage right now.

Of all the men to fall into bed with her first night in town, of course he would turn out to be a cop *and* Zach's brother.

Of course he would.

Putting his phone back in its cradle, Dylan turned and sighed, half smiling up at her and bringing to mind all sorts of naughty memories.

Whoa, girl. Keep your mind on the matter at hand, and not on his, er, weapon.

28

She crossed her arms and arched a brow at him. "So it's Detective Collins, is it?"

He stood. "Pleased to meet you, Ms. King."

"Funny. You remind me of this guy I know, only I don't think he ever mentioned his name."

He glanced around, seemed satisfied no one was paying them attention, and lowered his voice. "Poor communication seems to be a real problem here. He doesn't remember you mentioning you were a psychic either."

She tilted her head and considered him. "Oh, dear. I thought you only referred to yourself in third person to pick up women. This is a real problem for you, isn't it?"

He did not look amused as he reached for his jacket and brushed past her. "The only real problem I see here is that I don't have time for this crap."

She hurried to keep up with him as he pushed out the door and headed for an unmarked car that had seen better days. He turned his head once he reached the vehicle, looked at her, and sighed as he opened the driver's side door. "Get in. We're going to check on the coroner's report."

She had to brush aside a fast-food wrapper and bag, but she slid into the seat beside him without commenting on his sudden lack of manners.

"Your car?"

"Detectives aren't allowed to use personal vehicles on duty." His gaze skimmed over her doubtfully. "Seems an experienced police consultant would know that."

She couldn't help it. She had to roll her eyes. Oh, the fun she could have with this man, winding him up. He hadn't been nearly so uptight last night.

"I'm not an idiot, detective. I was simply wondering if this was your mess or someone else's." She picked up a discarded receipt

29

on the seat beside her. "I have to wonder about any man who eats a simple ham omelet sandwich when the enormous omelet sandwich on their menu is so much tastier." She handed him the receipt, which he promptly crumpled and tossed over his shoulder into the back seat before starting the car. "Oooh. Messy. Another strike against you. Didn't your mother teach you better than that?"

Speaking of…where the heck was his mother? Rebecca still hadn't made an appearance, even though every effort Alexandra had made to close herself off had been futile. She'd seen a few ghosts wandering around, but none had tried to make contact with her. Only that pesky guy from the bar last night, and the young woman from the café this morning.

As she buckled up, she took stock of Dylan's features and began to notice a slight resemblance to Zach. Both men had thick, dark hair, blue eyes and a strong jawline, but Dylan's face was longer than his brother's. Oh yeah, she could see it now, in the daylight, and felt like slapping her forehead and murmuring "D'oh!"

She'd slept with her boss's little brother.

Oh, Alexandra, how do you get yourself into these things?

He directed the car into traffic and caught her looking at him. "I'm gonna ask you some things, and I expect the truth."

"Who wouldn't?"

His chest moved beneath a deep breath. "Why are you in Charleston?"

Ah, heck. Of course that would be the first thing he asked.

"I'm looking for someone." There. That was the truth.

"Who?"

Well, crap. "A friend's brother. I've been led to believe he's in trouble." *Please don't ask for a name.*

"What kind of trouble?"

"I have no idea. That's partly why I'm here. To figure it out." She flexed her hand in a circle motion. "My information so far has come from … my special abilities."

He sent her a narrow-eyed look before focusing on the road again. "Mind telling me what your abilities are exactly?"

She shrugged. "I'm a psychic medium. Any dreams, visions, or voices I hear are from the spirits feeding me information."

"And there are ghosts everywhere, all of the time?" He scoffed. "So all ghosts are crime-fighting ghosts? Is that what you're saying?"

"Most have the same personalities they had when they were alive. There are plenty of ghosts who keep to themselves, just as there are plenty who like to help if they see an opportunity." She pursed her lips as she considered his words. "Although I have met some who consider themselves vigilantes of a sort. I met this one guy last year who died on Halloween. I swear, he loved that he'd died dressed as Batman. He used to—"

"Spare me the ghost stories," Dylan growled. "When did you get here?"

"Last night." She felt her face warm. "I checked into my hotel, went to the bar to grab something to eat, and you know the rest."

He grimaced and glanced toward his window, hiding his expression from her. "So you're ditching your search for your friend's brother to help us with this case, for free?" He shook his head. "Sorry, honey. Something doesn't smell right here."

"Probably that left-over omelet sandwich. I'd toss that bag soon if I were you."

His lips twitched. "I wasn't talking about the omelet and you know it."

Her muscles bunched in that way they always did when she met a skeptic a-hole hell-bent on dismissing her, and nothing she said or did could persuade him to the opposite.

Where the heck was Rebecca? Alexandra would have given anything in that moment for his mother to share some information to really freak him out.

"I don't expect you to understand. I have a question for you now."

He nodded. "Alright."

"What does that grim reaper drawing have to do with the woman who was murdered in the cemetery?"

His jaw clenched, but he said nothing.

A series of images flashing in her mind momentarily disoriented her. The grim reaper cartoon she'd already seen this morning. An image of water. A woman's hand falling into water. Water flowing onto sand.

She blinked when the road came into focus again in front of her. She blew out her breath and glanced toward the back seat. She didn't see the dead young woman sitting back there, but Alexandra suspected the woman was hitching a ride and feeding her information telepathically.

This young woman must be the victim. That's why she was drawn to me, but she's new, still confused, probably scared. Trying to see if she can trust me before she reveals herself in full.

Alexandra returned her attention to the man beside her. "She wasn't killed in the cemetery, was she? Her body was just placed there after."

He shifted in his seat. "What?"

"She was killed near water."

Dylan shook his head and then laughed. "This is Charleston. Water is all around us."

A-hole.

Alexandra felt a little nauseous—that sometimes happened after such visions—so she placed a hand on her stomach and willed it away. "I can't begin to explain to you how this works, but when it happens, like it happened this morning when I saw the newspaper, it doesn't matter what else I have on my plate. I feel such a strong sense of urgency about this case right now. I had to offer my help."

Because Alexandra knew, deep in her soul, that whoever killed the woman found in the cemetery would kill again.

Soon.

Chapter Three

The sterile, gray-walled hallway was empty except for a handful of people dressed in scrubs, some carrying books or backpacks, as Dylan led Alexandra through a door marked MEDICAL AND FORENSIC AUTOPSY SECTION. She'd remained quiet as he'd pulled into the Medical University of South Carolina's parking lot, but her curiosity finally got the better of her.

"Is this a school or a hospital?" Alexandra asked.

"Both. It's a teaching hospital."

Her throat tightened. "Is this where the coroner's office is?"

"No."

An anxious feeling nestled in her chest and refused to leave. "But this is where he performs autopsies?"

Dylan didn't answer, which told her all she needed to know.

The bastard was bringing her to see the girl's dead body. Some warning would have been nice. She slowed her steps to a stop, and with a heaving sigh, he finally turned and acknowledged her.

"The staff here handles them and sends their report to our coroner. I don't have time to wait for it." He motioned her toward another door. "After you."

Great. He actually was taking her to the autopsy room. Goosebumps lifted the hairs on her arms at that realization. Alexandra had assisted other police, sure, but none had ever taken her to a morgue before. She wasn't sure she could handle it, quite frankly.

Dead people, no problem. Dead bodies, hell no.

Her feet wouldn't move, and she reached out a hand to grab the wall beside her. "I know what you're doing."

"Excuse me?"

"You're being mean and cruel, and trying to scare me away."

His eyebrows shot up, even as his shoulders relaxed. "What? You mean you've never seen a dead body before?" A smirk played at the edges of his mouth. "In your line of work? Come on. I thought psychics got their information from things like this. You know, touching stuff."

Touching a dead person in the autopsy room? Was he out of his ever-lovin' mind?

Oh, she'd seen plenty of dead people in ghost form, and a few times at funerals. She didn't particularly care to ever see one up close and personal after a medical examiner had cut it open.

The scent of some harsh cleaning chemical nearby assaulted her nostrils and sent her stomach on a gymnastics routine.

"Since what I do is new to you, I'll cut you some slack. I don't need to see a body in order to—" Ugh, she still felt nauseous from earlier. This wasn't helping. She waved a hand. "—to be able to communicate with the person. Spirits, at least young spirits, tend to linger near the person, place or object they valued most in life. Eight times out of ten, it wasn't their body."

Dylan's mouth pulled into a tight line as his eyes seemed to trace her features. Was she turning green? Man, she felt like she might be. "Fine. There's a chair in the office around the corner. Wait there. I'll try to make this quick."

Nodding, she hurried to find that chair before her mind and body conspired to faceplant her right there in the hallway. She found one in a small, empty room and dove for it. Her face grew

35

hot as her vision blurred and the room spun around her.

Oh, man. Not good.

Forcing deep breaths in and out of her lungs, she squeezed her eyes shut and lowered her head between her knees. Breathe. Breathe. Okay. Everything's okay now. She repeated the mantra over and over until the kaleidoscope of color behind her eyelids stopped. She slowly opened her eyes and sat up. This had happened before, most memorably when she'd been visiting a cousin after foot surgery, glanced down at the freshly stitched wound on the swollen limb propped on a pillow, and abruptly lost consciousness.

Given the assortment of strange and unnatural injuries she'd seen among the dead over the years, one might expect her to be blasé about the real ones, too, but nope, she was a first-class wimp when it came to blood and gore. Her mind had always been able to disconnect when a ghost manifested a slit throat or bloody gash, much the way many people did when watching horror films, but put her near a hypodermic needle or flesh wound, and she was horizontal in seconds.

She reached for the lightswitch on the wall above her shoulder and flicked it on. She yelped when she spotted the elderly woman sitting in the chair behind the desk across from her.

"Geez!" She held a hand to cover her racing heart. "I'm sorry. I didn't see you before."

The woman said nothing.

With cold, void eyes, the grandmotherly type just sat there, staring at Alexandra with absolutely no emotion on her weathered face.

Tha-thump. Tha-thump. Tha-thump.

The sound of blood rushing through Alexandra's ears intensified.

Oh no. Please, no.

Swallowing hard, Alexandra grabbed the arms of her chair. She'd met a lot of ghosts in her time and could easily distinguish between the living and the dead. Ghosts emitted sparkly auras, but living people had no auras at all that Alexandra could see.

Neither did this old lady. Alexandra's heart raced and her stomach did continuous somersaults beneath the ominous, intense stare aimed in her direction. Those eyes were…unnatural.

Ghost?

No, she didn't think so.

"What are you?" she whispered.

The old woman tilted her head and examined Alexandra even more closely. In a deep, gravelly voice, the woman countered with "What are *you*?"

Alexandra fingered the gold cross at her throat as she slowly rose from the chair, her gaze unwilling to leave the old woman. She said the silent prayer her grandmother had once taught her—By the power of Saint Michael and all the angels and saints, please keep me safe from harm—as she felt for the doorway behind her.

Hurrying out of the room, she glanced down both directions of the hallway, searching for the entrance she and Dylan had come through. Screw this. She'd wait outside by the car.

She spotted the familiar door and hurried toward it, but her feet came to another abrupt halt as figures down the hall turned toward her.

Nervous laughter bubbled through her chest when she saw not one, not two, but three more dead people standing in front of the door marked EXIT. They were all staring back at her.

Crap. Crap. Crap.

This wasn't right. Dead people shouldn't be hanging around the hospital-slash-morgue. They should be following their loved ones around or something. Not this.

They all advanced at once, chattering over one another so that Alexandra couldn't make out the details of what any one was saying.

"Help me! Please help me!" One man began begging as he reached for Alexandra's arm. His grasp was strong and determined. "My wife? Do you know where she is?"

"Where am I?" A middle-aged woman asked, pushing that man aside to clasp Alexandra's elbow. "My children. Do you know where they are?"

"Outta the way!" A stern-looking old man in a hospital gown knocked them both aside and pressed Alexandra closer to the wall.

Alexandra mentally exclaimed for everyone to give her some space. At least, she hoped she didn't yell the words aloud.

The three figures all fell silent and backed away, and that's when she spotted the fourth figure, standing behind them all.

A gargled, sickening sound was coming from the naked man. His face was mangled and bloody. No features were distinguishable.

He reached out a hand toward Alexandra, and she screamed.

***

"Not that I'm complaining or anything, but you guys almost never come by here when we're doing this. What gives?" Dr. Jeffrey Watkins removed the bloody gloves he wore and then washed his hands in the sink and flicked water off his fingers.

As one of five professors and medical examiners on the pathology staff at the university, Watkins was the only one Dylan had met, and he sent up a silent prayer of thanks for his one piece of good luck today. It would have sucked if he'd had to explain himself to someone new.

Dylan veered around the medical instruments that always gave him the heebie jeebies and tried not to look at the corpses barely covered on the examining tables a few feet away. The pretty, young autopsy technician Dylan didn't know gave him a brief smile and left the room.

"My captain wants this case solved, and soon." He gestured toward the body he was here to investigate. Candice Christopher. Twenty-two, a recent honors college graduate, and too damn young to be lying on that table. "I thought I'd come see if I could get a jump on that report."

He didn't mention that he'd hoped to shake the supposed psychic he'd been saddled with too. Guilt tugged at his conscience. Bringing Alexandra here had been a stupid thing to do, but the sooner he got rid of her and put his focus back on solving this crime, the better.

He'd have liked to have gotten to know her a little better, spend some more time in bed maybe, but that plan had been shot to hell and back.

Besides, the idea of someone pretending to be psychic sent his blood pressure up a few millimeters. Psychics made him think too much about his older brother, Zach, who was as dead to him as the bodies in this room.

A clang of metal in the sink snapped his attention back to the medical examiner.

"You're in luck. Charlie told me this one was a rush job, so we did this one first," Watkins said, mentioning the coroner both he and the police department dealt with regularly. "I haven't finalized our report yet."

"Did you find anything I should know?"

Watkins nodded and moved toward the body, slid the sheet lower and pointed out a small swollen spot on the woman's arm. "Same as the others. Our guy used a needle to inject about 10 milliliters of chloroform. She was dead of cardiac arrest within minutes. The rest was done to her afterward."

"So it's the same suspect?"

Watkins nodded and tugged the sheet back up. "This one was a little different. I found sand under the fingernails on her right hand and salt water in her lungs, but that's not what killed her."

"Water?" Dylan blinked in surprise, remembering Alexandra's words from earlier. "So she wasn't killed in the cemetery?"

"Hard to say for sure, but I doubt it. She'd been dead about eight hours before she was found."

What was he supposed to make of that? No way had she been in that cemetery eight hours before someone found her body. Some of the ghost tours trampled through that graveyard up until midnight, and her body had been found around two this morning by a homeless guy looking for a place to sleep.

That was a short window of time for someone to have carried a dead body off the street, positioned it grotesquely and gotten away without being seen. Someone had to have noticed something. Dylan made a mental note to check with the directors of the city's night tours to find out which one had last been by there and when.

The sound of a scream diverted his attention, and he turned just in time to see Alexandra burst through the double doors to the autopsy room. Her face was pale and her eyes were wide and crazed as she stumbled toward him. His hands reached out to steady her as she fell against him, her fingers clasping his arms with an iron grip. Her hair whipped around her shoulders as she glanced frantically behind her.

What the? Was she being chased?

"Dylan!" she cried, sagging against him. "Oh, thank heaven!"

"What happened?"

She squeezed his middle, but he was too preoccupied with figuring out what the hell was going on to respond. His protective instincts kicked into gear and he tried pushing her away and behind him, but she was stuck to him like a leech.

Watkins hurried to the doors, opened them and glanced both ways down the hallway. The other man's shoulders relaxed as he turned around, his expression just as puzzled as Dylan's probably was.

"I don't see anyone," Watkins said.

The tension began to seep from Dylan's muscles. "Sorry. She's with me."

Pushing herself away, Alexandra closed her eyes and shook her head, gesturing wildly. She danced around in the same spot, wiggling her fingers in that way little girls did when they were grossed out or had to pee. "No. No, you can't see them. One guy... his face is all..." she shuddered as she waved a hand in front of her face. "Mangled. He's dead. They're all dead. They all want..." She opened her eyes and looked at him. She'd stopped trembling. "Dylan, can we *please* leave?"

Her nose scrunched. The odor in the room was hard for most to stomach. Her pallor turned an unnatural gray. She looked like she was about to toss some cookies.

"Mangled?" Watkins repeated. He thumbed over his shoulder and started walking toward a second examining table, where a body was covered with a light blue sheet. "Are you here for this guy too?"

Watkins ripped back the sheet, and Dylan felt his stomach lurch. A man—or at least, he assumed it was a man by the width of those broad shoulders—looked like he'd been in one hell of a fight, eyes swollen and bloody, nose either missing or sunk in, and a deep gash in—

Dylan had to look away.

"This guy was in a boating accident. Not a homicide." Watkins threw the sheet back over the poor schmuck's face, but it was too late.

Alexandra made a squeaking sound deep in her throat and sagged against him. Her eyes rolled back in her head and her body went suddenly limp.

He caught her seconds before she would have hit the ground.

***

"Alexandra? Alexandra, honey, are you okay?"

The echo of a woman's voice and a warm, gentle touch on her cheek teased at the edges of Alexandra's consciousness like an annoying alarm radio set on low. She stretched out to hit the snooze button, wanting nothing more than to snuggle deeper into the darkness, but her fingers touched nothing but air.

"Alexandra, it's me. I'm here."

She knew that voice. Blinking her eyes open, she saw Rebecca Collins leaning over her. She sucked in a deep breath and reached out to hug Dylan's mother. The older woman engulfed her in return, rubbing her back and murmuring, "There. You're all right. You just had a bit of a scare."

The fog cleared and Alexandra remembered. The spirits harassing her for help, demanding attention, and Mr. Hamburger Face freaking her the heck out by physically shoving her against the wall when she asked him to leave her alone. He hadn't realized he was dead, and had gotten violent when she'd tried to coax that truth into him. And then the old woman had appeared behind them all, exuding malice and negativity as thick as cigarette smoke. It was almost as if the woman was controlling the dead people, commanding them to overwhelm Alexandra. Well, it had worked! Alexandra had lost it.

She'd never encountered anything like that old woman before.

She'd never encountered a lot of the things she'd experienced in that hospital. Only old, experienced ghosts could move or touch things with force. Hamburger Face hadn't even been dead twenty-four hours, but he'd shoved her against a wall.

How?

Pulling back now, she looked around. The cold, sterile medical room was gone. Dylan was gone. The familiar sight of Alexandra's bedroom surrounded them.

Her muscles sank with relief.

"I'm dreaming." She lifted a hand to touch her forehead. "This isn't real. That explains why everything's been so screwy."

She could have only been dreaming that she'd traveled to Charleston and found Dylan. Had she found him? She was so disoriented. She had no idea. She could have been having a serious nightmare—minus the erotic bits at the beginning with Mr. Delicious. Those parts of the dream, if she'd been dreaming, she hadn't minded at all.

"Honey, I need you to listen to me." Rebecca's hands felt solid as they cupped Alexandra's face, confusing her even more. Rebecca hadn't been dead long enough to master the skill of touch. "We don't have much time."

"Where have you been? I think I found your son." Yes, she knew she had. It was getting easier to recognize this delusion for what it was. The giant stuffed red monkey sitting on her nightstand was a dead giveaway. She didn't own any such novelty, as cute as it was. And her walls weren't blue either.

If this was a dream, then…

Alexandra grasped Rebecca's arm, something she'd only be able to do in a dream state. "Woman, where the heck have you been? I've been freaking worried about you!"

"I know, honey. I'm sorry." Rebecca's face tightened. "I need you to do something for me. Take Dylan and leave this place. Alexandra, you're in danger. You're both in danger."

"What do you mean?"

"I'm sorry. I'm so sorry. I didn't mean to put you in harm's way. I didn't realize he knew. I didn't know he would recognize you."

"Who knew? Knew what? What are you—?"

A gasp ripped from her lungs as her eyes flew open again, blurring into focus on Dylan's chiseled features so close to her

43

own. A man stood over his shoulder, peering down at her with a mixture of concern and curiosity. The coroner, or whoever he was.

"Alexandra? Are you all right?" Dylan's softly spoken question calmed the panic clawing at her chest at the realization of where she was. Her fingers touched cold metal. Oh. My. Word. Was she on a dissecting table? She tried to push up, but he stilled her.

"Easy." He pushed her back. "Trust me when I say you'd rather be lying on this table than the floor."

Her head spun. "Dylan?" She blinked away the haze and struggled again to sit up.

The smell of ammonia was strong, heightening her senses, bringing her closer to awareness. Dylan shifted one arm away from her and passed a pungent-smelling cloth to the man hovering around them. Sweet heavens. She'd passed out. Oh, look, a real mangled face, and wham, she'd been down faster than Marie Osmond that time on Dancing with the Stars.

How embarrassing.

"I'm sorry." She swallowed and moved to lower her legs to the floor, but Dylan kept her from standing.

"Give yourself a minute." The other man said. "Are you dizzy or anything?"

She shook her head and let her hand fall to Dylan's chest while she struggled to get a grip. *Um, I don't think I should be gripping him though.* The warmth of his solid abs reminded her of the sculpted muscles hidden beneath his shirt, so she moved her hand to his bicep instead and...oh my.

He really was in good shape. She didn't think she'd ever dated or known a man as cut as him.

"You work out a lot, don't you?" Oh, geez. Had she really just said that out loud? She bit back a groan.

His brows scrunched in confusion, but then a slow smile tugged at the corners of his mouth. "I try to keep in shape." He carefully guided her into a standing position. "Mind explaining what the hell that was all about?"

Sighing, she sagged against him, grateful for his warmth and support, no matter how temporary it might be. "Place is crawling with ghosts. They overwhelmed me."

His body tensed, and a chill replaced his body heat as he moved away from her. "I think it's time we headed back to the office." His hand on the small of her back pushed her forward a little. "Thanks, Watkins. Sorry for the dramatics. It won't happen again."

"Sure. No problem." The other guy was staring at her as if she'd just flown over the cuckoo's nest and landed in his cereal.

She couldn't blame him. Nice way to make a first impression, King. You ditz. She really needed to work on her fainting-at-the-sight-of-blood tendencies if she was going to be a badass private investigator.

Dylan practically dragged her down the hallway, his feet marching to an increasingly angry rhythm as he headed for the exit. His grip on her arm was punishing in its pressure. It helped refocus her on the physical. "What's your problem?" she demanded, tugging her arm free of his hold. "I'm the one who just passed out."

He whirled and cornered her against the wall. "You want to know what my problem is? Right now it's you. You might think this is some kind of game, but this is my job. A young woman lost her life last night, and while I should be out tracking down the person who did it, I'm stuck babysitting you. Do us both a favor, and give up the charade, all right?"

He'd just put Alexandra through a personal hell, and he was accusing *her* of playing games? She punched a finger at his chest. "Don't you dare get an attitude with me after the stunt you just pulled. You think this is a game to me?" She gestured toward the room they'd just departed. "She's not the first victim, and she won't be the last. I'm here to help you, you—you—" Her mind searched for the worst insult she could conjure. Gah, he was so frustrating! "You medieval dipstick!"

Shoving past him with a frustrated groan, she pushed the exit door open with such force that it whacked the outside wall hard and loud, causing a poor young woman on the other side to jump nervously and squeal in alarm.

"Sorry," Alexandra murmured as she walked past the girl.

She was debating whether or not to make a detour around Dylan's car and find a bus or cab when he caught up to her.

"Wait a second." He grabbed her arm again—she was getting tired of him doing that—and frowned down at her. "What do you mean, she's not his first victim?"

She scoffed. "Exactly what I said."

"How do you know?"

"I just know." She crossed her arms. "There was a man recently found dead in an alley. Same killer." She bit her lower lip as she remembered the cartoon she saw anytime she thought of the two deaths. "I keep seeing the grim reaper. It's like it's the killer's calling card or something."

Dylan said nothing, just stared at her for several uncomfortable seconds.

He finally relented. "Get in the car."

"Are you going to keep being an ass?"

"Probably. Would you just get in the car already? I want to show you something."

"What?"

"Something that will help me trust you or prove you're just taking advantage of the situation."

Ah, he wanted to test her. That she could handle. She was used to skeptics. She usually reached out to the nearest spirit, asked them to peek over the skeptic's shoulder, so to speak, and tell her whatever the answer was to his secret test. Piece of cake.

It was the uncertainty she felt over everything else that had happened that caused her to hesitate. It was as if everything she thought she knew about ghosts was turning out to be questionable. People came to her for help because she knew these things, dammit. How could she be so wrong? Was it this city? That old woman? What?

It took all of her effort to bury her pride and get in his vehicle. This wasn't about reuniting her new boss with his brother anymore. This was about catching a killer, and she figured she didn't really have a lot of choice in the matter.

One thing was certain though. As soon as she helped Dylan find the sadistic sonofabitch using Charleston as his personal playground, she was out of here.

The sooner, the better.

Chapter Four

How the hell was he going to pull this off?

Dylan rifled through the drawer, pulled out an old manila file, and then shoved it back in again. His idea had seemed like a good one on the ride back to the station, foolproof, even, but now that he was trying to figure out the specifics of it, doubts began flooding his mind.

His plan had been to give Alexandra some crumbs on an old case, one that had already been solved, and watch her flounder on the details, thus proving there was nothing extraordinary about her. When his plan worked, she'd hightail it out of here with her tail between her legs, and he could get down to business catching this killer.

But what if he chose a case that had gotten extensive media coverage, and Alexandra had caught some of the details on one of those forensics shows on cable? The case he'd originally intended to use went back in the drawer. It hadn't been high profile, but he knew reporters had picked up on it. Damn. It didn't help that his own knowledge of the solved cases here was limited. He'd only been here for a little over a year.

Maybe something older?

Detective Reedus walked past, and Dylan called out to him. As the bureau's senior detective, Reedus had been the first person to welcome Dylan on board and had worked in Charleston forever. The man seemed to know everything. "I need a case that's been solved without a lot of public knowledge."

Reedus tilted his head and frowned, so Dylan waved him closer and kept his voice low as he explained why he needed the file.

"Psychic?" Reedus perked up. "Ah, geez, Collins, don't tell me the Cap laid one of those on you." He reached into the drawer, glanced through some files and retrieved one. He cocked a smile. "Pretty clever idea you had to call her out. Mind if I watch?"

Dylan opened his mouth to say no but thought better of it after glancing through the file. "Did you work on this case?" He gestured with the folder. It was thicker than he would have liked.

"Damn straight. Did half the paperwork in there."

He didn't want to waste any more time than necessary. "Then come on."

Reedus walked into the conference room first, and Dylan almost plowed into the back of him when the older man suddenly planted himself on the carpet.

Reedus turned and backhanded Dylan's bicep. "My colleague didn't tell me he was working with a gorgeous woman. Collins, what the hell is wrong with you?" Reedus held out his hand and introduced himself to Alexandra.

Alexandra was leaning back in a chair and tapping a rhythm on the table in front of her with her fingertips as if she was bored out of her mind. Considering he'd shared his plan with her before leaving the room, he'd half expected her to be jumpy and anxious, knowing there was no way she could get herself out of this one.

The woman continued to surprise him.

She reached up and accepted Reedus's hand. "Nice to meet you, detective."

Dylan shut the door behind them. "Detective Reedus worked on this case and can help me determine whether or not you're

49

just pulling things out of thin air."

She sighed, and the sound translated as annoyed. She reached her hand across the table and wiggled her fingers in a gimme gesture. "Let's not waste too much time on this, okay? I'd rather be working on a case I can help on."

Surprised again, Dylan tried not to show it as he sank into the seat across from her. He pulled a plastic bag containing a necklace out of the folder. "It helps you to touch something that belonged to the victim, right?"

"It's called psychometry, and I can only do that if a spirit connected to the object is still here and willing to talk."

Yeah, whatever.

"I'm not gonna to share anything about this case with you first."

"Good." She snatched the necklace from his hand and looked down at the table. "Just give me a second to see what they show me."

"They?" Reedus asked from where he leaned against the wall watching.

Alexandra ignored him, staring at the oak tabletop as her fingers toyed with the chain of the necklace. Her eyes glazed over, and silence filled the room while she fondled the charm and chain alternately. Oh, man. She was good at this. Dylan wondered if she had a background in the theater and decided to ask her before she left.

Her voice was firm and confident when she finally spoke. "The victim was a man. He was tall. Mustache. Maybe 190 pounds."

Dylan glanced at Reedus and saw the older man's eyebrows shoot up in surprise. Dylan had been certain the necklace would throw her off on the gender. A small religious medal on a chain, it had struck him as being a bit feminine in appearance. Maybe he'd been wrong.

She took a deep breath. "I'm feeling something at my throat. Like I can't breathe." She looked up at Reedus. "Was he hung? From a tree? Like, a tree in his own yard?"

Reedus nodded and moved to take the seat beside Dylan. He leaned forward on his elbows and waited quietly for more.

Dylan shifted in his chair. How the devil was she doing this?

"He's dressed funny." She scrunched her nose. "Might be the seventies?" She shook her head. "It took you a while to solve this one. Hmmm. There was some speculation it had been a suicide, but it wasn't. That's why. Right?" She fingered the necklace and tilted her head, staring straight at the wall over Dylan's shoulder. "Your killers worked together. It was a lynching-type murder. Like a hate crime. Oh, I know." She blinked and looked at Reedus as if she'd just had a great epiphany. "He was gay. They killed him because he was gay. And they tried to make it look like a suicide."

Reedus glanced back at Dylan and gave him one of his I'm-impressed expressions.

Alexandra held the necklace out to Dylan. "The ringleader died about ten years ago, and his wife gave up the other two people involved. He'd bragged about it to her once when he'd been drunk. She had a guilty conscience."

Reedus chuckled and took the necklace before Dylan could. "Actually it was his sister and there were three arrests made, but you got everything else right. Good enough for me."

Alexandra shrugged. "No psychic is one hundred percent accurate. We're human. We make mistakes." She tapped the table with a finger. "But I'm glad you caught those guys. I see a history of domestic violence with them. Nasty stuff."

Surprise lit up Reedus's face again. "Yeah, one of the guy's wives led us to some evidence from the crime scene he'd kept. She was glad to get rid of him. Open and shut case."

"And you're telling me this didn't get any media?" Dylan asked.

Reedus shook his head. "Not much. The victim's family had disowned him because of his sexual orientation, and quite frankly, I think his father—a real religious asshole—was a bit relieved to be rid of him. They were ashamed, but fine believing it was suicide. No one on the force really took an interest in proving otherwise either. Times were different back then. If the killer's sister hadn't come forward, it would have remained a suicide."

"What about when it was solved?" Dylan couldn't believe this. There had to be some explanation for Alexandra's guesses.

"Sure, they ran a piece on the local news. I think it lasted about thirty seconds. End of story."

Dylan shook his head and addressed the woman across from them. "Tell me this. If you were getting your information from a spirit connected to that necklace, why weren't you one hundred percent accurate?"

She released a sigh. "I don't know, Dylan. My best guess is that it's like a radio signal. Every now and then there's some interference. I hear the information wrong or it comes across distorted because of something screwy in the transmission."

Alexandra held up a hand before he could voice his next thought. "Look, you gave me nothing, and I gave you a lot. I think you're just determined to find excuses, which is your prerogative. Stupid, but your prerogative. I'd really like to get back to the case I volunteered to help you with. Okay?"

Reedus chuckled and gestured toward her. "I like this woman, Collins. We should work with her more often."

Yeah, and Dylan knew why. All it took was a pretty face and a hot body to win Reedus's favor. He muttered a curse and put the bagged necklace back in the folder. Doubts nibbled at his conviction that she was a fraud.

Zach had been pretty convincing on TV, too. Don't forget that.

Zach. He didn't like the way he kept thinking about his brother today after working years to forget the bastard ever existed. He'd been twelve when his older brother had taken off, abandoned him and their mother as if they'd meant nothing, and Dylan had been a senior in high school when his girlfriend had pulled him over to her TV to watch a new show she'd become fixated on.

The Psychic Detective, starring Zachary Collins. "Gee, you kinda look like him, too," his girlfriend had commented before asking if there was any relation.

Dylan had been horrified to realize his brother was actually passing himself off as a psychic. Zach had never shown any ounce of having those abilities growing up. He'd known it was a scam, had been pissed as hell that the brother he'd once worshipped had been unworthy of his praise.

The word "psychic" had been a hot button for him ever since.

But maybe he was being too narrow-minded. Just because his brother was a fraud didn't mean they all were.

"Look," he told Alexandra. "I'm willing to listen to whatever it is you have to tell me." He leaned across the table. "But the second it becomes obvious to me that you're conning me, that's it. I'm done."

A beautiful smile lit up her face. "Sounds fair to me. Can we get started now? I mean, seriously."

"Wait here. I'll go get the file so we can go over what we already know."

If Alexandra King could help him solve this case, great. If not, he hadn't lost anything but a little time.

***

Alexandra's behind hurt from sitting too long, so she stood to pace the room while she once again studied the crime scene photos Dylan had shared with her.

She stared at the close-up photograph of Candice Christopher's face. She was the young woman who'd been standing outside the café, the spirit who'd been feeding Alexandra information about the case.

53

She flipped between pictures showing Candice's body positioned on her back, one hand covering her face, the other outstretched, and her jean-clad legs crossed at the ankle, and a second, more close-up picture of a tarot card. Dylan had explained that the card had been found next to the body, propped against a tombstone. There was nothing unusual about the card except what it represented. A grim reaper carried a scythe over the word DEATH.

"You okay looking at that?" Dylan asked, and she glanced at him, a little puzzled until she realized he was probably thinking of her penchant for fainting at such things.

"Yeah. Photos don't bother me." She flicked a dismissive hand and turned away. She focused on the first photo again. "He's obviously trying to send a message with the positioning of the body and this card. But what?"

Alexandra had tried closing herself off again earlier, and thought it had held this time. She hadn't yet opened herself up to information from the other side on this case. She'd wanted a moment to refresh her mind from the test he'd given her and look over the current files. But something was scratching at her consciousness, already trying to make itself known. She imagined a wall, the way her grandmother had taught her, and blocked it. Blocked everything. She liked to familiarize herself with the basic facts before she invited anyone else to weigh in on a criminal case. It helped her decipher the information she was given when she understood a little about it first.

"The other body was also positioned," Dylan said, sliding a different folder across the table. "Killers don't usually pose bodies, so yeah, I assume he's trying to tell us something. Since the positioning is so different on all three of these, I have no idea what it could be."

"When was the first victim found again?"

"Three months ago."

Hmm. That was when his mother had started making a menace of herself, insisting Dylan was in danger. Oh, but Alexandra would love to talk to her right now.

He spread open a file and tapped a report. "Second victim was end of August. Third victim was yesterday."

"So one every month? Any significance to the days?"

"What do you mean?"

"Were they found exactly one month apart or what?"

He shrugged. "Give or take a few days." His eyes narrowed. "You think he's on some kind of schedule?"

"I don't know, Dylan. It might not be a bad idea to see what days the full moons were on."

"Whoa."

She glanced up at him. "What?"

"I know two of them were killed on the night of a full moon. I didn't make that connection until now." He rubbed at the back of his neck and began pacing. "I remember the first one. Reedus made a comment about the full moon bringing out the lunatics. Last night, I noticed the moon looked full."

Alexandra reached for her phone and did an Internet search to verify the dates of the last three full moons. "Interesting. They were all killed on full moons."

"Let me see that." He stepped close and reached for her phone. Alexandra immediately grew aware of his warmth, his scent, his—

Stop it! He is your boss's brother! No more touching!

Dylan glanced up, a hint of a smile tugging at his mouth. His eyes danced with excitement. Excitement that quickly took on a new focus when he seemed to realize how close they were standing. He stepped away.

He cleared his throat. "This is good. This means he probably won't try to kill again until next month, end of October. Gives us time."

55

"Halloween." Alexandra reached for the newest file and skimmed the crime scene photos in it. A man's body was propped from the waist up against the wall in an alley, his legs sprawled out in front of him on the cobblestone walkway. Spray-painted in black next to his head was one word. Reaper.

"So that's his moniker," she decided. "He wants to be known as the Grim Reaper."

"Seems like it."

"Okay." She wiggled her shoulders to shake out the tension creeping in at that disturbing thought. "I'm going to concentrate now and see if I can find anyone who knows something that will help. I'm going to let them in now."

Dylan straightened from his position leaning against the table. "Let them in?" His voice was skeptical again.

She resisted the urge to roll her eyes. "Not literally. I don't ever allow them to take over my body. Now shut up so I can think for a minute."

He crossed his arms, but said nothing else. Man, he was sexy when he did that. All brooding and hot.

Focus on the case, not on Mr. Delicious.

Alexandra closed her eyes and thought of the wall she'd erected in her head. She cracked it open and felt an electric jolt course through her veins like liquid fire. The word COPYCAT flashed in her mind along with DEATH over and over again. Several scenes from various, violent slasher films played in her head, and she felt pleasure at seeing them.

This guy must really love horror movies.

She could feel warm breath tease her ear as a woman's voice whispered, "He's always been fascinated by death. He's fascinated by this city. It called to him, and he came. There was another... another he killed, just to see if he could actually do it."

Her eyes opened, but she saw no one standing at her side.

Clearing her throat, she repeated everything for Dylan's sake.

"Copycat?" He sat down on the edge of the table. "What the hell does that mean?"

"I'm just telling you what I'm getting. I don't understand it either."

"Go on."

She took a deep breath and paced along the length of the conference table. Nothing else was coming to her. The voice was gone, and so were the images. Slowly she completely lifted the wall.

Candice, you can trust me. I want to talk to you about your death. Will you help me catch your killer?

She spun at the end of the table and turned to pace the other way. The feeling of almost colliding with someone standing in front of her caused her to correct herself and step back. She lifted her gaze as her hands instinctively reached out to grab hold of the person she'd bumped into.

Candice Christopher was even more beautiful in death than she'd been in the college honors portrait attached to her file. Her long, red hair was pulled back from her face, and Alexandra recognized the clothes the younger woman wore as the same from the crime scene photos. The same clothes she'd been wearing at the café.

Okay. Here we go.

"What happened to me?" Candice's voice trembled.

Alexandra wished Dylan weren't in the room, because she never liked to converse with the dead with skeptics present. But this time, she made an exception.

"I'm so sorry. You're dead."

Candice's eyes lowered to the floor, and she nodded. "Yes. That's what I thought."

"Excuse me? I'm what?" Dylan said, and Alexandra shot him an impatient look along with a forceful "Shhhhh." Didn't he realize she wasn't talking to him? Geez.

"I'm trying to help find the person who did this to you," Alexandra said more gently to the ghost. "Can you tell me what you remember? Can you show me?"

Candice's unblinking eyes fixated on Alexandra's, and she nodded.

A flash of bright light temporarily blinded Alexandra, and she blinked her vision back into focus. The daylight was fading, the glow of orange glistening on the gray-blue ocean water just beyond the railing. Candice laughed over the backdrop of old beach music. A singer whined out the melody of "Good Vibrations" by the Beach Boys, and Alexandra turned to see a live band of young people playing on a makeshift stage while dancers whirled around her. She spun in a full circle and recognized that she was on a pier.

"I've really got to get home," Candice told someone, drawing Alexandra's attention back to her. "I'll call you later."

With a wave toward a group of three women, Candice began walking down the long dock, her flip flops making a distinct whack-whack sound against the wood. Alexandra followed, even though she knew her feet weren't moving. On and on the young woman walked, as if the pier kept on for miles instead of the thousand or so feet it probably was, the music growing more and more distant.

Candice reached the end of the pier, which felt deserted and bereft. Her flip flops quieted when she stepped on sand. She turned suddenly at the sound of an animal's whining. She bent and moved closer to the underbelly of the pier. The daylight had faded so much by now that only shadows could be seen.

Candice clicked her tongue several times. "Puppy?"

The whining continued, luring Candice deeper into the darkness as she cooed and pleaded for the unseen animal not to be afraid. The hair on the back of Alexandra's neck suddenly lifted as goosebumps chased each other down her arms. She wanted to yell at Candice not to move any closer, but it was too late.

Candice disappeared into the shadows, and Alexandra followed. A pair of gloved hands snaked out of the shadows and snatched the young woman by her shoulders, dragging her further under the dock. Candice's screams mingled with the howling horn and throbbing percussions in the distance as she fought against her attacker. She tore away from him and ran, sloshing through the surf beneath the pier, but the killer was fast and tackled her at the water's edge. Alexandra watched in horror as the dark-clad shape of a man plunged a hypodermic needle into her arm from behind and injected something into her system. Candice continued to claw her way toward the water, her movements slowing until eventually her head lowered into the ebb and flow of the ocean's edge. A bubble broke the surface, and then she went completely still.

"Alexandra!"

Alexandra felt a cough tear through her chest, and she realized she was clutching her throat with one hand and her chest with the other. Why couldn't she breathe? Dylan had both hands on her shoulder and was shaking her, hard.

"Alexandra! Are you okay?"

She struggled to pull air into of her lungs and whispered "Yes," feeling more than a little disoriented to see the plain beige walls of the conference room instead of the ocean and sand.

"What the hell was that about?" Dylan's fingers gripped into her upper arms. He tried to push her into a chair, but she resisted.

"I know how she was killed, and where."

He narrowed his eyes, but said nothing. Leaving no detail unmentioned, she explained everything she'd just witnessed. Dylan finally let his hands fall away from her.

He swore and turned on his heels.

"What?" she demanded. "You don't believe me?"

He placed his hands on his hips and spun back toward her. "That matches information I haven't had time to put in her file yet. She was last seen at Folly Beach Pier, but her car was found a block away from the cemetery, about half an hour away from the pier. A witness told us they saw her driving away, but maybe..." His voice trailed off.

"Maybe they saw her car, but not her." Alexandra stepped closer. "She was killed at that pier, Dylan. I know it."

He nodded. "It would explain the ocean water in her lungs."

"So you believe me?"

He stared at her for several seconds. "I'm keeping an open mind."

Happiness rushed through Alexandra at his hard-earned admission, although she didn't know why. It was always a high when someone came to appreciate her abilities, but she'd never felt so excited about it. Why did she care so much what this man thought of her? She barely knew him. Except in the Biblical sense.

There was a knock on the door, distracting Alexandra from her inappropriate thoughts. A uniformed officer opened the door and gestured at Dylan. "There's a call for you, Collins. Person insists you'll want to talk to him about the Christopher case. He refuses to leave a message. You want to take it, or—?"

"I'll take it. Transfer it to my desk." He told Alexandra, "Excuse me for a minute." And then he left her alone.

***

Dylan made it to his desk before the first ring. Snatching up the receiver, he barked, "Detective Collins. I understand you have some information about a case I'm working on?"

Heavy breathing was the only response.

"Hello?" Sinking into his chair, Dylan lifted his hand and rubbed at his forehead. He was tired. Damn tired. He was grateful it was almost six o'clock, and that Alexandra would be leaving soon for the day. He hoped. The woman was a major distraction on multiple levels, and he could use some distance right about now. Distance to regroup and think. And sleep. Man, he hoped he could sneak in a nap after a quick bite to eat. "Hello? Anyone there?"

"I'm here," a raspy voice responded softly. A man's voice. Distorted.

Dylan waited for more, but the heavy breathing was all he got. "Look, I'm pretty busy at the moment. Do you have information to share, or can I transfer you back to our front desk so you can be redirected to the right person?"

"I'm calling you about the Grim Reaper."

Every cell in Dylan's body snapped to alert. The Grim Reaper info hadn't been released to the public. "I'm listening."

"Are you, Detective Collins? Or are you too busy playing with your new girlfriend to appreciate my offerings?"

"Who is this?"

A sinister laugh trickled down the line. "None other than the Reaper himself, of course. I wanted to let you know how pleased I am that you brought in Alexandra King so soon. It pleases me very much."

Dylan looked around and spotted Reedus. He lifted his arm and snapped his fingers, then gestured to the phone. When Reedus got close enough, Dylan wrote on a piece of paper, *This might be our killer. Get me a trace.* He leaned closer to the phone and said, "Who?"

"I recognized her last night, when you met in the bar. Tell me, detective, is that how you pay your consultants? By sleeping with them?"

Dylan stifled a curse. Whoever this guy was, he knew a lot of information.

"Who says she's a consultant?"

61

"I don't have time for games. I have one demand to make, and then I have to hang up."

"Okay. I'll bite. What?"

"Release my name to the media. I want to see my name on the news by tomorrow. If I don't, you won't be pleased with the results."

A click preceded a dial tone, and Dylan swore. "Did we get a trace?" He directed the comment at no one in particular, but Reedus lowered the phone receiver in his hand and shook his head from across the room. He slammed his phone down.

"He was using an unregistered mobile, one of those prepaid ones." Reedus coughed as he hurried over. "We didn't have him on long enough to triangulate the call."

This guy was smart. Too smart.

How the devil had the caller known so much about Alexandra? Was she an accomplice to this whole thing? How else had the caller known who she was?

He swore again.

His gut told him she wasn't involved, but he'd have to run a more thorough background check after this. Where had she been at the time of the first murder? And if she wasn't an accomplice, then she was a potential target.

And neither scenario pleased him.

Chapter Five

Alexandra heard the buzz of her phone vibrating against the table and pulled her purse close to find it. Oh, man. Probably Hannah. She'd forgotten to check in with Hannah that morning, but when she glanced at the caller ID and saw a photo of Dylan's older brother on the screen instead, she immediately jerked her wide eyes toward the door.

What the heck was Zach calling her for? Now?

"Hey, boss," she answered and paced toward the other end of the room, never mind she was alone, the door was closed, and no one could hear her conversation anyway. "This is not really a good time."

"It's important, Alexandra."

"Ohhh-kay. What's up?"

"I hope you can tell me." His voice sounded tense. Almost accusing.

Crap. He'd figured out where she was and what she was doing. Or someone had told him. Probably Abbot, that devious cat, or Costello, Hannah's dog who was allegedly too dumb to keep a secret. Maybe it had been Charlie, Hannah's youngest pup, who adored Zach something fierce. It sucked having a pet psychic around when you were trying to—

"Something's going on with Hannah," Zach continued before

she could finish the thought. "She's acting kind of secretive. What do you know, King? Spill it."

Oh. Ohhh.

Crap.

She crossed her fingers behind her back and flat-out lied to the man. "I don't know. What do you mean?" She gave a quick look toward the door. Still closed.

"She excused herself last night to call someone, and now she's having a hard time looking me in the eyes." He made an annoyed sound. "What's going on, Alexandra? Before you answer, remember I sign your damn paychecks."

He made a good point, but Hannah and Hannah's best friend, Sarah, had welcomed Alexandra into their girls club with open arms. She'd never had two better friends in her life. Where did her loyalty lie? With the guy who'd gotten her fired from his TV show because he'd felt threatened by her since he hadn't yet realized his own abilities? Granted, he had made amends by giving her a job at his new firm.

She resisted a snort. No contest.

She uncrossed her fingers and began pacing. "I don't know what you're talking about, Collins. Why don't you ask the boys?"

The boys was how everyone referenced Hannah's pets because they were practically the woman's children. Alexandra suspected Zach was an empath—a rarity among psychics—but his abilities seemed especially sensitive to animals. He'd proven he could communicate with Hannah's animals time and time again.

"I have," he bit out. "They're not telling me and that makes me even more suspicious." He lowered his voice. "I gave Abbott extra tuna, but all he said was 'Maybe I know something. Maybe I don't.' I mean, what the hell?"

Alexandra bit her lip to keep from snickering. Hannah had said she was going to give Abbott extra tuna for a few days to assure his loyalty, and the cat and Zach had a tumultuous relationship anyway. Abbott probably spent his days planning how to get more tuna from Zach.

Under normal circumstance she would have never suggested this, but…

"Have you tried reading Hannah then?" Oh, this was too much fun. Alexandra had been teaching Hannah how to block Zach from picking up on her feelings, and Hannah was good at it.

"Of course I have. Why do you think I'm calling you? I'm not getting anything, except for a wall. Maybe I'm doing something wrong?"

Alexandra smiled, and her muscles relaxed a little. "Maybe you're just being paranoid, Zach. Did you ever consider that?" Oh, she was bad for toying with him like this. Bad, bad, bad.

He growled. "Just tell me one thing. Is she seeing someone else?"

"*What*?" Alexandra abruptly stopped moving, the question shocked her so much. Then she laughed. "You've got to be kidding me, Zach. Hannah would never cheat on you. For some insane reason, that woman thinks you're the male equivalent of a hot fudge sundae." She snorted to emphasize her disagreement with that assessment. His brother, on the other hand…

"Something's going on, dammit. I'm not an idiot." He grumbled like a caged animal, and she imagined he was pacing like one too.

Alexandra sighed. She needed to detour his suspicions a little longer without making the poor man completely neurotic. Dylan wasn't ready for a reunion with his big bro yet, and she wasn't sure Zach was in the right place either. She snapped her fingers as an idea came to her. "All right, Zach. Don't tell Hannah I said anything, okay?" She'd have to call Hannah and let her in on this jewel of a decoy. "You have a birthday coming up in a month, right?" She knew this only because it had been part of Hannah's argument for finding Dylan. Hannah hadn't wanted Zach to go another year without mending things with his little brother.

"Yeah. How do you know that?"

"Think about it, boss. Your birthday is coming up. Hannah's being secretive." Boy, she hoped he took the bait soon. She needed to get him off the phone.

"She's doing something for my birthday?" He sounded surprised, and as pleased as a kid on Christmas.

"Bingo. And she called me last night so we could talk about planning a party. You will deny all knowledge of this. Got that?"

"Well, yeah. I guess. You guys are really throwing me a party?"

She rolled her eyes. Men. They could be so easy to manipulate. "Zach, I've got to go. Don't tell Hannah I said anything, okay?"

He sighed. "Thanks, Alexandra. You're a good friend."

Why did he have to go and say something like that, making her feel as guilty as a loyal pup sitting beside the poo she'd left in her owner's shoe? Yes, she and Zach had become friends. Kind of. That's partly why she'd agreed to help Rebecca and Hannah find Dylan, but crap. Now they really were going to have to try to throw him a party.

Alexandra hated parties.

A click signaled the door opening behind her, and she spun around quickly, her eyes widening when Dylan stepped into the room, all hot and brooding.

"Er, thanks, boss. Sorry, but I really gotta run." She pressed END and stepped forward. "So, are we done for the day or do you have some more things you want to throw at me?"

Crap. Did she look as nervous as she felt? That had been a close call. Literally.

Dylan's gaze moved from the phone in her hand and looked her up and down. "You in a hurry to leave? You meetin' someone or something?"

"I sure as hell hope so." She reached for her jacket and purse and arched a brow at him. "I've got a hot date with the drive-through guy at McDonald's. Or did you forget we skipped lunch?"

He pushed a hand through the hair at his forehead. "Sorry."

She shrugged, because it really wasn't a big deal. She'd worked with enough cops to know that a few skipped meals were usually the last thing on their minds when working a case like this. She fingered the manila folder on the table. "Could I take a copy of one of the pictures? I'll bring it back tomorrow. Maybe I can try to get some more impressions of this killer. I don't know, Dylan. Something about him really scares me."

He moved closer, so close that the scent of musk and sandalwood teased her senses. "What do you mean? How does he scare you?"

She forced herself to focus on the contents of the folder and not on him. He was too distracting. Of all the men in the world, why did this one send her brain to mush with only a glance? "He seems dangerous. I think he enjoys killing, and I think he'll do it again. Soon. I don't think he'll wait another month."

His hand stopped hers from lifting the photo from the table. A zing of awareness shot from her fingers up her arm and warmed her in places she hadn't realized were cold. Their eyes met and held. If he moved just a few inches closer, his mouth would be near enough to—

"I'll go make a copy." His breath was hot against her face.

She leaned against the table for support after he moved away. A cold shower. That's what she needed. And a few hours alone, in her hotel room, to get her wits about her again.

It had been a heck of a day. She deserved a little relaxation time.

Dylan wandered back in. He had managed to shrug into his jacket in the time he'd been gone. He handed her a paper copy of the photograph. Not ideal, but she could work with it.

"Why don't you let me buy you dinner?" His blue eyes had softened, that cocky grin was back on his face, and just like that he morphed from skeptical cop back into Mr. Delicious.

Oh dear.

Tell him no. Tell him NO, Alexandra.

"Okay." She mentally face-palmed herself, but her brain and her mouth had reached an impasse. "I'm starving. Where do you want to go?"

"You've got a car?" When she nodded, he put his hand on her back and gently pushed her forward. "I'll follow you to your place, and then we can walk to it."

Intrigued, she found herself moving forward without arguing. She had the distinct feeling he was up to something, but that could be a bad call. He might only want to unwind a little himself. It would offer her a good chance to get to know him better, for Zach's sake, of course.

Now she just needed to decide if letting him unwind in her bed again was a good idea. For anyone.

***

The evening air was cool as a breeze blew against Dylan where he stood waiting on Alexandra to get out of her rental car and join him.

Fall in Charleston was one of the best times to visit in his opinion. Sure, he'd grown up in hot-as-hell Louisiana, but he'd never been one for the beach or for hot weather. Even so, when it was sunny here, the seventy-degree temperature in October was perfect. He smelled rain on the wind and figured it would blow in soon. Maybe his idea to walk down to Poogan's Porch was a bad one. He didn't want them to get caught in a downpour on foot.

"Ready when you are," Alexandra said, hurrying up to his side.

He glanced at the sky and made a decision. "This way," he gestured and began walking. Why the hell was he doing this again?

Right. To get to know her better and figure out if she was in danger from this madman or working with the killer somehow. He honestly couldn't fathom that she was an accomplice, but he almost preferred that idea to her being in danger. It nibbled at his nerves to imagine anyone threatening this woman. No idea why he cared so much. He barely knew her.

"You've had an eventful day," he said to make conversation and smiled, because it was true.

"No kidding. Been there. Done that. Let's *not* do some of it again, okay?"

"Which part can we do again, 'cause I kind of enjoyed some of it." Damn. Why had he said that when he'd promised himself he wasn't going to flirt with her? She was a consultant. Off limits.

She puckered her lips and hummed. "Yeah, I say let's avoid the morgue and that whole fainting at the sight of a dead guy part. Does that work for you?"

"Agreed."

She hadn't excluded sex, he noticed. Did that mean she was willing to have another go at it? His pants tightened at his groin and he quickened his step on the pretense of opening the door for her. He swallowed a curse. This was no good. He couldn't trust himself around this woman. Half the time when he looked at her, all he saw was the way she'd stared up at him when she was underneath him. Her eyes had been dark and drugged with passion and—

He felt a tug on his jacket and turned toward her. She was pointing up at the building. "Seriously? We were just here last night."

He forced memories of last night into the corner of his mind he rarely visited. "And you've got a problem with that? I come here most days after work."

"Men." She rolled her eyes. "Please tell me you live around here or something."

"Or something." He smiled.

"As long as the food is good, I'm game." She brushed past him and moved inside, glancing around as if she were scanning the area for someone. His earlier suspicions wiggled back to the forefront. Did she know someone here? Was she afraid of being outed for something?

The hostess must have recognized her. The tiny blonde co-ed Dylan knew as Jane welcomed Alexandra back and asked if she was dining or wanted to visit the bar and billiards upstairs again.

"Two for the restaurant," Dylan answered for her.

The last temptation he needed was a reminder of the sexually charged game of pool they'd played here last night. The first-floor restaurant was crowded but they snagged a table in the corner, which gave them a little privacy. A live jazz band was finishing a set on the makeshift stage on the other side of the room. He waited until they were seated to speak his thoughts.

"I'm surprised you opted to eat upstairs last night if it was your first night in town." Maybe it hadn't been, he thought. Maybe she'd been here before and he'd never seen her. He hung his jacket on the back of his chair and watched while she did the same before sitting.

She shrugged. "The hotel worker who recommended this place told me to eat upstairs for the harbor view."

"What'd you think?"

"Of the view?" She gave him a slow once over. "Impressive."

Now she was flirting back.

He was grateful for the interruption of the waiter who came to take their drink order. Alexandra surprised him by shutting her menu after barely giving it a glance, saying, "I'll have whatever you're having. You obviously know the menu."

Dylan ordered them both burgers and sweet teas and sat back

in his seat. The music was loud but not loud enough to discourage conversation.

"So tell me about yourself, Alexandra King. You're from Atlanta, right?"

"Currently." She leaned forward and met his gaze while her fingers toyed with a napkin.

"Where are you from originally?"

"I was born in Hawaii."

"Hawaii?"

She smiled. "After that, we lived in Germany for a while, then Florida and California. We lived in Australia for a year when I was 10. That was awesome." She snapped her fingers. "I did graduate from high school in Arizona. We lived there a few years. I went to college in Colorado and stayed there until I moved to Georgia about six months ago. What about you?"

The woman got around. "Born and raised in Louisiana. Moved here a couple of years ago." The music got louder, so he leaned forward and raised his voice. "Were you a military kid or something?"

"Bingo. My dad was a two-star General in the Army. He's retired now, so my parents are happily rooted back in Colorado, where they grew up together."

"Ah, an Army brat."

"Yes, I absolutely was, but my brother was more bratty. Trust me."

"Is he older or younger?" He loved that she was feeding him information so willingly. If it was true, she was fascinating. Absolutely fascinating.

"Older by about five minutes, but I'm convinced all the mature genes stayed in the womb with me."

"Five—?"

"We're twins." She held up her hand, palm toward him. "Before you ask, yes, Alexander and Alexandra, but we decided early on that was incredibly stupid, so he goes by his middle name, Matthew. No sense in two little Alexses running around causing chaos."

"So is Alex your nickname?" He'd wondered if it was.

She shook her head and wrinkled her nose. "Lexie. I prefer Alexandra. I think it makes me sound more sophisticated." She smiled. "My brother's friends turned me off the nickname in high school. They used to call me Sexy Lexie. After a while, it got old."

"Most women would be flattered."

"I didn't enjoy being objectified."

"So is your brother…?" He had trouble saying the word psychic.

She shrugged, following his hint. "He likes to pretend he isn't, but yeah, he's been known to see a few dead people now and then."

"So being psychic is a genetic trait?" Good thing his own brother was a fraud.

Her eyes glanced toward the band and wandered. "Could be. My grandmother had 'the sight' as people like to call it."

He considered her for several seconds. She licked her lips as she looked everywhere but at him. She seemed to lock onto something near the bar and stay, and she straightened a little in her seat. He thought she mouthed the word "Crap," but he wasn't sure. He followed her gaze but couldn't peg what she'd seen. She slapped the table gently and focused on him again.

"What about you? Any brothers or sisters?"

He leaned away and sat back in his chair. "Older brother. We're not close."

"In age or—?"

"I haven't spoken to him in a long time." Why was he telling her this? He never talked about Zach to anyone. He usually told people he was an only child. It was easier, less messy.

"What happened?"

He shook his head. "Woke up one day when I was twelve and

he'd left. End of story." He gestured to her. "When did you first realize you were…" He still couldn't say the word. It stuck in his throat like a bad piece of food.

She smiled and arched a brow at him. "Psychic?" The waiter appeared with their drinks, told them their food would be out in a few minutes, and disappeared again. Alexandra took a sip and leaned further across the table. "I think I always was. I would see people no one else could see. I never understood why they couldn't. Sometimes Matt saw them, too, but no one else did. One time, my parents were worried my dad was getting a transfer order. They worried about it for days. I had a dream about my uncle who'd died the year before, and I woke up and told them what he'd said to me. 'Yes, we're moving to California in three weeks.' My dad didn't believe me. He said no one had even mentioned California as a possibility. A few days later, he got the call. We were being moved to San Diego."

"How old were you?"

"Eight."

She knew how to tell a good story. He'd give her that. He took a sip from his glass and sat it beside his right arm. "How did you get involved with the police?"

"What do you mean? They obviously heard how awesome I was and came beating down my door, wanting my help."

"Really." It wasn't a question. He knew she was teasing.

"Of course not." She rolled her eyes. "I kind of…well. Matt and I went to college in Colorado so we could be close to our grandmother. When I was a freshman, this girl—Amelia Cosby, she was a senior—went missing. There were flyers all over campus. It was on the news. I was looking at one of the flyers one day."

"Did you know her?"

"No, but I'd seen her on campus." She waved her hand dismissively. "Anyway, I could see exactly where she was as clearly as if I

73

were there with her. I went to the police and—"

"You saw her in a dream or someone, meaning a dead person, told you where she was?"

"Exactly." She nodded. "It was like a vision. Kind of like watching a movie play in my head. I'm sure someone close to her on the other side showed it to me. That's usually what happens." She speared him with a pointed look. "Stop interrupting me."

His lip tugged up in a smile. "I'm a cop. It's what I do."

"Do it to someone else." She narrowed her eyes then grinned. "So I told the police," she continued. "I told them the area and the road she'd been driving on when she had her accident."

"And they believed you?"

"Of course not. I called Amelia's parents myself and told them too. I had to at least try. They were desperate, so they coerced the sergeant I'd talked to into checking the area. Good thing, too. She'd fallen asleep driving one night and gone over an embankment into some foliage so she was hidden from the road. When they found the wreckage, she was still alive, but barely. The news said later that another hour or two and she would have been dead."

"Now that's impressive."

"Yeah, well. A couple months later, the same sergeant who'd refused to listen to me called and asked if I would take a look at another missing person case. It sort of became a side job, helping him out every now and then. We eventually became friends. He told me I should give up on my accounting degree and use my real talents for a living, helping people. With hindsight, I could slap the crap out of him for that, cause I dropped out and have been living paycheck to paycheck ever since."

"What's his name?"

"Sergeant Byron Carter. Fort Collins, Colorado. You should have no trouble looking him up. I can give you other references if you want. It'll make your background check go a lot faster."

Feisty. He liked that.

Besides, she'd already given him a name. Amelia Cosby. Easy enough to fact check. He reached for his glass and stopped. It was gone. His gaze searched the table and found it sitting beside his left arm. He could've sworn—

He muttered a soft curse. He must have sat it there without realizing it. He needed sleep, and bad.

Alexandra's eyes were sparkling with amusement, and she was biting her bottom lip, trying not to smile, when he returned his attention to her.

She sure as hell was sexy when she did that.

He'd needed this. Needed to relax and smile and just have an excuse to look at her while she talked. He'd be back buried in this case soon enough. He liked hearing her talk, even if he wasn't convinced he believed half of it.

Her gaze seemed to be following someone as he or she moved behind him. The waiter? Good. His stomach was growling out a complaint. At least one part of his body would be satisfied tonight.

But no food was lowered in front of him. He spotted their waiter at a table a few feet away, so he glanced behind him to see who she'd been staring at.

No one he recognized.

"I have a confession to make," she said, snapping his attention back to her. She sighed and grasped her glass between two hands. He noticed she'd barely taken more than a sip. Didn't she like it? Looking at the table, she still nibbled at her lower lip. She needed to stop doing that.

Confession. Wait. What?

He braced himself for an admission of fraud, for the revelation she was involved in his case, for anything.

"I kind of cheated at our game of pool last night." She looked up at him through her lashes the way a little girl might when admitting guilt.

Not what he'd been expecting. "Yeah, I know. I've been trying to figure out how."

"I guess you could say I had a partner helping me."

What was she playing at? No one had been near them.

"And he's messing with you again now. Sorry about that. He's a very playful spirit."

He looked around. The next table over was a group of women.

"Um, he's actually sitting right there now." She pointed at the empty seat between them. Dylan was taken aback by the fact it was pulled out far enough for a third party. He could have sworn the seat had been pushed firmly under the table. Alexandra gestured toward the seat. "Derby Hat Guy, this is Dylan." She waved toward Dylan. "Dylan, this is, er, Derby Hat Guy. I don't know his name."

Was she for real? She honestly expected him to believe a ghost was with them right now?

"Oh! Sorry." She pulled an *oops* face. "He says his name is George." She glanced at the empty seat. "George? Really? I would have never pegged you as a George."

Okay, she was playing with him now. Joking around. Had to be. There was no way.

Dylan's smile fell from his face as the glass sitting in front of him slowly began to slide across the table toward the empty seat. He sat back, hands spread wide in disbelief just as their waiter finally appeared with their food.

Seeing the glass moving before abruptly coming to a stop, the waiter chuckled. "I think you've met our ghost. Not usually a tea drinker. Yeah, he loves our beer. He's always messing with the taps at the bar. Funny, right?"

***

The look on Dylan's face was priceless.

Alexandra said nothing as their food was placed in front of them. Their waiter rambled on about the antics of the building's resident ghost. He left the bathroom sinks running. He loved to brush up against the ladies dancing on Salsa night. He was quite a dancer, their ghost. And he was notorious for messing with people's billiard and dart games. Yeah, she'd learned that one firsthand.

Derby Hat Guy—er, George—looked delighted to hear himself described with such matter-of-factness.

Chuckling, he slapped the table and pointed at Alexandra. "Derby Hat Guy. I love that ya call me that. Maybe that's what they can start calling me here. Derby Hat Guy: He haunts our building. I love it." She noticed the bloody gash at his throat was gone today. She wondered why he was hiding it. Maybe he'd realized it freaked her out. He poked his thumb in Dylan's direction. "So ya two came back together. I'm not sure about this fella. We'll have to keep an eye on 'em and size 'em up."

We?

"So who's the other guy?" George put his hand in her fries, and she slapped him away. Her fingers touched cold skin as he snapped his fingers back. She would never get used to that sensation, of actually feeling them sometimes. The old ones, the ones who'd been around a long time, usually felt as solid as the living.

She waited until the waiter left to ask, "What guy?"

George gestured toward the bar. "The one who followed ya in. He's been watching ya the entire time ya've been here. Kind of creepy if ya ask me. Lots of negative energy around that 'un. Is he a friend of yours?"

Chapter Six

Someone had followed them.

The small hairs on Alexandra's neck tingled as they lifted. Goosebumps raced up her arms.

She stood and glanced at the patrons sitting at or near the bar. She recognized no one, but of course she wouldn't. The killer's face hadn't been revealed to her in her visions. Only his shape had been.

"What's going on?" Dylan stood and followed her gaze.

"George said someone followed us in and has been watching us."

"What? Where?"

He didn't doubt her? She couldn't allow herself time to process that fully, but she was insanely pleased by her realization.

"The bar." She turned to George, who was already up and moving. "George, which one is he?" she whispered impatiently.

The ghost weaved between the tables until he was close enough to specify the person. "This fella here."

A tall man was leaning over the bar, his back to them. He wore a knitted cap over his head. His shape was somehow familiar to her.

"I think it's that guy. The one wearing the black cap." She pointed him out for Dylan.

Dylan nudged her back toward her seat. "Stay here."

Gladly.

She sank back into her chair and watched anxiously as Dylan

pushed his way through a crowd of people who'd just stood to leave their tables. When the people dispersed, the tall figure at the bar was gone. Dylan spun around in a circle, searching the room for the man. He finally held out his hands and glanced back at her.

Alexandra looked for George in the crowd. Where had he gone?

"He went out the front in that crowd of people. He's on the street now." George said from behind her. Hand over her heart, Alexandra turned and saw him leaning toward the window, watching the activity outside. His expression was serious. "Who is he?"

How did she answer what she didn't know?

She glanced back at Dylan and saw that he was leaning over the bar where the man had stood. He picked something up and then spoke to the bartender. The younger man pointed toward the door, and Dylan sprinted in that direction and out of sight. Should she follow him? Who cared what he'd told her? Maybe he needed her help.

She turned to speak to George, wondering if he could leave the building, if he could follow Dylan, but he'd disappeared again.

Dammit. Why did he keep doing that?

Alexandra came to a quick decision. She was reaching for her purse and Dylan's jacket when she caught sight of George following Dylan back into the building. Ah ha! So he *could* leave. The ghost stopped and waved at her over the crowd gathered at the door, and in a blink, completely disappeared again.

Dylan stomped back to the bar and said something to the bartender. The lanky man retrieved something from behind the counter and handed it to him. A Ziploc bag? Dylan carefully picked an item up from the bar top and sealed it in the plastic.

Alexandra felt a presence beside her seconds before she heard George say, "The man's gone. What's going on here?"

"I don't know. I think he was dangerous." She looked at the ghost. "Can you describe him to me or show me what he looks like?"

"Sorry, hon. I didn't get a good enough look at his features. He didn't have facial hair. I can tell ya that much. Kinda young."

"How young?"

George mumbled a grumpy, incoherent response. It sort of sounded like "They all look young to me."

A woman at the next table giggled, and Alexandra realized she was the subject of other patrons' attention now. Of course she was. Who else talked to thin air?

George meandered to the woman's table. With a flick, he knocked the brunette's glass of water over, spilling it directly into her lap, before turning and sitting with a *hmmmph* in the chair beside Alexandra. Alexandra smiled at his gesture, and also at the way he scooted his chair closer, protectively, next to hers.

"His attention was mostly focused on you," George whispered. "I don't like it. I don't like the way he was looking at ya, now that I think of it." This playful, mischievous ghost was frowning? The situation must have been bad.

After speaking to everyone at the bar Dylan strode back to their table, whatever he'd picked up from the bar clutched in his right hand.

He sat down and glanced around the room. His expression was dark, almost furious as he stuffed the item into his jacket pocket. "Eat your burger," he ordered and moved to pick up his own. He took a bite and chewed hard.

She'd been nervously munching on fries while she watched him. She didn't think she could manage anything else. "What did you find? Wait. Shouldn't you call for backup or something?"

"Done," he barked around a mouthful. "Now eat."

Alexandra had lost her appetite and, quite frankly, couldn't believe Dylan wasn't still doing something to find the guy from the bar. What did he know that she didn't? Maybe she'd been reading the situation wrong. Maybe George had been mistaken. Maybe Dylan had caught the tall man outside and decided there was nothing suspicious about him.

"Tarnation." George finally sighed and reached for Dylan's coat. "I wanna see what's in that bag."

Alexandra gasped and nearly choked on the bite of food she'd just forced herself to swallow when George maneuvered the plastic bag out and tossed it onto the table. It landed softly on the wood between her and Dylan.

"What the? How did that?" Dylan reached for his jacket then stared at the plastic bag as if it were possessed. Alexandra reached for it as George hunched over her right shoulder to watch her thin out the bag and get a better look at what was inside.

A napkin.

Drawn in black ink on the white paper was a figure.

A figure of the grim reaper. Underneath was a scribbled message that sent chills up and down her spine.

GR loves AK.

***

Dylan spotted the patrol car outside the window and checked his watch. Only six minutes to respond to his call. He pushed another bite of his burger into his mouth, stood up and told the woman sitting across from him, "Don't you dare move from this spot."

Snatching the bag from Alexandra's fingers, he went to speak to the officers he'd called in to question witnesses at the bar. He'd spoken to a few already. No one had given him a clear description of the man who'd left the napkin.

The Grim Reaper.

He'd considered searching the entire restaurant himself, including the area outside, but he hadn't wanted to leave Alexandra alone for too long. What if the killer's plan had been to separate Dylan from her so he could swoop in and take her? *Hurt her.* He swore beneath his breath. Nothing that had happened in the past hour was within his comfort zone. Had a freaking ghost actually warned them of danger? Something—or someone—had moved his glass without touching it. And somehow the stupid napkin had flung itself out of his jacket pocket and landed on the table a few seconds ago.

"Has anyone patrolled the area yet?" he asked the young-looking officer who came through the door first.

"Yes, sir. I was in the area when your call came in. I didn't see anyone wearing a knit cap dressed the way you described. Jameson's in his car on the next block over, checking things out."

"Alright. Secure that end of the bar until a crime scene tech gets here to dust it for prints. Get some statements. Don't make a scene. We don't want this showing up on the eleven o'clock news tonight." He slapped the young man's back and gave similar orders to the officer who followed. He wanted the area searched. Maybe some of the businesses on this street had security cameras. They were going to find this guy.

Alexandra had her head down, her face blocked by her forearm, when he made his way back to their table. She looked rattled. Good. He wanted her aware of what was at stake.

The woman was in danger.

She lifted her gaze and attempted a wobbly smile. "Geez, Collins. What have you got planned for our second date? I could do without the whole serial killer following us around part."

Date? He couldn't help it. He felt his lips turn up in a smile. "Ready to head back to your place?"

"Don't you need to stick around and, I don't know, search for fingerprints or something?"

Reedus would be here soon to supervise the uniforms. His

priority right now was her safety. "No, we're good."

She'd only eaten part of her burger, and so had he, but he guessed they'd both lost their appetites. Maybe they'd order a pizza later. She shrugged her jacket on while he threw enough cash on the table to take care of the bill. Biting her lip, she turned away and murmured quietly, "Thanks, George. See ya later."

Then she squealed and bucked her hips forward as if someone had just spanked her behind. Her expression went from discouraged to furious in three seconds flat. She swatted the air behind her.

"Jerk."

Dylan's chuckle grew into a laugh when he realized the table full of people behind them was watching, and they all looked as confused as hell.

"Come on." He grabbed her arm and led her outside. He needed to get her somewhere safe, secure. Some place quiet. They needed to talk.

He kept his gaze alert on their surroundings. Wouldn't surprise him if the bastard was hiding in the shadows, still watching them.

Alexandra kept pace beside him on the sidewalk, not once attempting to dislodge his hand from her back. He liked that she was letting him lead. He liked it a lot.

They'd almost made it to her hotel when the sky opened up and rain began pelting their bodies so hard it stung his face. He swore and shoved her into an alley where an awning covered a doorway. He pressed her against the wall, shielding her with his body.

"I'm sorry." It was his fault they'd gotten caught in this. Probably his fault he'd made her a target for a madman too.

He didn't believe she was an accomplice. He'd seen her face when she'd looked at that napkin. Shock. Fear. Disgust. No way could she have faked those emotions.

She shivered and turned her gaze up toward his. "Don't worry about it." Her throat moved as she swallowed. "We should make a run for it."

Yes, they should. But he liked having her trapped between his body and the wall. Her warmth soaked into his front and his gaze fell to her chest. The rain had drenched her shirt, and the material was plastered to her breasts, highlighting the lacy bra she wore beneath. It was similar to the one he'd taken off of her last night.

"Dylan?"

He couldn't seem to help himself. He wanted one more taste of her. That was all.

"Dylan, we —"

He swallowed the words on her lips. His mouth moved over hers, his tongue dipping inside and tasting her sweet nectar. She tasted like sweet tea and something else. Something he could stand there for hours enjoying.

Her fingers gripped his hair and pulled him down into her. She was enjoying herself too. It was madness. They barely knew each other, but he wanted this woman more than anything. Her warmth was like a drug. He couldn't stop thinking about when he'd get his next fix. Heaven help him, he wanted more. And so did she. He didn't even have to ask to know that. Maybe if he got her out of his system, he could focus on his job. Maybe even catch this twisted sonofabitch.

He pulled back to catch his breath. "Stay with me tonight." He hadn't meant to whisper the plea, but it slipped out anyway. He wanted her close. He needed to make sure she was safe.

"Yes."

No hesitation. Excitement surged through his veins. "Your place is closer. We'll make a run for it. Ready?"

She nodded. Her dark eyes and languid expression told him that, oh yeah, she was more than ready.

Thunder crackled in the distance as they raced hand-in-hand to her door. Alexandra struggled to dig her room key from her purse. Her hands were shaking, from the rain or nerves or excitement, he had no idea. He took the keycard from her and pushed them quickly inside.

"You know, Dylan, we—"

"Stop talking." He grabbed her by her hips and pulled her front against his. Man, they were both drenched. He nibbled at her mouth, dipped his tongue inside and tasted her again. "We need to get you out of these wet clothes."

"Oh, and you're going to leave yours on? I don't think so." Her hands reached up and shoved his jacket over his shoulders. The material bunched around his elbows, and she tightened her grip, tugging him closer. Her lips crashed into his, and he chuckled. She wanted to be in charge? He was good with that. More than good. Her mouth was hot as it moved against his. She opened for him, and he deepened the kiss. Her hips moved against his in a way that felt positively indecent.

Urgency racked his body. His blood thrummed with the demand that he possess this woman. He wanted inside her. Needed to feel her come apart in his arms. Needed a reminder that not everything in the world was messed up.

He slung his damp jacket away, the arms pulled inside out, and watched her do the same before reaching for her. His fingers dug her shirt out of her jeans and slid against warm, slick skin. So smooth. He tugged the shirt over her head and tossed it aside before claiming her lips again. His hands dipped down to her ass and pressed her hard against him while he feasted on her lips. His erection was so tight it was painful.

Could she feel how hard he was against her? He adjusted so that his leg was between hers, pressing up. She pushed down against his thigh, squeezed against him. He sucked in a breath.

She ripped her mouth away, buried her head in his neck and made the sweetest whimpering sound he'd ever heard. Oh, yeah.

She wanted this just as much as he did.

He walked her backwards until her legs bumped against the sofa and she fell back onto the cushions. They could climb upstairs to the bed later. He took a few seconds to get rid of his clothes while she watched his striptease with dark, greedy eyes. Wearing only her bra and jeans, she looked like sin incarnate, lying there watching him, licking her delicious lips. He tugged her jeans over her hips, down her legs and threw them behind him. A splat sounded as the wet denim hit the wall. She chuckled as he crawled between her thighs—thighs that opened easily at his gentle touch.

"Someone's in a hurry."

"Only to get you naked." He trailed one hand down her chest, bypassing her bra for her panties. His fingers teased a path around her hip and back again, slid beneath the material and slowly tugged them down, letting his fingers dip inside her folds along the way, just enough to tease her. His tongue tasted her skin as he worked the material off her hips, down her legs, and flung them aside. He hadn't gotten nearly familiar enough with her body last night. As he recalled it, she seemed to like it when he licked around her nipples. This bra simply would not do for that.

"That wasn't a complaint," she said as she tried to move against him. Her voice was husky. Needy.

He pressed her down with his body and devoured her lips while his hands made short work of the bra. She made that soft whimpering sound again when his fingers cupped her breasts and played with the mounds, lifting them so his lips could enjoy them the way they both wanted.

She adjusted beneath him, tangled one of her naked thighs around his, slid her hand down between their bodies and wrapped her fingers around him, tried to press him into her. He sucked in a breath. He'd come too fast if she kept doing that.

He grabbed her wrist and pulled her hand away. "You can play later. Now it's my turn."

Before she could argue, he slid his hand down and stroked through her curls with two fingers. Her hands clutched at his biceps as her hips moved against him. Up and down he explored, finally pushing into her tightness. Her muscles squeezed him as he started to move with deep glides, up and down, teasing her depth a little more with each push.

"Please, Dylan."

He liked hearing her say his name like this. He caught her gasps with his mouth as her orgasm approached. He felt it build inside her like a vortex until she trembled beneath him, her muscles in spasm around his fingers as she jerked her head away and cried out.

He gave her a moment to recover while he made a quick search for the condom in his wallet. Sheathing himself, he settled back between her thighs and wasted no time sinking into her, knowing she would be more than ready for him.

"Sweet heaven, Dylan." She grabbed his shoulders and met his thrust. "You're too darned good at this."

This time he was the one to make a sound, groaning as she squeezed him deeper. She was so snug. So hot. Over and over he pounded into her, slow at first, then faster as she got used to him being inside her again. Her fingers left his shoulders and tangled in his hair as she pulled his mouth down to hers, even as her legs wrapped around his hips and held on for the ride. He'd wanted to give them both pleasure, but he didn't think he could hold on long enough. She felt too damn good. He tore his mouth away and groaned into her neck as his own release spilled out.

He didn't realize until after he came that so had she. Her cry of pleasure had been soft, but unmistakable in his ear.

He'd made her come twice. He felt pretty pleased with himself.

"Dylan?" Her voice was still raspy when she finally spoke again.

"Hmmm?" He kissed her shoulder and rolled so that his weight was off of her. Already, sleep nibbled at his mind.

"We need to talk."

Why did women always want to talk after sex? He pulled her close and was trying to get them both more comfortable on the sofa when she said, "That napkin," bringing him back to the present. "He wanted me to see it."

"Shhh."

Just a couple of hours of sleep was all he wanted now. As long as she was in his arms, she was safe. He didn't have the energy to think about anything else.

***

Alexandra awoke with a start.

Glancing down, she saw that she was dressed again and not in her bed. She was half-lying on the floor of…what was this place? This was some kind of stage. A theater, maybe? She knocked against the wooden floor. It was solid, but no sound came from the movement.

She was dreaming.

Pushing herself to her feet, she glanced out at the rows of seats facing her. Her heart gave a quick jump in her chest when she saw a man standing in the back. He was too far away and too hidden in shadows to see his face, but she recognized his shape.

The man from the bar.

The killer.

And he was watching her.

This is a dream. This is only a dream. He can't hurt you.

She needed to see his face. Needed something to give Dylan so he could catch this guy. She climbed from the stage and moved toward him. He waited until she was about twelve feet away to turn and move through a set of doors. Following him, she couldn't help but note the beautiful architecture of the building. It looked like something out of *Gone With the Wind*. As she entered what seemed to be a large, spacious lobby, she also noticed the darkness outside the windows. It was nighttime here.

The man quickly moved up a grand set of stairs. The soft carpet beneath her feet had a pattern lined with red. The man passed the second landing and continued up. There were three floors, she realized.

She followed him down a hallway, passed a large mirror that didn't show her reflection. She stopped and watched as he hesitated outside of a doorway. The door was brown. The trim around it was white, and the wall was red.

So much red.

The man glanced over his shoulder as if he felt Alexandra behind him. His face was still too shadowed for her to see his features. The hall was only lit by the dim glow of streetlights pouring through the windows outside.

Alexandra moved closer.

The man faced forward again and pushed into the room. He quickly shut the door behind him. Alexandra hurried to follow, but the door handle wouldn't turn for her. She slammed a fist against the solid wood and groaned in frustration.

A woman's muffled scream shattered the silence.

Alexandra jerked awake, chest heaving, blurry eyes struggling to focus. Beside her, Dylan mumbled and turned on his side.

She was awake. This was real.

And so was the feeling of dread heavy in her stomach.

Chapter Seven

Dylan's fingertips touched cold, bare wood instead of the magazines and junk that cluttered his nightstand. Had his alarm clock moved? He slapped his hand around the space, trying to muffle the sound of his radio.

"Eh-hem."

Warm fingers caught his and shoved something hard and cold into his palm.

His phone. Scrambling to sit up, he managed to take the call before his voicemail snagged it. "Collins."

Alexandra lifted her eyebrows and smiled as she cast a slow glance over his naked parts not covered by the sheets, then turned and moved away from the bed. He wiped a hand over his face. He distantly remembered trudging up the stairs and tumbling with her into her bed at some point.

She had clothes on. Pajamas. When did that happen? How long had he been sleeping?

There was no sunlight, only the dim glow of a lamp in the corner. Still dark outside. The aroma of coffee aroused his taste buds and helped pull him further out of his fog.

"Where've you been?" Reedus said. "I thought you were gonna call me to check on what we found at the bar."

The glowing red numbers on the bedside clock told him it was a little after midnight. About four hours had passed. He'd been sleeping heavy, too. "Sorry. I've been, uh, tied up with something."

Alexandra, who had curled up in a chair in the corner, cup of coffee in hand, smirked a little as she raised the mug to her lips and sipped.

"I'll bet." Reedus coughed and Dylan recognized the hiss and pop of a beer can being opened. "She wouldn't happen to be blonde, would she? Talks to dead people in her spare time? Did she tie you up or did you tie her up?"

"You're hilarious, Reedus." Dylan cleared his throat and shifted into a more comfortable position on the bed. Last thing he needed was word getting around he was sleeping with a consultant. He rubbed at his eyes. "What did you find?"

"Not a damn thing. Did you question the bartender when you were there?"

"Not for very long. Why?"

"He noticed the suspect was wearing those tight surgical gloves when he handed him his beer, so our suspect came prepared. No prints. Nothing."

"Wonder if the killer's OCD." Dylan brushed the hair back from his forehead and sat up, tossing his legs over the side of the bed and wondering where his pants were. "Can we get the bartender in with a sketch artist tomorrow?"

"Got him coming in at 10 a.m. *today*. You gonna be there, or are you still gonna be tied up with your girlfriend?"

Jackass. "I'll be there, don't you worry." Dylan ended the call and tossed his phone onto the bed. He spotted his pants hanging beside hers on the stair railing. She must have carried them up at some point. Stepping into them, he sent Alexandra a sideways look. Still curled up drinking her coffee. And smirking.

"Hey there."

"Hey." She arched an eyebrow at him. "Have a good nap?"

"And then some." He gestured toward her mug. "Got any extra?"

"Help yourself." She nodded toward a small coffee pot on the counter outside the bathroom. "I don't think I have any lids though. I'm sure you need to get home."

He plucked his shirt from the railing. "I could use a shower." Later, he decided. He needed a change of clothes more.

She tilted her head and watched him. Her eyes sparkled with interest as he shrugged into his shirt. "Are you married?"

He chuckled. "You wait until *now* to ask me that?"

"Excuse me. You're my first one-night stand. I'm not exactly sure what I'm supposed to say or do here."

He was glad to hear it. "I don't think so, baby."

"What?"

"I'm not your first one-night stand." He nodded toward her bed. "By definition, we're at least a two-night stand now."

She blew out her breath. "Next thing you know, we'll be living together."

He loved her sense of humor. He leaned down and tasted her lips, licking at the flavor of coffee she left on his mouth. "I could probably be convinced."

"Oh, really?"

"Do you do laundry?"

She mock kicked him in the shin. Chuckling, he fingered the sleeve of the silky pink pajama top she wore and wondered how fast he could get her out of it. "When did you get dressed?"

She shrugged. "An hour ago, maybe."

"Why?" He straightened and moved to the coffee pot. Her sigh carried across the room and mixed with the sound of the liquid pouring into one of the paper cups the hotel provided.

"I had a nightmare."

"Sorry. You had quite a scare earlier. That would do it for me."

He turned in plenty of time to see her rolling her eyes. "I don't have nightmares the way most people do, Dylan." She sat her empty mug aside. "I think I had a vision of the next murder."

Every muscle in his body tightened into painful awareness of what her words meant. The next murder. "It's already happened?"

She shook her head. "I don't know. Sometimes when I dream things, it's precognitive. Other times, it's already happened. I really have no way of knowing until after the fact."

Did he believe her or assume she was still trying to con him? Dylan knew the moment had come for him to make that choice. And it was a lot harder to do now that he'd gotten to know her better. And slept with her. Again.

He leaned back against the counter and took a sip of his coffee. He supposed there was no harm in giving her the benefit of the doubt. "What did you see in your dream?"

***

Alexandra wondered if Dylan was just humoring her again, or if he'd finally decided to be open minded about what she was capable of and what she could do for his investigation. Either way, nothing would change what she'd seen.

So she told him everything she could remember. Every detail down to the red walls and patterned carpet.

His brow furrowed as he listened, and he shifted so he could cross his arms. That was the classic I'm-Not-Giving-You-A-Chance stance she was used to from most men. But then he said, "That sounds like the Dock Street Theater."

Her shoulders relaxed on a sigh as Alexandra realized she'd been expecting the worst from him. He'd surprised her. That didn't happen often.

He moved to retrieve his phone, and she took the chance to wash her mug in the bathroom sink. She listened as he called and asked an officer on duty to go and check the theater for any signs of disturbance. When she re-emerged, he was sitting on the bed, putting his shoes on.

"I need to run to my place and get a few things. It'll just take a few minutes."

She crossed her arms and leaned against the wall. "You're coming back?" The idea sent a thrill of happiness dancing along her spine.

"Yeah, I'm coming back." He reached for his jacket and shrugged into it. "I thought we could go over some files since we're awake and will probably stay that way now that we've got caffeine in our blood."

Of course. His return was work-related. She should have known that. Idiot.

He closed the space between them, tugged her hard against him, and nipped at her mouth. Flames of arousal immediately licked through her body as her hands rested on his arms. How had this frustrating cop reduced her to one of those women who went weak at the knees with one kiss? Figure that one out.

"I don't like what I saw on that napkin. I doubt the captain would let me place a patrol on your hotel, so I'm keeping an eye on you until we either catch this guy or you leave town."

He pressed her hips into his and her mouth ran dry. She licked her lips. "I don't need a bodyguard."

"You've got one anyway." His look was wolfish as he stared at her mouth. "We'll discuss my payment later."

That sounded promising. "I'm aware you still haven't answered my question."

"What question?"

"Whether you're married or not."

"I wouldn't be here if I was." He frowned as he pulled away. "No girlfriend either. Just a stray cat I feed every now and then when she wanders up to my door."

She was glad to know her intuition was still on target there. "If it matters to you," she held up a bare hand, "neither am I."

His eyes danced with humor as he started down the stairs, keeping his focus on her. "I know."

She crossed her arms and leaned over the loft wall to watch him leave. "How do you know?"

"Background check." He rattled the doorknob as he squeezed through the door. "Make sure this locks behind me. I'll be back in ten minutes tops."

***

The Grim Reaper—that's how he thought of himself these days—glanced at the clock above his television and pressed the channel up button again on his remote control. It was almost time for the morning news. He hadn't slept all night, anticipating the Live 5 News logo and a quick lead into a breaking news segment. Almost time. His fingers drummed the padded armchair in excitement.

Would they call him the Reaper or the Grim Reaper? Reporters liked brevity, but he hoped they didn't shorten his moniker too much.

A soft thud outside his front door stirred his excitement in a different direction. Ah, the newspaper. He hurried to retrieve the Post and Courier, expecting to see a large headline taking up much of the front page. *Serial killer targets Charleston*. He hoped it was something like that. He liked the way that sounded.

Shutting the door behind him, he opened the paper and felt dumbfounded when the main headline read *S.C.'s jobless rate falls to 8.6% in September*. He quickly skimmed through all the pages, then skimmed again.

Where was the story about *him*?

He urged himself to calm down. Maybe Collins hadn't been

able to reach the newspaper by its deadline. Maybe the cop had decided to skip the newspaper altogether and give the TV news an exclusive.

Yes, that's probably what it was.

The chime of the newscast's theme song interrupted his thoughts and drew his attention to the television. This was it. The moment he'd planned everything for.

That pretty brunette he liked appeared on the screen. She must have been filling in for Margaret, the usual morning anchor.

"Good morning, Charleston. I'm Stephanie Rodriguez in for Margaret Dolan who is on vacation today. This morning police are searching for two men they say robbed a convenience store in Goose Creek and left a store employee fighting for his life."

What? The Grim Reaper turned the channel to another local news station. The male anchor was rattling off details about the same story.

He'd been trumped by armed robbers?

He settled back in his recliner and waited, feeling his blood simmer as each story became even more mundane and stupid. By the time the weather segment began, the truth was slowly sinking in.

Collins hadn't done as he'd demanded and revealed his presence to the news reporters.

Asshole.

Slamming his fist on the side of the chair, he stood and headed for his special room. The young cop wasn't going to cooperate. That's fine. But Collins would regret this.

They all would.

**

Dylan shut the door to his captain's office behind him and rubbed

96

his eyes.

Already he was getting pressure from the last murder victim's well-connected family to bring in a suspect. As if it were so easy.

He'd been going over the case files half the night with Alexandra and didn't have a clue who this killer was, or why he was doing this.

His thoughts went back to what Alexandra had said yesterday. *Copycat. He's fascinated by death.* She'd said the guy loved slasher films and got excited watching them.

If she was right, he should be looking at half the whackos that lived in Charleston. It was that copycat suggestion that worried him most. Were there two killers, or was one killer copying crimes from another city?

He'd asked Reedus to run a comparison through the system. The results wouldn't be back for a few more hours.

Alexandra was kneading the tension out of her shoulders when he made it back into the conference room where he'd left her with the case's files. He'd had to check his email and voicemail and follow up with a few calls on the other cases in his log. Then Capt. Deveraux had wanted an update.

"Sorry to leave you for so long." He poured them each a cup of coffee and then handed one to her. He wished he could massage some of the tension away for her, but he didn't dare touch her where he could be seen by his co-workers. He'd make it up to her later, in private. "Have you had any more clues or visions or whatever it is you do?"

She arched an eyebrow at him and pointed at a photo of the last crime scene. "Can we go here? I might be able to pick up on something there. There's something about this location that's significant to the killer." She flipped through another file. "Actually, all of the locations are significant. I just don't know how yet."

"Sure. Let me see if Reedus can send that sketch to my phone as soon as it's done. Give me five minutes."

Reedus was at his desk playing solitaire on the computer. Nice. Dylan tapped the back of his chair and perched on the edge of the desk. "You're busy."

"I'm waiting on results and a sketch artist to finish his job. Leave me alone." Reedus frowned at Dylan, but his eyes followed something behind Dylan, all the way toward the captain's door. "Why do I get the feeling that's not a good sign?"

Dylan turned and saw a familiar figure in a pantsuit step into the captain's office. He'd recognize Stephanie Rodriguez's sleek brown hair and feminine figure anywhere.

Dylan muttered a curse.

Rodriguez was a fierce reporter he likened to a terrier with a bone. Once she caught scent of the marrow, she became a serious pain in the ass to get rid of.

He'd also dated her for a few weeks after moving here, and she'd taken that as an okay to hound him for information on stories whenever a big one came his way.

She turned and pointed at him through the glass office, caught him looking and smiled.

He swore again.

The captain also caught his gaze and waved him forward.

Dylan glanced toward the conference room and took a deep breath. Alexandra would have to wait a few more minutes.

As soon as he neared the captain's office, he could hear Stephanie saying, "And I understand you've consulted a psychic, too. I'd love to talk to her."

"Out of the question." The captain gestured for Dylan to close the door. "Detective Collins, we have a bit of a situation on our hands."

"What kind of situation?"

Stephanie cast him one of her cat-like appraisals. "I got a very interesting call after my newscast this morning, Dylan. I have it recorded, and I plan to air it on tonight's newscast. I wanted to be courteous and give you a head's up."

A phone call? Dylan crossed his arms and glanced at the captain. The man was stone-faced.

"Ever heard of The Grim Reaper?" Stephanie asked and watched him close for a reaction.

Dylan shrugged. "Hasn't everyone?"

"Tell me this. Does Charleston have a serial killer on the loose? Is that who killed Councilman Burke's niece? Because I have a pretty convincing guy on tape claiming responsibility for her death and two more. He also said more would come, and you've consulted with a famous psychic on his case. Does any of that ring a bell, Dylan?"

"We want to hear the call," Capt. Deveraux said. "It's potential evidence in a criminal investigation."

She reached into her bag and pulled out a digital voice recorder. "I let you listen to this, you give me an exclusive on the story. Deal?"

"Or we could arrest you for withholding evidence," Dylan countered.

Her smile broadened. "Our attorney would have me out in time for tonight's news, and you know it."

Dylan wanted to warn the captain Stephanie's producer would never let her air the recorded phone call without more evidence to go on—frustrating woman was calling their bluff to dig for more information—but his superior sighed and reached out a hand.

"We give you an exclusive on the terms that you only release the information we want released. You got that?"

"I can do that." Stephanie dropped the recorder in the captain's palm and then winked at Dylan. "All you have to do is hit play."

The captain set the recorder on the desk, adjusted the volume and pressed the button. Stephanie's voice answered with a professional greeting. In the same distorted voice Dylan remembered from yesterday, a man said, "I murdered Candice Christopher, Gerard Nicolby and Jennifer Bradley, and I will murder more people by the week's end. My name is The Grim Reaper and I want people to know I'm out there, stalking the streets of Charleston."

There was a static-filled pause. Finally Stephanie answered, "I'm sorry. Who is this?"

"I told you my name. I want you to tell the people of Charleston there's a serial killer on the loose."

"Listen, pal. I'm a serious reporter. If there was a serial killer in Charleston, I'd know about it. I don't know what kind of hoax this is, but it's not a very funny one."

The call ended.

Stephanie reached for the recorder. "I hung up on him. He called me back not even ten seconds later."

"If you hang up on me again, I'll gut you like a pig." The Reaper's distorted voice was calm, which made it all the more menacing. "Call Detective Dylan Collins with the North Charleston Police Department. He knows who I am. He was supposed to let all of the news outlets know about me. Because he didn't, I'm taking matters into my own hands."

"Detective Collins?"

"Yes, your old boyfriend."

Dylan's gaze jerked to Stephanie's. How did this guy know their history?

"Did Dylan put you up to this?" Stephanie's voice changed. "I get it. He's playing a prank. Ha ha. Not funny."

"This isn't a joke." The caller breathed hard into the phone. "I positioned Candice Christopher's body. The police didn't tell you that, did they? Why don't you ask them how I positioned her, and ask them why they're so afraid of me that they called in Alexandra King to consult on my case? I'm very happy they did. I'd like you to give her a message for me."

100

"Who is Alexandra King?"

"Don't disrespect her by pretending you don't know who she is!" The calm was gone, replaced by barely controlled anger. Heavy breathing. Then, calm again. "Please tell her I'm glad she's here, and I look forward to playing with her."

Click.

Silence filled the room.

Stephanie reached across the desk and retrieved her recorder. "Now why don't you gentlemen begin by telling me what that was all about. And better yet, why did you bring in a psychic?"

Chapter Eight

Dylan had been gone for a lot longer than she'd expected.

Alexandra pushed out of her chair and paced the room, eager to exercise her limbs and exorcise the kinks that had worked their way into her muscles from sitting most of the night and morning.

She wandered over to the door and peeked into the department's work area. No sooner had she spotted Dylan than Reedus scared the crap out of her by barking in her ear, "Got the sketch back from the witness at the bar. Wanna take a quick look at it and tell me if you recognize him?"

Dylan's partner must have been standing right outside the conference room door. He shoved an 8x10 drawing in front of her before she had time to calm her racing heartbeat.

The man in the drawing looked average and completely unknown to her. A dark stocking hat covered his hair, and his eyes were shadowed.

"Doesn't look familiar to me. Sorry." She handed it back to him. "Who's that in there with Detective Collins?"

"A shark in high heels." He coughed and pulled out a handkerchief, wiped his mouth. "Stephanie Rodriguez. TV news reporter. If she's here, she's probably figured out something to do with this guy. Can't be good." Reedus puffed up his chest. "Guess I'd better throw myself into the feeding frenzy. We'll need her help distributing this. Wish me luck."

Alexandra smiled and watched as he went to the small office, knocked, shuffled inside and handed the captain the sketch.

"He likes the attention."

Alexandra's heartbeat, her whole body, jumped at the unexpected voice behind her. Turning slowly, she swallowed and stared at Rebecca Collins with wide eyes. Dylan's mother did not look like she normally did. She looked haggard and dirty.

Reaching behind her to shut the door, Alexandra asked, "Where have you been? I've been worried I did something to you."

Rebecca's eyes were dark and unfocused. As if she were in a trance. "I've been—" She shook her head, dazed. "Hiding from him."

"Who?"

Rebecca looked down, confused. "I don't know." Finally, she looked at Alexandra and her eyes were lighter, clearer, more normal. "He doesn't want me to help you. He doesn't want any of us to help you."

"Who's he?"

"I don't know. I just know he's dangerous. I know you and Dylan are both in danger now." Rebecca rubbed at her temples. "Why can't I remember clearly?"

Good question. Was she talking about the man calling himself The Grim Reaper?

He's fascinated by death.

Alexandra considered all she'd learned about this case and weighed it in her mind.

"Is he playing around with black magic? The occult?" That might explain it, or some of it.

Rebecca still looked a little dazed. "Yes. I think that's it."

Alexandra took in the spirit's strange appearance and thought back to how poorly she herself had been feeling since she'd arrived in Charleston. "Whatever the killer's messing with could be affecting us both." Black magic was not something Alexandra knew much about. She described the gray beams she saw shooting toward the sky every time she neared her hotel. "Rebecca, do you know what that is?"

"No, but I like to be near it. It makes me feel…strong. Alive."

An ache began forming at the base of her skull, so Alexandra tried to massage it away. This was all so confusing.

She would tell Dylan to check with any occult stores in the city, have him ask about regular clients. Maybe their killer had consulted with other psychics here. Maybe he was working with one. She got the feeling he was the type to be drawn to psychics.

He certainly seemed drawn to her.

"Where's my son?" Rebecca asked.

"In the other room. He's fine." She opened the blinds on the office window so Rebecca could see. Young ghosts could not see through things the way older ones could.

Rebecca visibly relaxed, then tensed again. "Don't tell me he's with *her* again." The disdain in the older woman's voice was sharp.

"Who?"

"That woman." The ghost pointed through the blinds. "She didn't love him the way he deserved. My little boy can do better."

"Oh." Ohhhh. Rebecca meant that Dylan and the reporter had been—"I see." She closed the blinds and moved away from the door.

A hot poker of jealousy seared at Alexandra's gut, but what sense did that make? She didn't have a claim on Dylan. So what if they were sleeping together? It was only temporary.

Which reminded her. How much had Rebecca seen of Dylan and Alexandra since she'd been here?

"Rebecca, have you been watching me this whole time?"

The older woman frowned. "No. Not always. It's like sometimes there's this wall I can't get beyond, like you're pushing me away. Other times, I've been hiding. I go check on Zachary."

"Hiding from who?"

The door to the room pushed open, startling Alexandra again. She normally wasn't this jumpy. What was that about? She blew out a breath and forced a smile for the man they'd been discussing.

Dylan stepped into the room and closed the door behind him. He looked unhappy. "Sorry. Change of plans."

"No problem. Anything I should be worried about?"

He shook his head but his sour expression didn't change. "Something I should worry about." He turned away from her and rubbed at his forehead. "The media has gotten wind of this. They know about you. They know about the link between the killings."

"They? Or she?"

He turned back toward her. "You saw?"

She shrugged. "I saw enough."

"The killer called Stephanie Rodriguez. She's the reporter who came to us. I wouldn't be surprised if he didn't call others. I guess we'll find out soon enough."

"He likes the attention," Alexandra repeated Rebecca's earlier words and glanced toward where the ghost had been standing. She was gone again.

"Yeah, I think so." Dylan took a deep breath. "He told her your name. He even got angry when she didn't know who you were, as if he were insulted on your behalf."

"You're kidding." It wasn't like she was some famous mystic or something. She'd been featured on a handful of TV shows in very minor capacity. Nothing to write home about. Certainly not enough to pay the bills. "I got some information from the other side while you were gone. I don't know if it'll pan out, but I think the killer has been dabbling in the occult, and not in a good way. I'd suggest checking with local stores to see if anyone suspicious turns up."

"Should be easy enough. We only have a few." He half smiled. "Makes sense. He left a tarot card at the last crime scene. Thanks. I'll check on it."

There was a knock on the door and Reedus stuck his head in. "Collins, there's a guy out here wants to talk to you about the Christopher case and the alley murder."

"Both of them?"

"Seems to think there's a connection." Reedus lifted his eyebrows. "Want me to send him in here?"

Dylan met Alexandra's startled look. "Yeah."

The man that walked into the room a minute later reminded Alexandra of a lumberjack. With shaggy auburn hair and a full, neatly trimmed beard, he wore jeans, a flannel shirt, a faded old sports coat, and was about the size of an ox. One of his giant hands was curled around some sort of book.

He reached across and engulfed Dylan's hand with his free one. "I'm Jason Murray, a professor of history at the College of Charleston."

"Detective Dylan Collins." Dylan pointed to Alexandra behind him. "This is—"

"Wow." The professor's eyes lit up with excitement as he stared at her. "You're a psychic medium." He snapped his fingers before reaching across to shake her hand. "I've seen you on TV."

He had? Alexandra uncrossed her arms and stepped forward, forcing a smile. She felt Dylan's gaze watching her. "I should come to Charleston more often. People know me here." She shook the man's hand. "Alexandra King."

"Right. You were on that show. Um, what was it called?" He tapped the side of his head.

Don't say The Psychic Detective. Say something else.

"Sixty Minutes." Her voice was a desperate rush. "I was on Sixty

106

Minutes once. Everyone recognizes me from that."

The man nodded slightly but looked confused. "It was—"

"Sorry to be curt, Mr. Murray, but why is it you wanted to speak with me?" Dylan inserted, pulling out a chair for the man. He gestured for her to take a seat across from him. "I've got an appointment I need to keep in a few minutes."

"Sorry." The lumberjack professor shuffled awkwardly into the chair. "I'm not sure it's even relevant, but a few of the other tour guides and I have been speculating on ideas since that young woman was murdered in the cemetery. I decided one of us should probably come forward and tell you our theory."

Alexandra glanced at Dylan. His eyes were narrowed. His lips were pursed. "What other tour guides?"

"Sorry." The man laughed softly and scooted closer to the table. "I own a ghost tour company, you know, something on the side, and sometimes after tours the guides from all the companies will get together for a beer and chat."

Dylan nodded. "Go on."

Alexandra focused on the burly man sitting across from her. He slid the book he'd been carrying across the table and tapped his hand on the cover, almost protectively. "I started my tours 12 years ago, after I wrote my first book about the ghosts of Charleston. Now there are at least four other ghost tour companies here." He reached up and scratched his beard. "Point is, if you're looking for an expert on the city's history or its alleged ghosts, I'm your guy."

A sudden image of the word PIRATE flashed in Alexandra's vision, and she said, "You know a lot about pirates."

Murray slid even closer to the table and smiled at her. "Yes. You've read my book?"

No, I think I'm reading the dead person attached to you.

She shrugged. "No, sorry."

"Oh." He looked at Dylan. "She's right. I talk about pirates a lot on my tour." He reached for his book and began flipping through pages. "When that man was found murdered in the alley off State Street, it caught my attention. That's one of the stops we do most nights. See?" He spread the book open, slid it toward Dylan, and tapped at an illustration underneath the heading *The Ghost of Black Billy*. The illustration was almost identical to the crime scene photo Dylan had in his files. A pirate lay sprawled in a half sitting position, his back slumped against the building wall, his legs spread eagle in front of him, a dagger sticking from his chest. "That's not the only one."

Dylan pulled the book closer. "What do you mean, not the only one?"

The professor stood, reached across the table, and flipped to another page. "The cemetery where the woman was found dead a couple of days ago." He stopped on a page and tapped. "The Crying Woman's Ghost. It's one of the stops on our tour. Not always, but sometimes. We like to change things up for repeat customers. Keep it fresh, you know?"

A black and white photograph seemed to show a transparent woman leaning over a grave, sobbing. Alexandra blinked and felt disoriented. The sound of weeping was as loud as if the woman were doing so in Alexandra's ear now.

"What's her story?" she asked.

"Jasmine Carter. She lost her husband and her two year old son to the Spanish influenza in 1919 and was so grief stricken, she climbed to the church's bell tower and flung herself off. She landed in a twisted mess on one of the graves. To this day there are sightings of her roaming the same cemetery. Usually, people hear her crying."

Poor woman.

Twisted mess. Alexandra thought back to the crime scene photos of Candice Christopher's body. It had been positioned in a twisted

108

mess in that same cemetery.

Copycat.

It made sense now.

"When did you get the idea all of these were related?" Dylan demanded, his voice taut with something she couldn't describe.

"Yesterday, when I read about that girl's body being found in the cemetery. Plus, there was an officer sitting there last night and none of the tours could go through. The same thing happened last month with the alley. It all got some of us to thinking. I don't know if it's related, but that woman who hung herself in the gardens at The Battery a few months ago, that spot is on the tour, too."

Dylan reached for the book, held it up. "Can I keep this?"

"Sure." Murray's chest suddenly seemed a little bigger.

"Great." Dylan glanced at Alexandra then back to the man again. "Think you can make me a list of all the stops on your tour? Any of the ghost tours, actually."

Murray sank into his seat again, seemingly happy to help. "Got any paper and a pen?"

Alexandra was bursting to talk to Dylan about this in private but the professor took his sweet time, listing about twenty stops when all was said and done. As she watched the man's large hand scribble names and streets that made no sense to her, one of the locations on the list jumped out at Alexandra.

The Dock Street Theater.

That feeling of oh-my-gosh-this-is-really-happening disoriented Alexandra for a few seconds. It always did, no matter how many times her information proved accurate or began to tie together in any way that made sense. She was always a little bit surprised.

Judging by Dylan's reaction when the man left, so was he. He released a ragged breath and looked a bit shell-shocked as he rubbed at the back of his neck. A cloud of disbelief floated across his features. "I feel like I've stepped into a freaking episode of

The X-Files or something. Am I seriously chasing a guy who kills people because he's obsessed with ghosts?"

Alexandra moved to her feet. "Not ghosts, I don't think. Death."

Dylan held up his hands. "That's supposed to be better?" He brushed past her and reached for her jacket. "Lunch is on me, then we'll go visit those occult stores you mentioned earlier. Maybe you can help me decipher all of that mystic crap I'm sure they're gonna spout me."

"Mystic crap?" She slid her arms into the coat he held out for her.

"All of that devil crap." He swore. "Tarot cards. Psychics. You know."

A tiny zing of hurt raced through her chest at his words. Maybe she'd been wrong in thinking he had decided to be more open-minded, at least where she was concerned.

"Devil crap?" Disbelief tinted her voice. Was he trying to imply something about her faith? "My family happens to be very religious, Dylan. My grandfather was a Catholic priest."

"Mine was a preacher. I'm pretty sure he always said not to dabble in the occult." There was no malice in his tone. He sounded matter of fact.

She wasn't going to fight with him on the subject. She knew she'd never win. People feared what they didn't understand. It was a mindset she came up against all too often in society, and one that always stung.

Her grandma had taught her to arm herself with knowledge and ignore the bigots who condemned her for the ability she couldn't control.

Still. That didn't stop her from glaring at Dylan as she tugged her long hair from the collar of her jacket. Oh, how she would love to mention his brother right now, but she couldn't.

And just like that, her anger dulled. Because she still hadn't told him the real reason she was in Charleston.

"You okay? You look kind of pale all of a sudden."

"Yeah." She pretended to straighten her clothes so she didn't have to look at him. "Let's eat. I'm starved."

But when she looked up, Dylan's attention was on something else. He swore, so she followed his gaze to the television situated in the corner of the bureau. At least a couple of uniformed officers were standing, staring up at the midday news.

The sketch that had been drawn this morning was shown with *Serial Killer in Charleston?* on top of it. Someone turned the volume up so the anchor's voice could be heard saying, "An unknown male contacted our news station this morning with a message for the city's residents. The man who called himself The Grim Reaper claimed responsibility for the death of 22-year-old Candice Christopher, niece of City Councilman Charles Burke, 34-year-old Gerard Nicolby, and 26-year-old Jennifer Bradley, and promised more murders can be expected. The North Charleston Police Department could not be reached for comment."

"Collins! My office!"

The command from Dylan's captain was expected, but Alexandra still winced in sympathy for the man at her side.

Dylan's chest heaved beneath a sigh. "There's a deli around the corner that delivers. Emily at the front desk can give you the number. Order me a turkey sandwich on wheat and whatever you want. This is probably gonna take a while." His hand squeezed her arm in apology as he pulled away. He glanced toward the TV and his expression fell again as he froze in place. His face lost all color.

Alexandra returned her attention to the television in time to see stock footage from the only episode she'd ever done of *The Psychic Detective* playing, with the words *Psychic called in to consult on case*.

The screen captured a perfect image of her and Zachary Collins standing together as they discussed evidence.

Well, crap.

111

Chapter Nine

A lot had happened in the last four hours and Dylan's brain hurt from trying to process it all. All hell had broken lose in the media. The captain had created a task force to calm the uproar that had followed. A brief press conference was held to announce the facts and address rumors already circulating among worried residents.

And Alexandra knew his freaking brother.

He wished he could wander back to his desk and pop one or two or five of the headache pills he kept there for days like this.

Then again, he couldn't remember a day like this.

He tried to focus on what the captain was saying to the small crowd assembled in the conference room and not on the woman sitting three seats away from him. Awareness lifted the hairs on the back of his neck and he knew Alexandra was watching him again. Tough luck. He wasn't ready to find out the full extent of her deception yet. It was too much. All of this. Too damn much.

"Detective Collins will be leading this task force." The mention of his name drew his attention back to his boss, standing at the front of the room. "Unfortunately, we're now under the scrutiny of the media and the public, but I have no doubt this team can track down this psychopath before he strikes again. We do have the privilege of a consultant on this case. Ms. King has already provided us with several leads to follow up on and which some of you will be assigned. I expect her to be treated with respect. Collins, do you have anything to add?"

About Alexandra? Hell no.

He stood and rubbed at the stabbing in his temple as he glanced around the room. His task force consisted of three uniformed officers he barely knew, the head of dispatch, Detective Reedus, and Alexandra. He wasn't counting the Deputy Chief who'd shown up to observe how things were progressing.

Placing his hands on his hips, Dylan took a deep breath and conjured up his best game face. "I've asked Emily to make copies of the sketch we have of the suspect as well as any other important documents from the files. Take those packets home. Study them. Work your beats. Ask your informants for help. Dispatch has also set up a special hotline for the public to call in with tips. We'll be dividing up the leads that seem most credible. I want to thank you all for your help in advance. We'll probably be putting in a lot of extra hours on this one, so if you have a problem with that, let me know now. Any questions?"

No one responded, so Dylan glanced at the list of names his captain had handed him thirty minutes ago. "Officer McCormick?"

A fresh-out-of-the-academy-looking young man raised his hand.

"I want a full background check on Jason Murray, a history professor at the College of Charleston. Talk to his colleagues. Find out if there's anything suspicious there worth looking into. Also, I want a complete list of all the companies operating ghost tours within the historic district. I want to know who the guides are and background checks on all of the employees. Find out if any of them have noticed repeat customers, anyone who has taken the same tour more than twice."

"Yes, sir."

He tapped his finger on the next name on the list. "Officer Graham. There's a list of tour stop locations in the packet you've been given. Follow up with the property owners to inquire about any suspicious activity or people they've noticed lately. Talk to the neighbors. Find out if there are any security cameras in those areas and what we need to do to get that footage. You get any leads, report to me or Reedus immediately, okay?"

The female officer—one of the older members of his team—nodded. "Absolutely."

"Finally, Officer Vinson." His gaze skirted over Alexandra as he hesitated in assigning the third officer his task. He'd worked with Vinson on a few cases. The man was a solid cop with ambitions to work homicide someday. "Our suspect seems to have a fascination with Ms. King, so I'm assigning you to her. I want a full background check on her and anyone she suggests, and I expect you to ensure her safety at all times. McCormick, you're his backup. You two can work out your schedules so that at least one of you has eyes on her until we catch this guy. Anything she needs to assist on this case, give it to her. Understood?"

Both officers chimed in "Yes, sir."

Dylan had never led a task force before—or been on one, for that matter. He'd expected pushback, maybe some grumbling from the older officers who thought he was too young and inexperienced to head the team but, so far, he'd gotten none. Even Reedus seemed happy to sit back and let him take the helm.

"Um, but—" Alexandra's muttered protest mixed with the shuffle of her pants sliding against the chair in which she sat. Dylan glanced in her direction and tried to keep the chill out of his voice. "Yes, Ms. King?"

Their gazes locked. Her jaw muscles clenched before she huffed through her nose. "Can I speak with you in private, Detective Collins?"

That was the last thing Dylan wanted.

Captain Deveraux stepped forward again. "I think we're done here for now. We'll meet back up for a status update tomorrow, two p.m. Thank you, officers. Let's catch this guy." He gestured for Reedus to follow the other members from the room. "We'll give you two some privacy." But the captain's narrow-eyed expression as his gaze darted from Alexandra and back to Dylan again suggested he knew their private conversation wouldn't be work-related.

Awesome.

Dylan waited until the door shut to even risk a look at the woman now standing too close for comfort. She knew his brother. She knew Zach and she never said a word. He didn't believe in coincidences. She had to know the connection between him and Zach. The hot rush of anger filled his veins again. Did she have any idea how much control it was taking for him to keep his cool?

She said absolutely nothing for so long, the silence caused the air to feel even thicker.

"Well?" He forced himself to meet her gaze.

"Call me crazy, but you've been avoiding me all afternoon. Why?"

She was kidding, right? "You didn't mention you knew the great Zachary Collins."

Her throat moved. "Dylan, I should have told you the first day I came here that I knew your brother."

"Damn straight." His mouth pulled into a half smile, which tugged at the pain at his temple. "How is Zach? Still an asshole?"

"Eh. He grows on you."

He doubted that. "He still playing at being a psychic, or is that a stupid question?"

She bit her bottom lip. "Dylan, your brother really *is* psychic."

"You forget I grew up with him. You can't feed me those kind of lies and expect me to believe them. I know better." There was

115

a lot more he wanted to say, but the fear of raising his voice so his co-workers could hear held him in check. Barely. "Did he send you here?"

"Zach has no idea I'm here." She sighed.

"Then why are you?" He stepped closer and lowered his voice. "Yeah, I figured out that whole spiel about coming to Charleston to find your friend's missing brother. You came here to find *me*. I get it. But why? What does he want? A kidney or something?" He drifted his eyes up and down her figure. "Did he think sending a hot blonde to sleep with me would win him brownie points? Please tell me you're not sleeping with him, too."

Her palm connected with his face hard, and stars exploded in his vision. His cheek stung like the devil. Damn. The woman knew how to deliver one hell of a slap. He'd give her that.

"Zach. Did. Not. Send. Me." Her eyes were wild now with anger and some other emotion he couldn't define. "Your mother pestered me until I gave in and tracked you down because your brother is as stubborn as you are and wouldn't do it. I am not sleeping with Zach, nor did I ever plan to sleep with you."

His attention caught and held on what she said before that last bit. "My mother?" Now she was just starting to sound crazy and desperate. He pushed his shoulders back. Met her gaze. "Lady, my mother died three years ago."

"Exactly."

Was she trying to say she had communicated with his mom beyond the grave? Uh uh. No way. The woman had just lost what little credibility she'd had left as far as he was concerned. He made to move past her. This conversation was over.

"She's here now."

His hand stilled on the doorknob.

"She said to tell you, 'The picture you've been looking for is in the trunk in the attic.'" She sighed, the sound carrying heavy in the air. "And she wants you to know she loves you very much."

Dylan let the words sink in, then pushed them aside. What picture? He had no idea what she was babbling about. He had a job to do.

He pushed the door open and chanced a look in her direction as he left the room. "Do us both a favor and leave town, Alexandra. You've done enough damage, don't you think?"

***

Alexandra didn't know which was worse.

The distraught ghost crying loudly in the chair beside her, making enough pitiful sounds to rival a soap opera diva, or the sour feeling deep in her chest—the one she hadn't felt since Grams had died.

Then her phone rang and, seeing the caller ID, she had a third option to throw into that mix.

Taking a deep breath, she answered, "Hey, Zach."

She leaned back in the chair and rubbed her eyes. Just as she'd feared. Some reporter had tracked down and contacted Zach for a comment about her. Not just any reporter. Stephanie Martinez, the shark in heels herself. Alexandra was tired of secrets, so she spent the next ten minutes telling her boss everything. Almost everything. She left out the part about Dylan being the lead detective and the reason she'd come to Charleston in the first place. She wasn't sure she could handle being reamed by Zach, too. Not right now.

Zach was quiet for several seconds. "I don't feel good about this." She imagined he was pacing his office. "Maybe you should cut your vacation short and come home where you'll be safe."

"What makes you think I'm not safe?"

"Gut feeling."

In the psychic arsenal department, Zachary Collins' gut feelings

117

were the equivalent of stealth bombers. You never saw them coming, and duds were rare.

Fantastic.

"I think you're overreacting. I'm fine."

"If you're telling me everything, and I don't think you are, I'm not overreacting."

Rebecca quieted her crying and leaned closer to Alexandra. "Is that my other son?"

"Yes." Alexandra shifted away from her.

"Yes? Yes, what? I'm not overreacting?" Zach said.

"No." Oh geez. She could only handle one conversation with a person at a time. "I've got a personal situation I need to deal with, and then maybe I'll come home. But not until I make things right."

"Am I supposed to know what you're talking about?"

"Zach, I'll keep you informed, okay? Just trust me."

Her boss surprised her by caving in fairly easy, which was a good thing, because Officer Terminator—seriously, Vinson reminded her of the robot guy from the second movie and had yet to smile—returned with a stack of papers in his hand. Background checks, no doubt.

"What did Zachary say? Is he all right?" Rebecca grabbed Alexandra's arm and squeezed. Ice pinched into Alexandra's skin, and she tried to pull away from the older woman's grip without looking like she was having muscle spasms.

Wait. What?

Alexandra glanced down at her arm in confusion. She shouldn't have felt that touch. Rebecca was too young a spirit to have already developed that skill.

"Just a few questions, Miss King, and we can head out for the day." Vinson skimmed the papers. "I see that you're divorced. Any reason your ex might be causing trouble for you?"

She focused on the officer. Last she'd heard, Seth had moved to a base in Alaska with a new wife and a kid on the way. "No, absolutely not."

"Not a bitter divorce?"

"Not especially." Seth had been Matthew's friend. He and her brother had gone through basic training together. They'd married too young. Drifted apart. It happened a lot with spur-of-the-moment military marriages dealing with long distance and too much time apart. She'd been relieved when he'd told her he wanted out because she hadn't had the heart to tell him first.

"Tell me about this restraining order against Kevin Alred."

She bit back a groan. Stupidest thing she'd ever done had been to get involved with that loser. "An ex-boyfriend. He didn't take it well when I ended things."

"He got violent?"

Harassing phone calls. Following her to and from her job at the call center where she'd worked at the time. The last straw had been finding him inside her apartment one night, after she'd already taken back her key. "He threatened it, but I got off lucky."

He scribbled something on a piece of paper.

Rebecca's raspy gasp caught her attention. Alexandra was turning her head to see what Dylan's mother was carrying on about now when she spotted the elderly gentleman standing close to the officer's desk. His skin carried that gray pallor of someone who had been dead for many years, and she knew immediately the man was not alive.

Another freaking ghost. Wonderful.

The word FATHER flashed in her mind. Officer Terminator's dad?

She shifted in her seat, angling one leg over the other.

"My son will die if he gets involved with you. Please leave him alone!" The gravelly warning was as much of a wheeze as it was a spoken statement. She focused on the officer and tried to ignore the elderly man. Maybe he'd go away without encouragement.

What did he mean, his son would die if he got involved with her?

Father pounded his fist on the side of the desk, causing it to tremble slightly. One of Vinson's pens started rolling from the vibration, and he frowned as he reached to stop it with his hand.

How the devil had the ghost done that?

"You've got to listen to me." The voice was stronger, not as wheezy this time.

Oh, boy.

Alexandra reached up to finger her hair, made sure Vinson wasn't watching her, and managed to shake her head. *No.* She absolutely was not going to engage this ghost in front of Dylan's precinct. No way.

"Alexandra, talk to him." Rebecca's cold fingers pinched through the cloth at her forearm again. "He just wants to help his son, too."

She pulled her arm away and shifted legs again. She had to bite her tongue to keep from saying, "Helping your sons is what got me into this mess, lady." She should have never come to Charleston, but that was a done deal. She'd fix things and move on. Without getting involved with more dead people!

The old man puffed out his chest and raised his fist, his expression fiercely angry now. Oh, no. Surely he wasn't going to pound the desk again?

Crap. He was.

As soon as his fist connected with the wood, Alexandra sprang to her feet and deliberately bumped against Vinson's desk to cover the action. She blew out a breath. "Sorry. Bathroom break. When you gotta go, you gotta go."

She didn't give him time to respond. She spun on her heels and headed for the ladies room. If they knew what was good for them, Mr. Grouchy Ghost and Rebecca would be there waiting for her.

She wasn't disappointed. After a quick inspection of the two stalls she rounded on the old man, jabbing a finger into his very solid chest.

"What the heck is your problem, mister? What do you mean, your son will die?"

He rubbed at his chest as if she'd irritated the spot. "Dangerous," he wheezed. "He's too dangerous. Too powerful now."

"Who is?"

It was Rebecca that answered. She grabbed the old man's arm and looked toward the door. "Oh no. He's here."

"Who?" Alexandra had never seen such fear overtake anyone's eyes—living or dead. Both ghosts moved toward the wall.

A bump against the outside door caused Alexandra to start and spin in that direction. Hand on her stomach, she waited for someone to finish pushing the door open, but it remained shut.

Bang.

One of the stall doors behind her slammed against metal.

"Hello?"

Crap. Had she not seen someone? No. She'd looked in both stalls. Empty. She knew it.

But now one of the stall doors was shut.

She leaned over and peeked under the door. A pair of old, black shoes, black slouchy socks and the hem of a black dress were visible.

The hairs on the back of her neck lifted as she straightened. Alexandra's heart began to race and butterflies hatched in her stomach. A wave of nausea swept from her gut upward.

Casting a glance around her, Alexandra realized the two ghosts had abandoned her. They'd said *he*, not she. That was a woman in the stall. Nothing to worry about. Probably just another ghost, seeking a handout from the living freak she was.

The shuffle of clothing being shifted indicated movement. The creak of the stall door opening felt as ominous as it sounded. Deep in her gut, Alexandra knew this was off. This wasn't a normal ghost. But she couldn't move.

She fingered the gold cross at her throat as she stared at the stall, her gaze unwilling to leave the old woman's dead, black eyes as they became visible.

It was the same old woman she'd encountered at the hospital, when she and Dylan had visited the autopsy room.

A growling sound echoed in the small space. It sounded a lot like the word "Leave."

No one had to tell her twice.

Alexandra raced back to Vinson's desk, grabbed her jacket and purse, and told the cop to drive her to her hotel. Scratch that. She amended the request to include a stop at the grocery store on the way.

She only made one purchase. Salt.

Shutting herself in her room, she made a clear line of the white powder along the edges of her space. Along the door. Along the windows. Everywhere. Salt kept the spirits away: both good and bad. She'd only ever advised people to use it, and it had worked for them.

She prayed it would work now.

Chapter Ten

Alexandra averted her gaze from the suitcase she'd packed last night and instead focused on her reflection in the door-length mirror in front of her.

She took a deep breath and smoothed the material over her thank-you-heaven flat stomach. *Perfect.*

She'd paired a flirty plum-colored dress with her knee-high black leather boots because she knew she looked damn good in the outfit, and she'd need that confidence to push herself out the door and head-on into battle with the black-eyed whatever-the-heck-she-was old woman that had scared the crap out of her last night.

Her grandmother had always chided Alexandra for being too stubborn for her own good, and she guessed she was proving Grams right again. Okay, so she'd packed her bags and checked flight information last night. Big deal. She'd only let the fear take rein over her actions for about fifteen minutes before she'd let another emotion take control.

Who did this crazy old woman think she was messing with?

No way was Alexandra going to run from her or anyone else, including Dylan Collins.

And that was another thing. Who did *he* think he was? They'd had two bouts of roll-over-and-make-me-beg sex, and he could walk away as if it meant nothing?

Granted, she wasn't expecting a ring or promises, but surely he owed her the courtesy of giving whatever this pull was between them a chance? And giving her a chance to explain why she'd come to Charleston looking for him.

Then again, he'd completely cut his own brother out of his life easily enough. Maybe walking away was easy for him.

Focus on the task at hand.

She had two items on her to-do list today: figure out what or who the creepy old woman was and if she was the same presence that was scaring Alexandra's ghosts, and force Dylan to listen to her arguments in Zach's favor.

She hoped her knock 'em dead outfit would kick-start his lust and distract him long enough to accomplish that.

Anything else she accomplished would be Nutella. Mmmmm. She loved Nutella.

There was a knock on the door, so she grabbed her trendy faux leather jacket—it was the only one she had brought with her—and went to greet Detective Reedus. He'd called her an hour ago to let her know she'd be tagging along with him today, hitting up occult shops before visiting the scenes of the crime.

She wondered what Dylan was doing and how long she should wait to ask. She had no idea if the older detective knew she'd been sleeping with his partner or not.

Reedus whistled when he saw her. "Damn, woman. You knew I was the one picking you up and not Collins, right?"

Okay, maybe that secret wasn't so secret.

Closing the door behind her, she shook her head and turned to him. "Don't flatter the man. I came here on vacation. My wardrobe is limited. Gotta work with what I've got." A small twisting of the truth. She slid her sunglasses on and glanced around the parking lot. "What happened to Vinson?"

A little worm of worry wiggled into her brain after the warning the younger officer's father had given last night.

"Just left. You're stuck with me now." He started moving toward an older model Ford. "Ever been to Charleston before?"

She climbed in beside him. "Nope. First time."

He pulled out a notebook, flipped through the pages and grunted. "Only found three stores under the occult listings. Guess we'll start with the closest."

The closest turned out to be more of a comic book store than an occult shop. It sold some incense but graphic novels lined the walls and, boy, the look the owner had given her when she'd asked if he was familiar with black magic had been priceless.

The second store had closed months ago, but stepping into the third felt like winning the lottery. A neon sign and well-lit doorway announced The Mystic Corner, and it wasn't a comic book store.

Alexandra hadn't gone inside many occult stores—that just wasn't her thing—but stepping inside this one reminded her of the one and only time she'd stepped foot inside a Voodoo store in New Orleans. This place had everything a tourist or voodoo-priestess-wanna-be could hope for.

Customers had to walk past the novelty T-shirts, key chains, coffee mugs and jewelry at the front of the store to get to the meat of it. A fake palm tree stood prominently in front of the checkout counter, shielding a wall of incense and candles that led to another wall of books. A display of various crystals, Ouija boards and other occult paraphernalia nestled near the back of the shop. A smaller section underneath a hand-painted wood sign proclaimed HOODOO.

Alexandra resisted the urge to press her lips together and whistle. It wasn't often she ran into people who knew hoodoo. Voodoo, yes. Hoodoo, not so much.

"Can I help you?" A deep voice boomed over Alexandra's shoulder, and she turned to see a tall man in his mid-to-late twenties behind the register looking completely disinterested in whether or not he could actually help them.

There was something about him that caught and held her attention. He was fair looking, not really her type, but...there was a spark of interest in his gaze when it brushed over her that went beyond sizing up a pretty girl. He also had an unusual tattoo on his neck. Some kind of rune, she thought.

Interesting.

Reedus stepped up to the counter and flashed his badge. He launched into a round of twenty questions: had anyone suspicious visited the store lately? Did they have any regular customers? Had anyone bought tarot cards lately? On and on.

Alexandra listened to the young man's stoic responses as she browsed the line of books.

"Lookin' for 'nything in 'tickluh?"

She'd been so involved in trying to listen and browse at the same time that she hadn't noticed the short black woman at her side. The older woman spoke with a strong accent Alexandra couldn't pinpoint. Kind of Cajun, but not exactly.

She guessed by the woman's African attire that she must have been native to some part of that country.

"I'm not sure." She glanced back at the books. "Do you have anything on ghosts or demons?"

"Yaas." She reached for a book that looked old and expensive. "What kinda problem are yo havin'?"

Of all the questions she could ask.

Alexandra kept it simple. "I just know it's negative."

The woman tilted her head and narrowed her eyes as she examined Alexandra's features. She nodded and slid the book back into its place. "Leggo." With a gesture of her hand, she spun and started walking toward a doorway marked off by a beaded curtain. Had she meant "let's go?"

Alexandra glanced toward the counter where Reedus was still talking to the young man. She supposed he'd come find her when he was ready.

Pushing through the beads, Alexandra emerged in a brightly lit room that looked like any ordinary office except for a bookshelf filled with bottles of spices and roots and other herb-type things.

The black woman started humming as she pulled a few bottles from the shelf.

"Excuse me?" Alexandra cleared her throat. "Are you a voodoo priestess?"

"Hoodoo." The woman turned and winked. "Yo know 'bout Gullah?"

Gullah? Er, sounded vaguely familiar.

The woman shuffled across the room, picked up a piece of paper from the desk, and handed Alexandra a flyer. By the time Alexandra had finished reading the brief history of Gullah and hoodoo—a creole African-American culture and religion native to the eastern coast of the United States —the woman had gathered several herbs and roots and was mixing them together in a bowl.

"Me name Bob-ra."

Barbara? Alexandra stepped forward and extended her hand. "Alexandra."

"Meemaw, what are you doing?" A different young black man pushed through the beaded curtain.

The woman waved him away, but nodded at Alexandra. "This un's special."

The young man seemed to grow taller as he glanced over Alexandra's figure. "Is there something I can help you with?"

She sucked in air, smelled something like garlic, and nodded.

"I'm a psychic medium, and I was hoping your grandmother could help me figure out what type of presence I've been encountering."

"What's a look like?" She continued to grind ingredients in a bowl.

"Meemaw, I think you can drop the accent." The young man smiled at Alexandra. "She seems cool."

His grandmother cackled and turned to place her hand to Alexandra's forearm. "I'm sorry, child. Sometimes I forget myself. Gotta put on a show for the customers. Know what I mean?" She winked and turned back to the mixture she was concocting.

The woman had been putting her on!

Alexandra shook her head. "You're not really a hoodo priestess."

Barbara waved a dismissive hand. "Oh, yes, I am. Learned it from my mama." Her voice was clear and Southern now. "Go on. Tell me what you've been seeing. I'll see if I can help."

Alexandra briefly described the old woman with her dark, empty eyes and went ahead and mentioned the other ghosts' warnings, too. "I don't understand, because whatever I'm seeing is an old woman. Yet I keep being warned about 'him.'"

The woman froze, her grinding coming to a halt. "It's making you see what it wants you to see. It's taking a form it knows will unnerve you." She began grinding, harder. "That means it's smart and powerful. Not good."

Alexandra glanced at the young man. His eyes were wide. "Demon," he repeated.

The curtains made a clacking sound as he disappeared through them in a rush.

"Here. This will keep it away from you." Barbara poured the contents of the bowl into a pouch, tied it, and handed it to Alexandra.

The curtains clanked again as the young man reappeared with a book in his hands. "My grandmother is a root doctor. What she made you will act as protection. Keep it on you at all times." He flipped to a page and tapped one finger on an illustration. "You said the spirits were afraid of it. Demons can influence both the living and the dead if they're not crossed over. Makes sense they would be afraid." He met her eyes. "You should help them cross on."

Alexandra had never experienced a demon—her Grams had said they were incredibly rare. "No. I don't think this is a demon."

"You know a lot about demons, do you?" Barbara mocked. She looked Alexandra up and down. "I don't think you know as much as you think you do."

Alexandra tried not to be insulted, and granted, the old woman with dark eyes was as scary as hell. But in all of her research and her experiences, demons were the spiritual equivalent of red diamonds. Even her paternal grandfather who'd been a priest, God rest his soul, hadn't believed they were as common as Hollywood pretended they were.

"I've had spirits present themselves to me as something they're not before." Alexandra crossed her arms. "How can I be sure this thing isn't just some negative spirit with too much power?"

"Does it have an aura?"

"Well, no." Alexandra took a deep breath. "Look, I know she's not a ghost. How do I know she's not a living person who needs help? What if this old woman has been possessed by something?"

"By a demon?" Barbara looked amused.

"I don't think she's a demon." Alexandra repeated the words as much for herself as the other woman. Her conviction was starting to waver.

"Do you even know what a demon is? Do you know where they come from?" Barbara was looking at her as if she was a child who'd failed a basic exam.

Alexandra threw her hands up. "Enlighten me."

Barbara's lips twitched before thinning into a serious line. "Tell me this, Miss Know-It-All. The oldest ghost you've ever met, how powerful was he?"

Alexandra's mind immediately went to the soldier she'd encountered as a young girl out exploring in the hillside of Germany. Before she could answer, Barbara asked, "What was his personality like?"

She shrugged. "He was scary. He seemed—"

"Cruel? Insane?" Barbara interjected. "And he was powerful enough to move things and hurt people."

Alexandra nodded.

"He was almost finished transforming then." Barbara tilted her head and skimmed her gaze over Alexandra's expression. "When a dead person doesn't cross over, they start to turn into something else. The longer they're here, the more powerful they become. Their minds become affected. Warped. It's an unnatural process."

Alexandra thought she was following. "Wait. You're telling me that demons are ghosts who haven't crossed over?" She scoffed. "There would be so many demons if that was true!"

"Why do you think you have your gift? It was given to you so you could help uphold the natural order. You and people like you are meant to help convince the dead to cross over if they've missed their first chance. Who knows where they go, but they're not meant to stay *here*."

The explanation felt far more comfortable than it should have given everything Alexandra had been raised to believe, and that in itself was an uncomfortable feeling.

Barbara chuckled. "Uh huh. I see the light bulb finally coming on for you, girl. You know it's true, deep down."

Alexandra reluctantly nodded. "So how long do ghosts have before they…transform?"

Barbara fiddled with the large beaded necklace resting at her cleavage. "It depends on the spirit. Some are able to resist it longer than others. If a weak-minded person dies and doesn't cross over, it could be only a matter of years before they turn into something worse. The stronger the person's mind when they die, the longer they tend to remain in spirit form."

George seemed reasonably sane, and so did Rebecca, except... she'd been looking sick the last few times Alexandra had seen her.

Barbara clucked her tongue and reached for the newspaper lying on the desk. "I've been reading the paper. That's why you're really here. This man killing these poor people is being influenced by this demon you keep seeing."

"How do you know that?"

Barbara pursed her lips. "Please, child." She waved a dismissive hand. "You ain't the only one around here who has visions."

"Does all of this have anything to do with the gray beams I keep seeing shooting toward the sky?"

"You can see that?" Barbara looked surprised. "Girl, maybe you have more abilities than I thought." She nodded. "It's not natural. We think it's giving the dead more power. Making them stronger. Probably helped create this demon."

And that didn't sound good at all.

Barbara's eyes narrowed on her. "You didn't use salt, did you?"

Alexandra blinked. "I used it to repel spirits last night. Why?"

The old woman cackled and turned away, shaking her head. It was her grandson who explained the reason.

"Salt can attracts spirits—it doesn't always repel them." He looked her up and down again. "How long have you been doing this?"

Oh, come on. They were yanking her chain now. Hand on her hip, she shook her head and held up a hand. "I've been doing this for a long time." She'd been to conventions. Exchanged notes with others. Read lots of books. Had long conversations with the dead about these things. "I worked with a priest once who told the family being affected to place table salt around the doorways."

Barbara's cackle grew louder. "White salt?"

Alexandra's smile dropped. "What else would I use?"

"Black salt repels the negative," the grandson said. "White salt tends to attract it."

Well...crap.

"You gotta lesson to learn." Barbara shook a finger at her. "That's why you're here. You don't know all you think you do."

"Apparently not." Alexandra touched the cross at her neck. White salt attracted spirits? And she'd all but bathed in it last night? Okay, that was seriously creepy. And a tidbit she'd definitely file in her mental need-to-know please-verify box. Maybe she should consult further on this with the demonologist she'd met last summer at a convention. The guy had a stellar reputation. He might be able to give her more answers.

"How much for the, um—" She held up the pouch the old woman had given her "—this stuff? And the book?" She gestured to the leather-bound edition the young man still held.

He named a price for the book that made her head swim. "That's free or it won't work." He gestured to the pouch.

The beads clanked and Reedus stuck his head through. "King." He nodded toward the way he'd come. "We need to go. Now."

She hurried to pay for the book as Reedus stomped toward the exit. The tattooed young man behind the counter returned her gaze with a knowing smile as she handed him some cash. She grabbed her change and the book, and her boots clacked against the concrete of the sidewalk as she raced to catch up with the detective.

"Find out anything?" He opened his car door and pushed inside, leaving her to follow suit.

Oh yeah. Loads. "Not really. You?"

"Got a few names to check out. Regular customers." He turned over the engine and then settled a blue light on his dash.

"What's going on?" Alexandra had barely buckled herself in before she was slung toward him as the car shot out of the space.

"Looks like you're gonna have a chance to visit a fresh crime scene today. We just got another one."

***

Dylan took in the gruesome sight before him and ran a hand through his hair. "Geez."

A woman hung from a noose, her limp body dangling in the white arched entryway leading into the old city jail. A person driving to work had seen the morbid picture and called it in a couple of hours ago. No one who'd been questioned so far—not even any of the residents living in the apartments across the street—had seen or heard anything suspicious.

One of the coroner's assistants ambled up to Dylan with a clipboard. "Can we go ahead and remove the body now?"

He nodded, hardly able to say the word, as he scanned the crowd of onlookers. A lot of cops believed killers showed up at crime scenes to enjoy the results of the chaos they'd created. All Dylan recognized were a couple of reporters.

They'd just finished zipping the body bag when Reedus's old clunker came into view as it parked down the street. Dylan blew out a breath and moved to his haunches to examine a fresh-looking set of footprints around the side of the building that one of the officers had found. He was in no hurry to see his partner because he knew Alexandra was with tagging along with Reedus today.

"Get pictures of these footprints." He squinted up at the four-story building that rose into the sky like some kind of archaic fortress in desperate need of repair. "I spotted some fresh tire tracks on the other side of the building. Get some shots of those too."

The officer scurried off to obey, and a familiar cough grew closer until Reedus's gravelly voice greeted, "What have we got this time, Collins?"

Dylan narrowed his eyes against the late morning sun as he again looked up at the historic building. "Caucasian female. Early forties. Hung in that archway over there." He straightened and turned to the two newcomers. "So far not a lot of obvious evidence."

Reedus shielded his eyes with one hand as he glanced up at the old jail. "Don't tell me the psycho was copycatting a death here."

Nodding, Dylan allowed himself to glance at the woman standing a little ways behind Reedus. His heart skipped a beat. Sweet heaven. She looked as sexy as all get out, dressed in that short dress wearing those notice-me boots. He directed his thoughts away from that assessment and concentrated instead on filling his partner in on the situation.

"Lavinia Fisher would be my guess." He turned and started walking back toward the entrance, knowing they'd follow. "I read that professor's book last night. Did some research on the computer. This place has quite the reputation among ghosthunters. I was about to do one more walk through inside, make sure we didn't miss anything. Place is damn creepy."

"Fisher?" Reedus repeated the name as if he were trying to recall it.

"Supposedly the first female serial killer ever documented. She and her husband were held here until their execution in the early 1800s."

"Let me guess. By hanging, right?" Reedus coughed into his handkerchief and tucked the small cotton sheet back into his pocket.

Dylan stopped walking and turned to face the older man. "You had that cough checked out yet?"

Reedus waved his hand and pushed past him. "Just my emphysema acting up."

For the first time Dylan noticed Alexandra wasn't with them anymore. He glanced around and spotted her hanging back near the sidewalk across the street, in front of where a group of curious onlookers stood behind a barricade.

Dylan swore. Didn't she realize she was potentially in danger? Wandering off from her protection wasn't exactly smart. Frustrating woman. She was gonna be the death of him yet.

He hurried over to where she stood. "What do you think you're doing?"

At least she had the decency to blush. "Waiting."

"For what?"

"For Reedus to finish so we can leave."

He put his hands on his hips and considered her. Boy, this lady was something else. "Don't you want to do your psychic mumbo jumbo and see if you can pick up some leads?"

He regretted the words as soon as they were out. She'd actually given him some good leads, known some facts she shouldn't have been able to, and made him question his disbelief in psychics. He shouldn't let his anger over her knowing Zach cloud his objective. Especially if she could contribute to solving this case.

He needed all of the help he could get.

Alexandra crossed her arms and jutted her chin forward. "I think I'll sit this one out."

He realized they were within hearing distance of the crowd. He grabbed her arm and tugged her forward. She dug in her heels and didn't let him pull her very far. She might not want to be near him either, but she needed to act like a professional and help him out.

She pushed close to him, lowered her gaze to the ground, and whispered, "Dylan, I'm not going in there."

He scrunched his face in confusion. "Why not?"

"Because it's packed to the rafters with ghosts, and they're waiting for me. I won't be able to deal with it. There are too many of them. I get overwhelmed with that many. Dylan, please."

She *was* scared. The slight tremble in her voice was echoed by her body as she pressed against his side. Well, hell. That didn't seem like her.

He forced himself to take a step away from her. Otherwise, he was afraid he'd put his arm around her and pat her back. "Okay." He sighed. "She appears to have been killed outside the actual jail. Can you pick up anything out here?"

"I can try."

"That's all I ask." He gestured her forward. He wouldn't push. Either she wanted to help, or she didn't. Her choice.

She took a deep breath and took a few timid steps. Her face winced. "I don't think she was killed here." A few more steps. She stopped and looked around, but her eyes didn't seem to see him or anything else. "Did she work for the government? Maybe the Department of Transportation?"

"No. She was a teacher at a local high school."

"Okay." Alexandra frowned and shook her head. "I don't think she knew her killer." She bit her bottom lip and hesitantly reached out a hand to touch the side of the entryway. "Was she stabbed? I'm feeling a stabbing pain in my stomach." She pressed her other hand to her middle.

"There were no visible stab wounds. No blood." He was starting to lose his patience. Was she wasting his time? He was trying hard to remain open-minded here, but she wasn't making it easy. "Can you see where she died?"

She sucked in a breath, blew it out again slowly. Several seconds passed. "I'm seeing a parking lot. I think he followed her to her car. There wasn't much of a struggle. It was quick. She didn't even have a chance to process what was happening. A hand over her mouth from behind. A pain in her stomach. Then nothing."

"Describe the parking lot."

She closed her eyes. "It's a garage." She shook her head. "I keep seeing a picture of a king."

136

"A king?" He shuffled on his feet. "Like wearing a crown and everything?"

She opened her eyes and looked apologetic. "I'm also seeing a big plant bowl with writing on it. I know that sounds crazy, Dylan."

"Maybe not as crazy as you think." He turned and called McCormick over. The young officer had been one of the first on the scene. He looked anxious to leave. "Check the Francis Marion Garage on King Street and see if we can find the victim's car. Let me know what you find."

Once McCormick was gone, Dylan turned to Alexandra and explained, "Marion Square is a park off King Street. There's a fountain that kind of looks like a bowl there. Maybe that's what you're seeing."

She lifted her hand to shield her eyes as she looked at him. It was unnerving, the way she considered him so closely. "Thank you for believing me."

He wasn't sure he did, but it was worth checking. "I need to do a walkthrough before I leave."

"Have fun." She glanced up at the building, then grabbed Dylan's upper arm to keep him from moving forward. "Don't go to the third floor. Let someone else."

He glanced down at her hand on his arm and she released her grip.

"There's a really mean ghost up there. Big guy. You remind him of someone he didn't like when he was alive, and I don't want you to get hurt."

Was she serious? He glanced up at the darkened, barred windows on the third floor. A shiver ran down his spine. It was almost like he felt someone watching him now. Crazy how a suggestion like that could play tricks on the mind.

"Dylan?" Her voice cracked. When he focused on her, a timid smile lifted her mouth. "Can we talk later?"

They needed to talk, but he didn't know if he was ready yet. He didn't answer.

"I'll send Reedus out. Don't wander off, or I swear I'll bend you over my knee next time I see you." He emphasized the threat with a pointed finger.

He was headed up the pathway when he heard her yell, "Promise?" He almost stopped in his tracks. He imagined she was grinning, but he didn't allow himself to turn around and make sure.

That dress. Those boots.

Crazy woman was gonna be the death of him.

Chapter Eleven

"*Pssst.* Guess what?"

Alexandra glanced up at McCormick. The young officer had a huge smile on his face as he glanced furtively around while leaning against the desk she was using at the moment. "Hmm?"

"I found the car. Just like you said."

She perked up. "Really?"

He nodded. "Collins told me you led us to it. That's what they're in there talking about." He gestured to the conference room where Reedus and Dylan had disappeared with Capt. Deveraux a few minutes earlier.

"Why aren't we in there?"

"Beats me." He shrugged and leaned closer. "So how do you do it?"

"It?"

"You know. How do you know stuff?"

She'd be a millionaire a hundred times over if she knew the answer to that. She glanced around and gestured for him to lean closer. "Brussels sprouts."

He jerked back to look at her. "Huh?"

"I love them. Most people hate them. I think there's a correlation in there somewhere."

His eyes widened until she rolled hers and shook her head to let him know she was joking. He chuckled. "I'm serious."

"I wish I knew. Things just come to me."

"For the record, I'm a believer." He thumbed his chest. "One time, my older sister was in a car wreck. I was in the middle of class in high school, and I got all agitated for no reason. I knew something was wrong. I had this feeling, ya know? Afterward, when my dad picked me up from school and told me what had happened, it gave me chills. It's like I knew. Ever since then, I try to keep an open mind about things like this."

She smiled. "Thanks, McCormick." She glanced around the office. "Have you seen Officer Vinson yet?"

"Nah, but I talked to him a few minutes ago. I'm gonna take your shift tonight. He's gonna patrol his beat and see if he can't shake down some info. When you get ready to leave for the day, let me know, okay?"

Nodding at him as he walked away, she slid a hand inside her purse and fingered the small pouch inside it. She'd realized she'd left the hoodoo concoction in Reedus's car earlier, retrieved it and shoved it into her bag. She hadn't seen a single ghost since. She'd actually been worried about Vinson, since she hadn't seen the cop yet. She was glad to know he was okay. The warning from his father that he would die if he got involved still haunted her.

Out of the corner of her eye, she caught the conference room door opening. The three men came out, but only Dylan and Reedus walked toward her.

"We found the last victim's car. You're good, lady." Reedus gave her a thumbs up.

Two compliments from different cops in as many minutes? She tried not to beam beneath the praise. "And?"

"Forensics is going through the vehicle now." Dylan sat on the edge of her desk. "They'll let us know if anything important turns up. The captain is impressed."

But not him? Alexandra realized his opinion mattered more than anyone else's and felt a tiny zing of hurt at his lack of agreement.

Reedus glanced at his watch. "I've got a report to write up, and then I'm gonna head over and see if I can't get a jump on the findings from the ME." He looked at Alexandra a little sheepishly. "That means medical examiner. You wanna come? See if you get anything from the body?"

After what had happened last time she was at that place? A shudder racked her frame. No thanks.

"Alexandra knows what an ME is. Trust me." Dylan seemed to be fighting a smile. "You wanna go see him again, Alexandra? Tell him hey?"

Jerk.

"No, thank you, Reedus. But there is something I'd like to ask you in private before you leave. Okay?"

The older man's brow scrunched as he looked between her and Dylan. "Yeah, sure. I'll come find you." He tapped a knuckle on the edge of her desk as he walked past. "Good job on that car."

Dylan said nothing for several seconds. Finally, he shifted to his feet. "We're drowning in calls from people who've already heard about this last victim. I've got to go prepare a statement for a press conference the captain's called for this evening."

A perky blonde officer from a few seats over called out Alexandra's name, followed by Dylan's. "There's a guy on the phone, insisting to speak with Alexandra King." She stood up from her chair. "I think it might be the guy you're looking for."

Dylan swore beneath his breath. "Send the call to my desk."

"Wait!" Alexandra grabbed his wrist before he could get far. "Let me talk to him. Maybe I can keep him on the phone." Or pick up information in another way. "Please?"

The precinct had fallen quiet. Nervous energy hummed in the

air while she waited for Dylan's decision. He nodded. "Okay. Patch the call over here. I want it recorded. Get me this guy's location. Reedus, Graham, follow the trace pronto." He sat on the edge of the desk again. She felt others crowd behind her. "We're putting it on speakerphone."

The phone rang and Dylan snatched the receiver before she could. He hit a button and a slight buzz could be heard. Dylan pointed at her.

She leaned forward. Took a deep breath. "This is Alexandra King."

A strong breath rasped into the phone, startling her. Dylan pressed some buttons to lower the volume as another Darth Vader breath blasted through the speaker.

She cleared her throat. Tried to sound slightly annoyed by the lack of response. "Hello?"

"What did you think of my latest kill? Good, wasn't it?" The person's voice was metallic, as if being distorted by some kind of device.

What was she supposed to say to that? When she hesitated, Dylan made a circling motion with his hand. *Keep talking.* She tried to block out their audience. "I'm not sure good is the word I would use. Who are you?"

"You know who I am."

"The Grim Reaper?"

"Yes."

"What's your real name?"

"You can call me Reaper. I like the idea of you shortening my name. It seems more intimate that way."

The way he said that last bit sent chills up and down her spine. "Why did you call me?"

"It's a lot easier to find a victim than it is a listener, Alexandra. I want us to be friends. I think we'll work well together. You're not afraid of death either, are you?"

She glanced up at Dylan. How long did he need for a trace? "You want to talk, talk. Go ahead."

"I knew who you were as soon as I saw you, Alexandra. I've seen you on TV. Helping the police in other places."

"Really? What other places?"

"Colorado. California. There are clips of it online. I've watched them all. I know you're a real psychic. I can tell."

So her biggest fan was a total nutjob serial killer? Awesome. "Have you ever used a psychic before?"

"Yes. She wasn't real, though. I found out. I made her pay for it."

"Made her pay how?"

Silence.

"Did you see Lavinia Fisher today? Was she pleased by my offering to her?"

"Who?" Oh yeah. That was the woman who supposedly haunted the old jail, Dylan had said.

"You know who she is. You're stalling, trying to trace the call and find me. It won't work." A sound that resembled snickering followed.

"Why are you killing these innocent people?"

"Because I can." Darth Vader breathing again. "I want you to tell me what they say to you. That's why I was happy when I saw the police had brought you on. What did Lavinia say? Tell me."

"I didn't see Lavinia's ghost today."

"You're lying."

Click.

Her gaze sought Dylan's. "Did we get him?"

He picked up a hand radio and barked, "Reedus, anything?"

Static chirped, then a response, from right behind them. "Yep. This is the phone number he called from. Look familiar?" Reedus held up a sheet of paper with ten digits written in big, black marker. Even to Alexandra, the number seemed slightly familiar.

Dylan swore and moved to his feet. Alexandra frowned as she watched him rush to his desk and pick up his cell phone. "Didn't I have him on long enough?" she asked Reedus.

"We had a lock on his number the minute he called in. We just needed you to keep him on the line until we could get to his location."

"Then why—?"

"The number he called from is mine," Dylan said. "My mobile. And it's right here." He held it up for her to see.

"Techs say he spoofed the damn number this time," Reedus growled. "Threw the system off."

Dylan tossed his phone back onto his desk. "Did we get anything on his location at all?"

McCormick stepped forward and shook his head. "Sorry, sir."

Dylan lifted a hand to the back of his neck. Shaking his head, he walked over to where some boxes sat in a corner and kicked them so hard one slammed into the water cooler and threatened to topple the thing.

Reedus walked over and put a calming hand on Dylan's shoulder, whispered something she couldn't hear in his ear.

Alexandra looked away. Lord, she was frustrated too.

She felt someone move closer and then heard McCormick say in a stage voice, "Anyone can use that spoofing software online. My brother-in-law did it as a prank to me last year. My phone sent a message to my entire family telling them—" A flush crept up his tanned neck as he looked down at her. "Well, it wasn't funny."

Alexandra had never heard of it. It made her feel inept. She was learning a lot from this case, and she'd only been here a few days.

Composed again, Dylan waited until everyone had returned to normal activity to walk back over to where she still sat. He planted his hands on the edge of the desk and asked quietly, "Did you pick up on anything during the call?"

Nothing, and that was strange. "Only that he's seriously deranged. I'm so sorry, Dylan."

The faint scent of his cologne enticed her senses, and she realized how much she'd missed his closeness. A shiver raced along her nerves. She wished he'd hold her. After that phone call, she needed a hug. She suspected he did too.

He pulled away. "You did good handling that. I've got to go take care of some things now." He hesitated. "You okay?"

No. Not really. "I'm fine. Thanks."

He nodded and walked away.

***

Dylan loosened the tie that'd held a death grip around his neck for the past half hour and tried not to groan when he realized at least one of the reporters had followed him inside the station after the press conference.

Stephanie Rodriguez's high heels clicked against the tiled floor as she targeted him in her sights. Her poise carried purpose and determination. "Dylan! I want to talk to you."

As if this day weren't already bad enough. Now he had to deal with her, too. Freaking great.

He dropped the file he'd been carrying onto his desk and rounded on her, his gaze skirting the other desks for a glimpse of the other woman in his thoughts. He didn't see Alexandra and figured McCormick must have already driven her back to her hotel.

Good. He didn't need an audience for this.

"I told you everything I intend to during the press conference, Stephanie. Don't even try it."

She feigned hurt, coming to a sudden stop beside him and placing a perfectly manicured hand over her heart. "Dylan. I only wanted to check on you."

"On me?" He dropped into his chair and settled at his desk. Maybe if he seemed busy, she'd leave.

She perched herself on the edge of his desk, her killer legs offering a bit of a distraction from the jumbled-up mess inside his head. "I know you haven't been here that long, and now you're heading up a task force? I can't imagine what kind of pressure you're under."

Something in her voice seemed sincere, so he decided to take her at face value. "I'm handling it. Thanks."

"Why don't you let me buy you dinner?"

He arched a brow. "*You* want to buy *me* dinner?"

"We're still friends, right? I swear you can unload on me, and I promise—Girl Scout's honor—not to use any of it in my story." She held up a hand, her thumb and pinky finger held down. "No ulterior motive. Besides." She reached out and ran a finger up the back of his hand. "I'm sure you could use a break."

For a minute, he was actually tempted. Not by her supposed gesture of friendship, but by her. She was sexy. She'd been good in bed. She had about as much interest in a long-term relationship with him as he had with her. He'd love nothing more than to sink inside a willing female body and lose himself again for a few minutes.

Problem was, wrong female.

The idea of taking any woman to bed other than Alexandra left a sour feeling in his gut. What kind of sense did that make? He barely knew the woman.

"Thanks, but I've got some phone calls to make. Maybe another time."

She sucked in a deep breath. "I can take a hint." She moved off his desk, but placed a hand on his shoulder. "You've still got my number. Call any time. Day or night. Bye, Dylan." She winked at him, the movement of her hips accentuating a great ass as she walked away.

Oh yeah. He was an idiot.

"Eh hem." He felt the pressure of a hand settling on the back of his chair. He turned and lifted his gaze from Stephanie's backside to a pair of sky-blue eyes. Alexandra stood there, a knowing smirk on her beautiful face. She flapped some papers in front of him. "I got a few more impressions from looking at today's crime scene photos. Made you some notes."

He grabbed the papers and glanced over them. "Anything important?"

"Don't know. Is it helpful I think the victim's favorite food was sushi?"

His lips twitched as he looked up at her again. "Probably not."

She shrugged and took a step away. "I'm headed out. Need anything else from me before I leave?"

"No. You've been here all day. Go get some rest. Relax."

She seemed to hesitate. "When are you leaving?"

Please don't ask me to have that *talk before you go.* He glanced at the clock. "I'll try to get out of here by eight. Long day. Still have plenty to do before I can head home."

"Don't work too hard." She winked at him and walked away, her walk mimicking Stephanie's exit from minutes before. When she reached McCormick's desk and picked up her purse, she flipped her hair dramatically and sent him a sexy look over her shoulder. And winked again.

Minx.

He couldn't help it. He laughed.

That woman was something else.

147

Chapter Twelve

Dylan pushed a slice of out-of-this-world delicious supreme pizza into his mouth and stepped back to figure out how to tackle this latest problem.

The wood on the mantle over the fireplace had been rotted through. He'd bought a restored antique mantle piece to replace it, but he'd apparently screwed up and measured the damn thing wrong. It didn't fit. Too thick.

Piece of crap had cost him almost an entire paycheck. What was he supposed to do now? He'd hate to take it back—it had taken too long to find one with this look—so maybe he'd see if he could shave a little off the bottom. Repaint it.

There was a knock on the door, and he glanced at the alarm clock sitting on the coffee table. It was close to nine. Probably the old guy from next door, coming to complain about the little bit of hammering he'd just done.

He shouldn't have done it so late, but he'd found that beating the hell out of stuff at night and on weekends helped release some of the frustration he felt when he got snagged on a case. Helped clear his head so he could think.

Tossing the uneaten portion of pizza slice back into the box, he ran a hand through his hair and dusted off his pants. His jeans were ragged and his wife-beater was stained with sweat. Hardly presentable attire for company. It would probably fuel the old guy's opinion Dylan did not belong in the neighborhood.

He opened the door and blinked in surprise.

Not the old guy at all.

Alexandra pushed her hand flat against his chest and shoved him quickly out of the doorway and back into his house before shutting the door behind her. She whistled and pointed up. "Holy crap, Collins. You live *here*?" She meandered into the living room and did a complete rotation as she looked around.

"What are you doing here? Where's McCormick?"

She thumbed over her shoulder. "Outside in the car. Told him I wanted to visit a friend. Didn't tell him it was you."

Of all the stupid things!

Did McCormick know where he lived?

She looked at him and chuckled. "Calm down, hot stuff. I asked Reedus for your address. FYI. Pretty sure he already knew about us. I don't think McCormick has a clue you live here. I mean, seriously? On a cop's salary?"

The three-bedroom townhouse on East Bay Street was nestled among historic buildings worth millions. It was a rich district. He understood why she'd question his ownership. He just prayed McCormick wasn't outside running a check on the property owner out of curiosity.

He made sure the blinds were closed tight. "I bought it at foreclosure." About six months ago, he'd been seeing a pretty little real estate agent who'd turned him onto the idea of buying the place, fixing it up and making a profit. He'd put all of his savings into the deal, and it had been nothing but a headache ever since.

She used the end of her boot to lift a piece of the rotted mantle he'd left lying in the floor. "Oh yeah. Looks like a bit of a fixer-upper." She arched a brow at him as she let the piece slide back to position. "You never mentioned you lived a block away from my hotel. No wonder it never took you long to run home and be back."

"Why are you here, Alexandra?"

He had a hunch he already knew. She was still dressed in that sexy-as-hell outfit, and when she slid out of her jacket to reveal even more flesh, heaven help him, he almost didn't care what her reason was. She could paint rainbows and clowns on his ceiling as long as he could stand here and watch her do it.

"Figured this was the only way I could get you to listen to me." She moved some papers out of the way and flopped onto his sofa, looking as comfy as if she owned the place. She picked up one of the files. "Do you always bring your work home with you?"

"Not always. Sometimes it follows me." He shook his head. Aside from shoving her out into the street in front of McCormick, he didn't have many options here. Cunning move on her part. Might as well sit back and listen to the woman. Enjoy the eye candy. Maybe if he put up more resistance, she'd end up stripping to get his attention. His lips pulled up in a smile at that idea. "Want some pizza? There are a few slices left."

"What kind?"

"Supreme." She'd probably scrunch up her face and say something negative about having too many toppings.

"Mmmm. Gimme." She popped off the sofa and hurried over to the table. "I didn't manage to snag any dinner. I'm starved."

She helped herself to a piece and bit into it. Her eyes rolled to the back of her head in ecstasy. "Ohmygosh. This is the best pizza ever."

He grinned and moved to get her a drink. "Afraid all I've got here is water. Haven't been to the store this week."

"Typical man." She carried her pizza slice as she walked around the room. "Mind if I look at the rest of the place?"

"Looking for ghosts?"

She shrugged. "Sorry. Habit. Especially in an area like this. I'm

150

sure you probably have a couple, at least."

He hoped not. "Help yourself."

Her boots clicked against the hardwood floors he still needed to have refurbished. He knew exactly where she was as she moved room to room.

She finally reappeared in the living room, licking her empty fingers. "Not a single ghost. So weird."

He handed her a glass of water and tried to ignore the way his nerve-endings danced with excitement when their fingers brushed. What was he? Fifteen again?

He forced himself to move to the other side of the room, away from her. He leaned against the doorjamb separating the living room from the small room he used as an office and crossed his arms. "Might as well get this over with. Why don't you just say what you came to say, Alexandra? I've got a lot of work to do here."

She glanced at the plastic spread in front of the old fireplace. Took a sip of her water. "I want to talk about Zach."

"I don't." The mere mention of his brother's name had his temper rising. "You have no idea what happened there."

"Enlighten me."

"None of your business."

She shrugged. "I'll tell you what Hannah has confided in me, and we'll go from there. According to her, Zach—"

"Who's Hannah?"

"Hannah is Zach's girlfriend. You'll love her. She's the best." She sank onto the sofa again. Crossed her legs. "Anyway, as I understand it, Zach ran away from home when you were still a kid. He didn't get along with your stepdad. Guy was a real a-hole or something. You—"

"That guy was a great dad to me after Zach left. The only a-hole in this scenario was my brother."

She hesitated at that comment. Good. No telling what lies his

151

brother had been spilling to try to make himself come off more sympathetic than he was. Ray hadn't been a saint, but he'd always treated Dylan well.

She licked her lips. "Dylan, didn't you see Zach before he left? I mean, that day."

"Of course I did. I'll never forget it." He'd thought back to those last moments so many times he'd lost count. He used to lie awake at night, wondering if it had been something he'd done wrong to make Zach want to leave.

"How did he look to you?"

"Like hell. He'd gotten into another fight at school."

She cast her eyes down. "Got into a lot fights, did he?"

"From what I remember."

She crossed her arms and lifted her gaze. Said nothing. Dylan shifted to the other side of the doorframe. Why was she looking at him like that?

He clenched his jaw. "Go ahead. Say whatever it is you wanna say."

"Did it never occur to you that Zach wasn't really getting into a lot of fights at school? That maybe someone else had done that to him?"

He scoffed. "Who? Ray?" He shook his head. "If Ray had hit Zach, Zach would have told me."

"Maybe Zach was protecting you."

He pointed at his chest. "Ray never laid a finger on me."

"There are other ways of protecting someone. You were how old? Like twelve, right? And Zach was only sixteen or so? Your big brother. What do most big brothers do?" She bit at her bottom lip. "Dylan, your mother came to me because she knew why Zach left. She's validated everything Zach told Hannah. She's told me most of this herself."

He shoved away and walked into the office, fists clenched. This was outrageous. His mother had never said anything about this when she'd been alive. She wouldn't have—

"Dylan, I won't pretend to know how screwed-up your family situation really was, but I do know what Rebecca has told me."

She knew his mom's name was Rebecca? Of course. Zach could have told her that.

"My mother was a good woman. She would have never let Ray hurt me or Zach and just stood by. *Never.*"

"But she did. And she spent the rest of her life dealing with that guilt, which is why she's still hanging around, trying to make things right." He heard the click-clack of her boots then felt her hand on his shoulder from behind. "She made a mistake. She told me she tried to make things with Ray work because she didn't think she could take care of you on her own, financially."

His mother had hinted as much, especially after she'd filed for divorce and kicked Ray out.

"Did you know Zach sent her money?"

He half turned. "What?"

"He sent her money to keep your house out of foreclosure. That's why he took the job on TV. Not because he wanted the money for himself, but because he needed it for *you.* He kept sending her money, to help you go to college, and that's what eventually gave her the courage to leave your stepdad. She tried to fix things with Zach when she was alive. It just never worked out."

"Then she tried. He didn't." He turned and faced her. "He could have come home at any time."

That's what Dylan had always believed.

Maybe he'd been wrong.

There had been times when Ray had come down hard on Zach for stupid stuff. Zach had always taken it on the cuff and not acted like it was a big deal. And Zach *had* tried to contact Dylan. He'd been so angry at his brother, he'd never responded to the

153

calls or letters.

His mind flashed back to a few days before his mother had died. She'd been on morphine for the pain and calling Zach's name over and over. He'd finally picked up the phone to call and tell Zach to get his ass back home, but he'd gotten a disconnect message. Man, how he'd hated his brother then for not being there.

Their mother had squeezed Dylan's hand. "Oh, Zach! I'm so sorry for what I did! So sorry, son. Please forgive me."

At the time, he'd assumed she'd been blaming herself again for driving Zach away. But maybe—?

"Dylan." Alexandra's hand moved to his face. "Are you okay?"

He felt the hot threat of tears behind his eyelids and moved away. "I'm fine. Is that all you wanted to say?" He rested his hands on his hips. Took a deep breath and faced her again.

"You're a good detective, Dylan. I just wish you could look at this information objectively, as if it were a case involving someone else. What would your gut tell you then?"

That everything Alexandra had implied was true. That the stepfather had driven the older son away. That the mother had displayed signs of guilt throughout her life that had been mistaken for other emotions.

"He waited *years* to get in touch with me, Alexandra. That part is all on Zach. That's the part I've always had the hardest time forgiving."

"I don't blame you. I'd be pissed too. You should give him hell about it. You deserve better."

He turned away and rubbed the back of his neck. His head needed to be in this Grim Reaper case. Not on old family problems or sexy female psychics determined to drive him to the grave.

"Is my mother...still with you?"

Silence. He turned again and looked at her. Alexandra was biting her lip. "Um, not at the moment. She's been coming and going as she pleases."

He nodded. He didn't know what to believe about that.

"That's not all I came here to talk about, Dylan."

He blew out a breath. She was changing the subject. Thank heavens.

"Okay."

She took a step closer to him. "I wanted to talk about us."

Aw, hell. Talk about leaping out of the volcano and into the lava. She really wasn't going to go there now, was she?

One look at her face told him all he needed to know.

She most certainly was.

***

Alexandra took a step back, not at all certain she was ready for this, but crap, who was she kidding? She was here. She'd lose her nerve if she didn't go ahead and get it out.

She lifted her chin and met his wary gaze. "You hurt me, but you know what? You don't really know me, so let me fill you in on some things so you won't make that mistake again."

He didn't turn away and seemed to be listening. Good.

Crossing her arms, she moved toward him. "I get that you're good-looking man who probably sleeps with every pretty little thing that bats her eyelashes at you, but I don't normally fall into bed with every guy I meet."

A flush ran up his neck. His expression darkened. "I don't sleep with—"

"Just listen!" She pointed at him, and he shut up. "I've certainly never slept with your brother. I mean, gross. Totally not my type, thank you very much." She shook her head and rotated on her heels. "And another thing, it's your prerogative not to believe in what I can do, but I would never—ever, *ever*—pretend I could talk to someone's dead mother unless I could. That's just wrong."

She rounded on him again. "You know what else? I like dead people. I can talk to them better than I can living people. They're usually pretty good listeners once they've forced you to listen to all of their crap. They don't give half bad advice either. "

"Really?" His lips twitched.

"Uh huh." She turned back toward the wall and kept on with her pacing. "I also go to church. Not as much as I should, I'll give you that, but I am not some freaking devil worshipper and you pissed me off when you implied I was. I even used to sing in the choir until I moved to Atlanta. Still haven't found a new church there, by the way, but I'm working on it."

When she twirled and looked at him this time, at least he had the decency to look sheepish about questioning her faith. His eyes dropped to the floor.

"Last thing." She stepped up and poked his chest. "I like you. Maybe more than like you, and I don't know what the heck to do about that because you keep pissing me off with your stupid assumptions about what kind of person I am. Plus, I'm not planning to stay and that's a problem. Maybe not for you, since you're a stud who probably can't wait to jump into bed with the next —"

He tugged her forward so fast, her words got lost in a gasp that he quickly swallowed with his mouth. His hot breath brushed her cheek when he pulled his lips away just as quickly.

"Anyone ever told you that you make a lot of assumptions yourself?"

Her breath hitched and she stiffened in his hold. He chuckled at her reaction, then thrust his tongue right back inside her pliant mouth. Oh, wow. He was good at that. So good. She curled her fingers into the silk of his hair, pulled him down, deeper, and lost herself in the sensation of his kiss. What had they been talking about? She had no idea.

Shifting away, he used his lips and teeth to nibble a path down the column of her neck. Grabbing her ass, he lifted her and took them to the nearest wall.

"I really like this dress." His voice was raspy as he managed to tug the top half down, exposing her naked breasts. She was suddenly very grateful she'd taken her bra off before coming here. "I like how you look in it."

"Really?" She was practically purring now. The man had barely kissed her and she was already ready for him. "Would have never guessed."

He blew a hot breath over one rigid nipple before tasting it. She was so distracted by that sensation she almost didn't catch him sliding one of his hands between them, struggling to free his erection. She heard the rip of a zipper, felt her hips and legs jostled as he shoved his jeans down. Oh, my. Someone was in a hurry. Maybe she should have left her panties at the hotel too. He lifted her higher, sucked her breast inside the moist cavern of his mouth, and she groaned.

"Dylan."

"Shhh." His tongue tangled with hers again. She moaned and was practically breathless when he pulled away. "I need to be inside you. Now."

"Panting here. Pretty good sign I'm okay with that." She'd be a hypocrite after calling him promiscuous if she let him go much further without, um, "Protection?"

He laughed quietly against her neck then licked the shell of her ear. Pulling back for a second, he framed her face with both hands and met her gaze. He brushed the hair away from her cheek.

"I don't sleep around, Alexandra. I'm no monk, but I'm careful who I take to bed. Always careful to use something."

Why was he telling her this now? Trying to ruin the mood? Couldn't he see how desperate she was for him at the moment? She tried to pull him closer, but he held back.

"I don't have any more condoms."

Oh. His gaze never left hers, but she could feel how hard he was against her. There were other ways of taking care of that little, er, *big* problem, but his husky plea haunted her. *I need to be inside you.* She needed him inside her, too. Like, soon.

"One, I'm on the pill." She pointed at her bag on the floor behind him. "Two, you left an unused condom beside my bed. I stuck it in my purse."

His eyes lit up with a happy, naughty gleam right along with his smile. He set her on her feet, swiped her purse from the floor, and watched as she fumbled like a virgin on prom night until she found it for him. Flicking her hair out of her face, she tossed the bag down with a clunk and yanked him forward again by the material of his shirt. She slid the condom into his hand as his mouth hovered over hers. "Only one. Better make it count."

A gasp stalled in her throat as he pressed her to the wall again, kissing her hard before pulling back again. He slid the condom on in record time.

One of his very talented hands found its way up her dress, between them, his fingers teasing the skin at the edges of her underwear before sliding beneath, inside her.

"Mmm, already wet."

No kidding. She wrapped one of her legs around the back of his thigh and pressed him into her. "Don't stop."

"Like this?" He whispered the words against her lips, slipping his fingers under the elastic of her panties, inside her. Her head fell back against the wall as he drove hard against her clit.

She was almost there when he jerked at the material at her hips, shoving the panties down and out of his way. His fingers bit into the back of her thighs as he lifted her higher. Her arms and legs knew exactly what to do. They held on tight as he positioned his cock at her opening and pushed inside. She bit her lip so hard, feeling him throbbing there, she almost drew blood.

He shoved into her. She pushed back. On and on, they rocked together.

"Dylan." She breathed into his ear. "I'm almost there."

He drove harder until she came, and then answered her cry with a moan.

Panting, he buried his face in her neck, squeezed his arms around her waist. "Man." He lifted his head and kissed her. "I wasn't lying. I'm safe."

"Better be."

His chuckle vibrated against her ear. "Did you really imply I was a man whore?"

Heat crept into her face. "I was angry. I'm sorry. That was pretty…unforgivable."

"I wonder why I can't ever seem to take things slow with you. For the record," he lifted his gaze and met her own, "I like you too. More than I should."

"Oh." She swallowed. "What are we gonna do about that?"

His cell phone sang out the first strands of an annoying rock song. He groaned and pulled away from her, reaching to tug up his jeans. She found her feet but couldn't seem to leave the support the wall offered her limbs. Completely satiated. That's how she felt. A good, long nap would be Nutella.

She straightened her clothes as Dylan snatched up his phone and shot her an apologetic look over his shoulder.

He went still at whatever the person said. "Which one? Where?"

Her happy mood began to evaporate. Oh no. Not another murder.

He ended the call. "It's Reedus."

"Reedus?" She'd seen him a couple of hours ago. He'd been on his way to talk to the medical examiner.

Dylan moved past her. "He's in the hospital. I'm sorry, Alexandra. I've got to go."

159

Chapter Thirteen

"Here. Coffee?" Alexandra nudged Dylan's shoulder with her elbow and indicated the extra cup she'd gotten for him from the vending machine.

It was after midnight and it had been a long day. She was sure he needed the caffeine as much as she did to stay vertical at this point.

Glancing up from the hospital's waiting room seat, he smiled sheepishly and took the cup. "Thanks."

She reclaimed the chair beside him. "Relax. The doctor said he'd let us in to see him after they got him settled in his room." Reedus had been ambulanced to the hospital after collapsing during his visit with the M.E. When Dylan had gotten the call about it, Alexandra had assumed his partner had been the latest victim of the Grim Reaper, but not quite.

"When he started coughing the other day, I told him to go to the doctor." Dylan swore softly. "Pneumonia? Does it come on that fast? How did it get into his bloodstream?"

Alexandra shrugged. She didn't know. She'd never had the stuff, thankfully.

She glanced around the waiting room sparsely decorated with people. One man had spread himself across a row of seats in a sort of makeshift bed. Another couple sat closer to the television. Since Reedus's children lived outside the state, she and Dylan were his only visitors. Alexandra was glad she'd insisted on coming. Not only had she grown fond of the gruff older man, but it was obvious Dylan was uncomfortable being here. His knee bounced to some unheard rhythm, and every two minutes, he would shift in his seat. The only time he hadn't seemed preoccupied with his thoughts was when his phone rang. It had been blowing up with calls from other officers seeking information throughout the night, so she expected the older detective would have a roomful of cops visiting him tomorrow.

Alexandra reached out and placed her hand on top of his. *He hates hospitals because they bring back bad memories of seeing his mother in one.* It was as if someone had whispered the words to her, but she knew only she had heard them. And she knew they were right.

Dylan turned his hand up and linked his fingers with hers. "I'm glad you came. Sorry you're not getting any rest."

"I'm worried, too."

Several more nail-bitingly slow minutes passed before the lanky man in blue scrubs who'd identified himself as the doctor treating Reedus reappeared. "He needs his rest, but he did ask to see you before we turned you away," the doctor told Dylan. "Try not to get him too excited."

The man led them to a two-bed room where Reedus was the only occupant. His complexion was pale and he looked more haggard than he had only a few hours ago. Hanging back in the doorway, Alexandra placed her hand on Dylan's arm. "Why don't I give you a few minutes with him? I'll wait right here where you can see me."

His expression was so vulnerable when he met her gaze it almost broke her heart. His eyes looked sad and stressed. His mouth was pulled tight with worry. Oh, Dylan. He obviously cared for his partner a lot. "All right, but stay where I can see you."

She nodded and found a spot against the hallway wall to lean against. She cradled her coffee between her hands and smiled when Dylan made sure the curtain on the glass window looking into the room was pulled all the way back. She waved through the glass and winked at him. Nope. She had no plans to leave this spot.

It was interesting how much you could learn about a person from their body movements when you were watching them. Dylan had his hands on his hips as he looked down at his partner. His forehead was crinkled. Every now and then he'd nod. In her experience, that pose meant the person was a good listener. That he was open and willing to hear what you had to say.

"Alexandra King?"

Alexandra started at the unexpected voice and turned to see a man in blue scrubs pointing and smiling at her.

"You probably don't remember me. I'm Dr. Jeffrey Watkins. I'm one of the medical examiners at MUSC. Last time I saw you, you were—"

"Oh, right. I fainted on your floor." Heat spread across her cheeks as she laughed self-consciously. Pushing away from the wall, she reached out her hand to formally introduce herself. "Yes, I'm Alexandra."

Instead of accepting the gesture, he stepped back and held up his hands. "Sorry. Probably don't want to do that." He gestured toward the room. "I was kind of in hurry to come check on Reedus, I can't remember if I properly washed my hands if you know what I mean. You're not the only person lately who's passed out in my presence."

"Don't take it personally. Doctor says he has pneumonia. Me, well, I'm just not good around blood."

He nodded and gave her kind of a funny look. "Yeah, I saw you on the news last night. Sorry. I had no idea who you were when you, uh, came to the autopsy room the other day."

A sour feeling started churning in Alexandra's stomach. She didn't know why exactly, but she knew it wasn't because of anything she'd eaten. She tried to make herself more open to whatever was causing it, but nothing else was coming through. Was that stupid hex bag keeping her so closed to the other side she couldn't pick up on anything?

It was so frustrating.

She glanced toward Dylan and saw that his gaze was focused on her now. He said something to Reedus and moved away.

When Dylan moved, that's when Alexandra saw her.

Saw *it*.

The old woman with the creepy black eyes sat in the chair beside Reedus's bed. The spirit's expression was void of any emotion. She just sat there, staring back at Alexandra.

Waiting.

Someone touched Alexandra's shoulder, and she jumped about three inches off the ground. "Hey, you okay?" Dylan asked.

Sucking in air, she nodded and looked between the two men. "Yeah. Fine." The poor medical examiner was probably going to go home and tell his family about how utterly weird and neurotic that lady psychic helping the police was.

Dylan didn't look as though he believed her, but all he said was, "I need to talk to Watkins for a few minutes. Why don't you go say hey to Reedus? Maybe he'll listen to you if you tell him to stay in that bed and get well."

She glanced back toward the bed Reedus occupied. The chair beside him was empty.

No one else can see this thing. Only you. You're the only one who can fight it. Now buck up and go in there.

She nodded and moved slowly into the room, hesitating when she came to the small bathroom right inside. It was eerily dark. Was the old woman hiding in there now?

"Still wearing that dress, I see." Reedus croaked out the comment. "Looks a little wrinkled. Guess you and Collins—" He started coughing, so Alexandra hurried to his bedside. His left hand was extremely warm when she lifted it in hers. "Sorry, doll. Can't talk too much."

"Good." She smiled down at him. "I can't imagine what kind of things you'd say on medication with that dirty mind of yours."

He chuckled and began coughing. Right. No jokes. Couldn't make him laugh.

She glanced around the room, that weird feeling gone from her belly. Her muscles relaxed. It was gone now.

She squeezed Reedus's hand and met his droopy gaze. "I'm sorry, Reedus. I didn't realize you'd been sick."

He coughed into his other fist. "Snuck up on me a few days ago."

A few days ago. "When did you first notice it?"

"When did we find that body in the cemetery?" He looked over her shoulder and frowned. "Right around when you showed up, I guess."

Seriously? Alexandra knew certain spirits, even the good ones, could make people physically ill. She'd seen it time and time again. The old creepy demon had just been in Reedus's room, so maybe...?

Holy crap.

Was the demon making Reedus ill? On purpose?

"What's goin' on inside that pretty head of yours now?" Reedus asked.

She bit her lip, reached down into her purse and pulled out the pouch Barbara had given her. Should she? Giving it to him would leave herself exposed again. Maybe that had been the demon's plan.

Alexandra steeled her shoulders. She had to give him the bag to see if her theory was correct, had to see if she could help him. His condition had gotten so much worse in only a few hours. She couldn't be selfish.

"Reedus, I know you think a lot of this is hocus pocus, but will you please do me a favor?" She put the pouch in his palm. "Keep this on you. I think it will help you recover a lot faster."

He lifted the pouch. "What's in it?"

She really needed to find that out for herself. "It wards off negative spirits. Just promise me you'll try it." At the very least, hopefully it would keep him safe from Creepy Black Eyes.

He started coughing, but nodded. "Where am I supposed to put it?"

Good question. "Just keep it near you. That's good enough." She hoped.

"Might as well." He put the bag on the table beside him. "Ain't got nothin' better to do."

Dylan came back into the room and asked if she was ready to leave. She nodded and tried to give Reedus a hug. "Let me know if I can do anything for you."

His hearty chuckle suggested an inappropriate reply was swimming around that brain of his, but he didn't say anything.

Once they were in the elevator, Alexandra took hold of Dylan's hand. Poor man looked tired. He was rubbing his forehead, too.

"Got a headache?" she asked.

"Yeah. This case has been giving me lots of 'em." He forced a smile and squeezed her fingers. "How are you holding up?"

"Eh." She shrugged.

He let go of her hand when the elevator stopped. He'd snuck out the back of his house earlier, and she'd told McCormick she'd gotten a call from Dylan letting her know about Reedus. The young man hadn't seemed too suspicious about taking her to the hospital. Dylan had told McCormick to go grab something to eat when he'd dropped her off. Whether or not they'd fooled the young cop, she had no idea.

"McCormick will take you back to your hotel. Try to get some sleep." She spotted the patrol car sitting at the entrance. Dylan must have called the younger officer when she'd been talking to Reedus. She guessed that meant they weren't spending the night together.

Disappointment flooded through her. And fear. When she realized she'd just given away her best source of protection to Reedus, her heartbeat fluttered in her chest like a fly caught in a spiderweb. McCormick would be outside the hotel, but he could only protect her from what he could see. She'd be alone inside, and vulnerable to what he couldn't.

"Alexandra?"

Dylan was watching her, his forehead crinkled in concern. She was tempted to admit how scared she was to be alone, but there were cleansing techniques she should perform. Things that might keep her safe. Things Dylan probably wasn't ready to witness. "Sorry. Just tired." She lifted her gaze to his. "Will I see you tomorrow?"

"Of course." One side of his mouth lifted. "You'll be riding with me tomorrow."

Relief soothed away some of the disappointment she'd felt. "Good night then."

"Good night." But he walked her to the car, opened the door for her, and leaned down to tell McCormick. "I'll be picking up Miss King around eight-thirty. If you have a chance, can you call in and have someone make sure that printout of ghost-tour employees is on my desk when I get to the office. We're going to pay some of them a visit."

"Yes, sir."

"Appreciate it." Dylan nodded and closed her door. McCormick probably didn't see the sexy way Dylan winked at her when he stepped back, but Alexandra caught the gesture.

It gave her hope that he wasn't completely pulling away from her again.

Eight-thirty couldn't come fast enough.

***

Dylan couldn't sleep, so he found himself staring inside his empty fridge sometime around three a.m. What he wouldn't give for a cold beer and some chips right about now. Scratching his chest, he shut the door and glanced toward the mess he'd left in his living room. There'd be time for that later. He needed sleep, but it didn't come easy.

A helluva lot had happened. His mind was on information overload, pinging from one subject to another. How had the Grim Reaper known his cell phone number? Did the killer have inside connections? Reedus had pneumonia. Would he be okay? Zach had left home because he was tired of being a punching bag for Ray. Was that true? Ray was dead. He couldn't get his side of the story. Should he approach his brother now with questions about it, or let Zach make the first move?

And why the hell hadn't he let Alexandra stay here for the night? He had a feeling having her next to him in his bed would have helped settle his racing mind. Funny, since he still wasn't one hundred percent committed to believing everything she'd told him. He couldn't argue with her effect on him though.

Strange how fate threw people together sometimes.

He couldn't help but wonder what kind of relationship she had with his brother, but thinking about it too much made him feel agitated. Thinking of Zach always had that effect on him, but he really didn't like the fact that Zach had known Alexandra first. Didn't like thinking her loyalties would always sway to his big brother's side.

But hadn't his own, once upon a time?

167

His thoughts pinged back to the day Zach had run away from home.

Zach had used their mom's truck to pick Dylan up from baseball practice. Dylan had been tossing his ball back and forth between hands as he complained to Zach about being made a short stop although he wanted to be pitcher when a loud *bam* had proceeded his entire body being thrust forward against his seatbelt. A second later, Zach had been right there, checking him over, his face shadowed with worry and concern.

Dylan's brow furrowed now. Zach hadn't had a black eye or bloody lip then, and it was past the end of the school day. Yet when Dylan had found Zach packing a duffle bag a couple of hours later, his big brother's lip had been busted and there had been a wicked gash over his eyebrow.

"What happened, Zach?"

"Nothin'," Zach had said. "Got in a fight today at school is all."

Had Ray blamed Zach for the accident and taken it out on him even though Zach had been sitting at a red light at the time? Even though neither of them had been hurt?

He swore. It was all starting to make sense. How had he never made that connection before?

Blowing out a breath, he found his wallet and pulled everything out looking for the small photo he'd always carried in it. It was a picture of him and his brother taken about a year before Zach had left home. When he'd been younger, he'd looked at the picture a lot. He hadn't even thought about it for years though. Where was it?

She said to tell you, 'The picture you've been looking for is in the trunk in the attic.'

The memory of Alexandra's words slammed into him with the force of punch in his solar plexus. She'd claimed the words had come from his mother. He laughed nervously. He hadn't been looking for a picture, had thought she was crazy, but now—

Fifteen minutes later, Dylan sat on his attic floor with the picture in his hand.

Any doubts he'd had about Alexandra King were gone, right along with any hope he'd had of sleep.

***

Things were getting more difficult, and yes, he knew he only had himself to blame for that.

The Grim Reaper tugged off the gloves and hat he'd been wearing and tossed them onto his dining room table. He carefully retrieved the hypodermic needle encased inside his jacket pocket and hid it in a cookie jar. He lived alone, so no one would bother it but him.

His kill tonight had been a failure. He'd had to postpone it when he'd done a preliminary walk past his planned site of display and seen a patrol car parked in front of the area.

He'd walked past each of the sites on his list. Police were watching each one.

Not to worry.

Charleston was full of haunted locations. Either the police would give up and leave a site vulnerable, or he'd find a lesser known location to use as his playground.

Leaving the TV volume turned up loud so he could hear it, he stepped into the next room and felt his heartbeat begin to race, the sound thrumming in his ears, drowning out the early morning news anchor's voice. His plan was precise. The least disruption could ruin everything.

He turned on his lamp and leaned over his desk where the map was spread out with his notes marked cleanly in the corners. Each location was important. He'd spent months determining them and verifying that they matched his drawing to the degree.

Five locations. Five points on the map.

He'd only managed to mark off four so far, including the one the police hadn't yet linked to him. His first. It had been his test run. Excitement chased away his anxiety as he remembered how easy it had been.

He'd been so afraid, that first time, but he'd gotten away with it. No one had ever suspected him.

Now he only needed one more. One more death to complete the pentagram on the map. One more victim before he could move onto his grand finale.

His original plan had been to make Collins his fifth but now his plans had changed. Hearing the TV news reporter say the same name he'd been considering only seemed to validate that he already knew who the fifth victim should be.

"No one at the private security firm where Alexandra King works could be reached for comment."

Alexandra King.

She'd make the perfect fifth. A fitting tribute.

And figuring out how to lure her into his trap would be exactly the challenge he needed to occupy his thoughts until the police got lazy.

His lips tugged against the small scar on his cheek as they spread into a smile.

Now all he had to do was plan, and wait.

Chapter Fourteen

"Tell me again why we're here." Dylan held the door open to the Mystic Corner and gestured Alexandra inside.

"I never told you why. I just told you to trust me." She smiled as she pushed her sunglasses to the top of her head and brushed past him. Truly, it spoke volumes that he hadn't grumbled too much when she'd asked him to drive her to the occult store after picking her up this morning.

Dylan sighed and glanced around. "Charming place."

He reached to touch one of the small shrunken heads hanging on a display, his hand hesitating before pulling back and sliding into his pocket. He kept one eyebrow arched as he skimmed the section of antique-looking Ouija boards. Alexandra didn't have to be psychic to read his mind. He thought this place was as strange as a fish on a bike.

The friendlier of the two young men she remembered from the day before was stacking items on a shelf. Alexandra moved closer and tapped him on the shoulder.

The young dark-skinned man did a double-take then smiled when he recognized her. "Hey! Meemaw said you'd be back."

Did she now? "Rex, is your grandmother available?"

He glanced over her shoulder at Dylan. His smile dimmed, but he nodded. "Just go in the back. I think they're expecting you."

"They?"

He only nodded in reply.

Alexandra hurried to the back curtained-off room, expecting that Dylan would follow. She'd decided it would be better for him to see certain things firsthand rather than attempt to explain anything about the black-eyed demon lady.

Barbara was leaning over, churning at the contents of a small marble bowl and murmuring what sounded like a prayer from the Bible. She didn't look up as Alexandra then Dylan stepped into the small space.

The young sandy-haired man with the neck tattoo sat on the corner of the desk, not the least bit surprised to see her. He gave her a slight wave. "Name's Connor."

She waved back. "Alexandra."

Barbara raised her voice when she said, "Go on. Ax'me."

Alexandra turned her attention to the black woman and smiled. "You know why I'm here."

"Chil', I 'spect ya last night." She stopped churning and reached for a pouch. "Ya need annuddah one, right? Gave yours away?"

Alexandra rolled her eyes. "You know, Barbara, I have a much easier time understanding you when you're not putting on."

Barbara cackled in that quirky way she did. "Don't spoil my fun, child." She lifted her gaze toward Dylan. "Introduce me to this fine-looking man of yours."

She did, stepping back to allow Barbara to accept and then cling to Dylan's handshake a little longer than was appropriate. Her brown eyes danced with mischief as she looked him up and down carefully. "Mmmm-mmm. Seen you in a dream. You're hunting him, aren't you?"

"Excuse me?" Dylan said, taking a step closer to Alexandra, his gaze zeroing in on the bookshelf where mason jars with hand-written labels revealed an assortment of strange ingredients. Gum

Arabic. Lovage root chips. Cinnamon oil. A bunch of other things Alexandra herself didn't recognize.

"Calls himself the Reaper." Barbara turned her back to them and began cleaning up the area she'd just been using. "Saw that in my dream too. Plus, it was on the news this morning."

But Alexandra's attention had caught and held on that mention of a dream. "Barbara, what did you see in your vision?"

"Saw you and him." She turned and nodded at Dylan, then shifted back to her work. "You're getting closer to finding the man you're looking for. You're figuring it out. Only a matter of time now."

Alexandra hadn't figured out a darn thing when it came to the killer. Well, other than he was a real nutjob who probably had a demonic parasite steering his ride on the crazy bus.

"Did you see the killer in your dream? Can you tell us anything about him?" Alexandra stepped closer.

Barbara shuffled around the desk and returned some items to a drawer. "He's surrounded by the darkness. Too much darkness. Couldn't see his face."

Alexandra wondered if the frustration building in her chest was the same as what her clients felt when she was unable to give them absolute information from her visions and feelings. She sympathized enough to know Barbara was only telling them what she did know. Which wasn't much.

Barbara pushed a drawer closed and straightened. Her caramel eyes locked onto Alexandra's. "You be careful, child. He's gonna come after you, and ain't nothing you can do to stop that but be prepared."

Dylan's body pushed against Alexandra's as he stepped forward. "What do you mean by that?"

Barbara's hands found her hips as she looked Dylan up and down again, her expression surprised. "I mean what I said."

Dylan didn't back down. "How should she prepare?"

The older woman gestured to the bag Alexandra now held and addressed her directly. "Keep that close. Keep your fine man closer." She tapped the side of her head. "Keep your wits about you."

"Can I get—?" Alexandra's words were interrupted by Barbara's.

"Only one bag this time. No more."

"Why not?" Too late, she realized she might have sounded like a petulant child.

The older woman chuckled. "Out of ingredients."

Alexandra bit her bottom lip to keep from asking for a list of ingredients so she could replenish them for the woman. She'd hoped to get protection for Dylan, too, but she sensed she'd be overstepping if she asked for a recipe. Alexandra held up the small pouch the woman had given her and smiled. "Thank you. I'll find a way to repay you for this."

The young man in the room—Alexandra had all but forgotten he was there—straightened and held out a piece of paper to her. She took it and saw a phone number scribbled on it.

"It's my number," he said. "You might need it."

Dylan's hands on her hips tugged her back against him. "Why would she need it?"

Oooh. Jealous, much? Alexandra smiled as she tucked the paper into her purse.

"Have you ever heard of the Bellator de Lux?" Connor asked.

Alexandra recognized the words from her studies of Latin. "Warrior of light?"

His brow lifted. "Very good. It's also the name of an organization I belong to. I came to Charleston to help—" his gaze moved to Barbara's, "—with a peculiar anomaly. I think Miss King knows what I'm referring to."

Alexandra glanced up at Dylan and back to Connor again. "The gray beams?"

"It's a portal of some kind. I'm here to close it." He shrugged. "I haven't been too successful in finding it so far, but Barbara tells me you've seen it. When you're not so busy catching a serial killer, maybe we can chat." He gestured toward Alexandra's purse. "And I was giving the number to Dylan, not you. He's the one who'll probably need it."

"Oh." Alexandra dug the paper out and handed it to Dylan. It was her turn to feel the sting of jealousy until Connor leaned over and stage whispered, "Don't worry. I'm not gay. Just someone who happens to know a lot about exorcisms."

"Exorcisms?" Dylan's voice was amused now.

Connor crossed his arms. "When you find the killer, he's going to need one."

Barbara's hearty laugh drowned any chance Alexandra had for more questions. The woman shooed them away with a nod and wave of her hand. "Go on. You two got work to do."

Dylan waited until they were back in his car to speak again. After putting the key in the ignition, he sent her a sideways look that suggested he was not amused. "Do I even want to know what any of that was about?"

She shook her head and fought a smile. "Have you checked on Reedus today?"

He steered the car toward traffic. "First thing. He sounded better. A lot better."

Alexandra had already checked on the older detective, too, and she would have said he sounded *amazingly* better. Reedus had told her his doctors were dumbfounded at his progress. He'd asked, "You think this weird lil bag you gave me helped?"

Not that she discounted the power of medicine, but yeah, she did. Her theory had been right. Whatever was in that little bag worked.

She felt its slight weight in her hand and lifted it to her nose for a sniff. A touch of sandalwood. Maybe some sage. Nothing too noticeable. She'd worn jeans today, and it was a tight fit, but she managed to stuff the new pouch into her front pocket. Who cared if there was a slight, unflattering bulge? She wasn't taking any chance of dropping it or leaving it behind somewhere.

For the next two hours, she and Dylan met with different employees of ghost tour companies, trying to determine if any were suspect or had noticed any customers who were.

Nothing stood out.

Alexandra did notice something, though. There were no ghosts. And she'd specifically opened herself to communication before getting out of the car earlier.

"Lunch?" Dylan asked after they'd finished their last interview. "There's a great deli right around the corner."

Alexandra stopped and glanced in the other direction from which he'd gestured. She was starting to get a feel for the area. "Can we go back to the brewery?"

"You're kidding, right?"

She shook her head. She had another theory she wanted to test, but for fun, she lifted a hand to her chest and tried to look horrified. "But they have the most incredible soup. I've been *dreaming* about that soup."

Dylan came as close to rolling his eyes as she'd ever seen—was he mocking her now?— and motioned her to lead the way.

A few minutes later they walked inside the all-too familiar restaurant amidst the lunch crowd. Alexandra glanced around, looking for a certain dead person wearing a bowler hat. George was nowhere to be seen.

A host seated them and Dylan hung his coat on the back of his chair. "Bathroom break. Order me a burger if the waiter comes."

That had been her plan, but he beat her to it. She grabbed his wrist before he could get far, dug into her jeans for the pouch, and slid it into his hand. "Take this and don't lose it. Please?"

He pushed his hand back toward her. "Aren't you supposed to keep this close at all times?"

She gestured to the crowded room. "We're in a public place. I'm safe for the moment. Please, just take it. I need to talk to George."

Shaking his head in disapproval, he shrugged and pushed the small sack into his front pocket. "Don't move from this spot." He pointed at her chair. "I mean it."

She watched as he disappeared toward the restrooms, and waited. One. Two. Three…

"Been wonderin' when you'd turn back up." The familiar voice accompanied a warm breath on the back of her neck. She turned to see George sitting ridiculously close in a chair at the next table. He smiled big and leaned back away from her. "Did ya catch that guy ya were after?"

Never mind that. Keeping her voice barely above a whisper, she slid into the chair to her left so she was facing him and the window, and asked, "Why couldn't I see you when I came in?"

He crinkled his nose and pushed his hat back off his brow a little. "Sorry to be direct, lass, but ya stank. I was keepin' my distance."

"I stank?" She hadn't smelled anything nasty. What the heck was in that pouch?

"Have ya ever tangled with a skunk?" A shudder racked his very solid body. "Woo-wee. This is worse. Absolutely foul, if ya ask me. No thanks."

"You're still there, but you just chose not to come near me?" She'd been wondering if the ingredients harmed spirits or simply repelled them. Great. Barbara had given her Ghost Away.

George shrugged. "I smelled ya before ya came through the doors. I like ya, but uh, that odor is pretty ripe."

Ripe enough to repel a demon?

"George, do you know what a demon is?"

177

He looked offended. "Course I do."

"Tell me."

"It's just like the good Bible says—" She held up her hand, stopping him from launching into a religious tirade. He didn't know. She suspected not many ghosts did. Otherwise, they'd all be eager to cross over.

"Have you ever seen one in here?"

His brow came together. "What do ya mean?"

She briefly explained about the black-eyed old woman.

He scratched his chin. "Know what? I think I might have seen her too. Her eyes aren't black though. An older woman, looks like my granny, stern and scary. I try to stay away from her cause she seems like a handful."

"You aren't afraid of her?" Rebecca and the other ghost had seemed terrified. Terrified enough to skedaddle when the old woman came around.

George scoffed. "Me? I ain't afraid of nothin' much, miss. Besides, she's never been too interested in me."

"Does she come in often?" If the demon was attached to their killer, maybe they could trace a pattern out of his visits here and set a trap.

"Come to think of it, I usually see her on Wednesdays and Sundays, right before closin'."

Oh, she could kiss him! As luck would have it, tomorrow was Wednesday.

"Know what? There is something that scares me. That smell." George shifted in his seat. "Matter of fact, that fella ya came in with is about to head this way. Stinks up the place, so if you'll excuse me, I'll take my leave now."

"Wait!" She reached for George's arm before thinking of the consequences. The older couple at the table beside them was now openly watching her, she realized. She dropped his arm, smiled and picked up her menu. At least it was so busy the waiter hadn't appeared to take her order yet. She tried to speak through her teeth as she pretended to skim the menu. "I need to ask you a favor before you go."

"Make it quick then."

She gave up on the trying to talk-through-her-teeth thing. Too hard. "Can you ask around for me?" She knew most ghosts recognized one another for what they were. "Ask if the other spirits around here can help us find the man we were chasing the other night. I know they've had to see him. We need details. What does he look like? What's his name? Where does he live?"

"Who are you talking to?" Dylan asked.

Lowering her menu, Alexandra glanced up just as Dylan pulled his chair out and sat down beside her. She glanced around, but George was gone.

Dammit.

Dylan arched a brow as he pushed his menu aside. "Very funny."

"What?"

"I told you not to move from your seat. You moved to a different chair. Yes, I noticed." His eyes took on a more teasing glint. "Or did you simply want to sit closer to me?"

She winked at him. "I can see why you made detective." She sprang to her feet and reached for her cell phone. "My turn for a bathroom break. I haven't seen the waiter yet, so just order me…. whatever."

She didn't wait on Dylan's response. She hurried toward the women's restroom. As she got closer, she put her phone to her ear—she'd done this an absurd number of times—and pretended to be talking to someone.

"George? George, I wasn't finished. Where are you?"

There were too many people hanging around the area outside the women's bathroom to hear herself think, so she pushed through the bathroom doors, hoping for a little more privacy. There were three women in front of her, waiting for a stall. She got in line and wondered where her pesky ghost was hiding.

"George?" She kept her voice low, uncertain about the acoustics of the room. At least the two young women in front of her were chitchatting and ignoring her, with the added benefit of masking her voice with theirs.

"Just remember ya brought me in here, so ya can't call me a pervert." George materialized in front of the sinks and quickly became fascinated with a young redhead doing up her makeup in the mirror. "Hello, beautiful."

Alexandra rolled her eyes. "Pay attention to our conversation."

"I'm listenin'." But he continued to stare at the redhead. "Go on."

"Can you do what I asked?"

The redhead finished her makeup and moved away, and George glanced around, his eyes gleaming with delight. "Sure. Ask around. I can do that."

She named some of the locations where the killer had staged bodies to be found. The alley. The cemetery. The old city jail.

George scrunched his face when she mentioned the last location. "Not goin' in there, lass. Sorry. Bunch of bad characters in that place. I'll go to the others though."

"And Dock Street Theater. Do you know where that is?" She clung to the idea her dream had meant something. She simply didn't know what. Maybe George could help her figure it out.

"Yeah, sure." He leaned close to a brunette and sniffed at her hair.

"I'll come back tomorrow afternoon. Will that give you enough time?"

He pointed at a young blonde who came out of a stall. "That one comes in a lot. Always with a different bloke. I'm pretty sure money passes hands, if you know what I mean." He held up one hand and rubbed his thumb against his fingers as he waggled his eyebrows.

Could ghosts have ADHD? Cause she was pretty sure this one did.

"I don't *care* if she's a hooker." Stepping forward as the line shifted, Alexandra realized too late she'd spoken the words aloud. A little too loud.

The blonde turned and did a startled doubletake, her eyes wide with a hint of horror as she stared open-mouthed at Alexandra.

Alexandra smiled and looked away, pressing the phone closer to her ear. "She could, uh, be the Queen of England for all I care. I don't want her babysitting our kids." Oh, geez, that made no sense. Not a word of it. But the blonde seemed to snap back to normalcy and went to the sink to wash her hands, even if she did keep glancing at Alexandra in the mirror.

"You have kids?" George asked, focused on her, finally.

"No, I do not." Heat crept up her neck. She stepped forward as the line shifted again. The next stall was hers.

A slow chuckle erupted from him. "Oh, I see what you're doing. Clever."

"So tomorrow? Does that give you enough time?"

George shrugged. "Sure."

"Around noon?"

He nodded. "I'll see ya then."

Alexandra pretended to end her call and sent the ghost a pointed look she hoped told him, *We're done. Now get the heck out of the women's bathroom.*

***

Some of the tension evaporated from Dylan's muscles when he finally spotted Alexandra hurrying back to their table. He'd been about to abandon their seats to go check on her.

He didn't like what that woman had implied this morning, about the killer coming after Alexandra. *Ain't nothin' you can do to stop that but be prepared.*

The more he thought about it, he should have never let Alexandra out of his sight.

"Sorry." Her face scrunched in apology. No sooner had she sat down than a brilliant smile was highlighting the dimples in her cheeks. "I have some information that might help the case."

"Let me get this straight. You got information about this case from the women's bathroom?" He pointed his thumb in that direction.

He expected her to roll her eyes at his teasing and admit she'd called someone. Instead, she laughed, and the sound spread warmth through his chest. "Uh huh." Waving a dismissive hand, she leaned forward. "I need you to keep an open mind with what I'm about to tell you. Will you promise to listen without shutting me out again?"

He hated it when women started conversations like that. "Tell me."

She did. She started with a wildly imaginative story about first seeing a black-eyed old woman outside of the autopsy room and ended with the information she'd obtained from George. George, the dead guy who supposedly haunted this restaurant.

His first instinct was to back away slowly and call the mental institution. But this was Alexandra, the woman who'd been spot on about finding one victim's vehicle and knowing far too many details about Candice Christopher's murder. The woman who'd known exactly where his long-forgotten photo of his brother had been, days before he'd even thought to look for it.

He took a deep breath. "If this black-eyed woman is seen here regularly on Wednesdays and Sundays, then you think—"

"I think she's attached to the killer, and where he goes, she goes."

"What about Reedus? You said she's been attached to him. You think he's the killer?" He scoffed.

"No, of course not." She looked thoughtful for a second. "I first saw her at the morgue. I think maybe she was trying to scare me away then, didn't want me helping. I think she can affect anyone involved with the killer or this case if she wants." She nodded, as if agreeing with her own idea. "Yes, I think she's that powerful."

"What if the old lady is totally unrelated to our killer?" He threw a wild ball out into left field with his thoughts. "What if she attached to you at the morgue because you can see her, and that's how she got close enough to Reedus to make him sick?"

"She's not attached to me."

"How do you know?"

Her lips tightened into a line. "I just do. Dylan, I know I'm asking a lot here, but can't you trust me on this? Let's set up surveillance here tomorrow. What have you got to lose?"

His reputation. His credibility. He could give her a dozen options, but he kept his mouth shut. It was a tough call, ordering manpower because of a hunch. The waiter arrived with their food, giving him a short reprieve.

As soon as the server left, Alexandra was on him again. "About tomorrow. If I see the old woman hanging around anyone in particular, you can pull him in for questioning. What do you think?"

Sighing, he nodded. "It's as good a lead as any we've gotten so far." The killer *had* been at this bar the other night. And he'd been familiar enough with it to disappear quickly and without detection. Dylan took a bite of his burger, trying his best not to feel unreasonably pleased by her obvious happiness at his decision. He glanced around, trying to ground himself before his thoughts veered in the direction of why. "At some point, I need to take you someplace different to eat. This place isn't bad, but we've eaten here how many times?"

"Four. Not that I'm keeping track or anything." She slipped some soup between her lips, closed her eyes as she swallowed, and then pointed her spoon at him. "Do you cook?"

"Me?"

She pinned her gaze on him. "No, I'm talking to that plant over there. Of course you."

"Not to brag, but I grill a mean steak."

"I'd love one. Thanks. Before I leave?"

Was she asking him on a date? Considering they'd already slept together a few times, he figured it was a reasonable expectation. And strangely one that didn't send him into a cold sweat. "Plan on it."

"Oh, I am. And I want to do one of those carriage rides I keep seeing people do." Her sparkling eyes were soaking up the scenery outside the window now. "I want to go to Fort Sumter one day. Mmm, I love history. I love learning about stuff. You know?"

He grinned, imagining she had resources in that area most people didn't. The ghost that haunted this building was believed to be the spirit of a cotton merchant who'd died in the 1800s. Her invisible friend George?

"I can't believe you sent George out to snoop around for us." That really was a brilliant idea, assuming spirits did haunt the entire city and she could talk to them.

An undead spy. Lord, had he gone crazy because he was buying into this?

She snorted as she dug into her salad. "You're only jealous cause you didn't think of it yourself."

"Guilty as charged." But his lightened mood was fading. A heavy worry settled in his stomach, flavoring each bite of his food more and more bland until he finally stopped trying to force it down.

What if he was spending so much time following Alexandra's

leads that he overlooked a more credible one…and someone paid for Dylan's mistake with his or her life?

"Dylan?" Alexandra's hand covered his. She waited until his gaze met hers to add, "Thank you for trying. I know it's not easy."

He turned his hand up and laced his fingers with hers. Funny how her simple gesture had chased away his rising anxiety.

"We're going to catch this guy soon," she said. "I can sense it."

He hoped so. He couldn't wait for this case to be closed. Couldn't wait for things to get back to normal. Only, he knew normal for him didn't include Alexandra King. As soon as they solved this case, she would leave.

Well, they might enjoy one day, maybe two, together, and then she would leave.

Why did that realization leave him feeling so empty inside?

Chapter Fifteen

Red. Like the color of blood.

Alexandra held still to examine the color of the walls around her. As she stared, paint began to drip down the large area. Not paint. It *was* blood.

A quick flash of latex-covered hands covered in red, holding a small knife, disoriented her vision. The buzz of a saw in the distance—the sound meant something. She knew it did. But what?

Her vision focused again on the walls, no longer dripping red. White trim separated a dark wood-stained door from the red wall directly in front of her.

Her hand trembled as she reached toward the doorknob.

A sense of urgency pushed her forward. She needed to look behind the door. *Now.*

As it opened into a dimly lit room, she knew why. A woman's body lay unmoving on the red-patterned carpet. She rushed forward, turning the woman's body over and—

"Alexandra?" The sound of her name was followed by the snap of fingers. "Wakey wakey."

She blinked until a man's blurred and shadowed features came into focus. Right in front of her face.

She yelped and dragged the bed sheets up to her neck as she scrambled toward the wall. "George! What are you doing here?"

She glanced around. Yep, she was still in her bedroom. At the hotel. She shoved her hair out of her face and glared at the pesky ghost.

George straightened and grabbed the lapels of his jacket with both hands. His mouth curled into a mischievous smile. "Not a morning person, are ya?"

"Gah! Didn't your mama teach you manners?" She scooted to the other side of the bed. "What time is it?" How was it already morning? Her eyes were gritty and full of sand. She snatched her cell phone from the nightstand and noted the time, plus a text from Dylan from almost an hour ago. He'd left her around midnight to go home, grab some clothes and shower. He hadn't wanted to wake her and promised McCormick was coming to stand guard outside.

It was only two o'clock.

"You scared the crap outta me, George. It's the middle of the night!"

He snorted. "Come on, now. Figured you were used to this sorta thing."

"Findin' a strange man leaning over me in my bed when I wake up? Not quite. Not in the middle of the night."

He narrowed his eyes on the clock on the wall above her head. "Oh yeah, it is still night, ain't it?"

She shook her head and fell back on the pillows. Her head was throbbing with a tedious ache.

He blew a noisy raspberry at her. "Here I was, doin' ya a favor by bringing ya what I'd learned earlier than promised. Alright then. I'll leave."

"Wait!" She huffed out a breath and tossed the covers aside. She'd gotten past the whole modesty in front of ghosts scenario a long time ago. And she really had to pee. "What did you learn?" She padded toward the bathroom, trying not to think about the fact she was still completely naked from a late-night romp with

Dylan. When George began to follow, she spun around and held up a hand. *Don't. Just don't.*

He turned and began pacing the other way. Alexandra moved into the bathroom, cracked the door—not that a door could stop him if he wanted inside—and called out, "I'm listening."

"I had a little look-see around like ya asked." His voice was only slightly muffled, but it reassured her that he was keeping his distance. "This fella you're looking for is quite the source of gossip among the others right now." The sound of glass clinked against glass in the other room.

"What are you doing?"

"Nuttin'. Nuttin' at all." He cleared his throat. "I ran into an old pirate fella in that alley you asked me to snoop around in. Saw the whole thing happening. Said this man y'all are interested in drove up in a car, carried out another fella, propped the poor soul against the wall, lingered for a bit, and then drove away. Simple as that."

She hurried to finish her business and then opened the door to ask, "Did he tell you what kind of car it was or what the man looked like?"

George was toying with the coffeemaker in the room. "I mentioned he was a pirate, didn't I? I don't think he really understands what a car is. Not every fella is as smart as ole George here." He tapped a finger against the side of his hat. "I've picked up a lot of know-how about such things over the years." Moving away from the coffeemaker, he zeroed in on the television. "Do you get any of those sexy pictures in here? Mind if I stay and watch one while you're out?"

"Sexy pictures?" She snatched the robe hanging on the bathroom door and groaned when she realized what he meant. It was too early to be dealing with ghosts right now. "No! You are not watching porn in my room."

He blew another raspberry at her as he sat on the end of her bed facing the television. "I might not give y'all the descriptions I managed to drag outta him if yer gonna behave that way."

Alexandra groaned and sank into the chair across from him. She could still be sleeping oh so good. She rubbed at her temples. "Gimme the descriptions, George."

"Bossy, aren't cha?" He waggled his eyebrows, tipped his hat, and fell back on the bed. "I pulled it together from talkin' to the others. Dark car. Two doors. Dodge Avenger, I'm told. Not a newer one. The fender was a bit rusty. As for the fella you're after, he was too much in the dark to see much of. Sorry 'bout that."

She perked up, but she was suspicious of his information gathering. "You got that much detail?"

"Bet your tush, I did. A poor kid lingers down near the cemetery. I think he was killed in a car wreck not too long ago, but he assured me he was a real gear head, although I don't have the foggiest clue what that means. Anyway, this rascal, Mike's his name. Nice fella. He assured me he knew his cars, and he's certain it was a 1997 Dodge Avenger. Said it's driven past several times since the police found that poor girl's body."

"Oh, George, I could kiss you!"

He sprang upright. "I'll take that as payment. Thank you."

Alexandra pushed out of her seat and planted one on his cheek. His skin was almost as solid as Dylan's. Barbara's warning about ghosts turning into demons if they stayed on earth too long nudged at her conscience. "Can I ask you a personal question?" He nodded, watching her warily as she sat beside him. "When did you die?"

"Eighteen thirteen."

She bit her lip. "Another personal question?"

He nodded, but pulled away from her a bit.

"Why are you still here? Do you want help crossing over?"

When a person died, they had one chance to move toward the bright oval portal that opened for a few minutes. She'd been told the hole felt magnetic to the dead. It kind of pulled them in. A spirit had to exert a lot of willpower to resist it, and if he did, he usually had a good reason.

Alexandra had been in her teens the first time she'd realized she could visualize a portal and make it appear, giving the ghost she was with a second chance to go through it.

George pushed to his feet. "Don't you go tryin' that on me, missy. I like it just fine here."

"How did you—?" She shook her head. "Never mind. I won't pry."

"How did I die?" He pulled at the collar of his shirt, and Alexandra recalled the deep, bloody gash she'd first seen at his neck. "Got myself in quite a bit of a mess. Couldn't see a way out. I'm not proud of what I did."

Snippets of his death flashed through her mind.

Poor George. He'd committed suicide by hanging. Alexandra suddenly understood his reluctance to cross over. His belief system probably suggested he'd go to hell when he did. He would need some counseling before crossing over, and that wasn't Alexandra's specialty. She'd met a couple of psychic mediums over the years who had degrees in psychology, too. She'd look one up when this was all done.

Her mind went back to her dream earlier. Alexandra's skin crawled beneath a sudden icy chill. She'd had the dream again, which meant Candice or another dead person had been sending her information while she was asleep. If George was here, then—

"What's wrong?" he demanded. "You've gone as white as a sheet."

"This isn't right." She hurried over to her purse, dumped its contents on the bed, and searched frantically for the pouch Barbara had made for her yesterday. "It's gone."

"What is?"

Maybe she'd put it in the nightstand. No, not there. "The Ghost

190

Away. It's gone. You wouldn't be here otherwise."

Her hands tore through the sheets, lifted the pillows, and searched her suitcase. The pouch was definitely not where she'd stored it.

George moved quickly around the bedroom, sticking his nose up and sniffing. He turned back toward her. "Perhaps your gentleman friend took it with 'em?"

"Maybe." But even as she hit send on his phone number, she knew there was no reason Dylan would have done so.

He answered on the second ring. "Alexandra?"

Her racing heart calmed a little at the sound of his voice. "Dylan, hi." She swallowed and reached to run fingers through her messy hair. "Question. Did you take the pouch out of my purse when you left?"

"No." He drew out the word. "It's gone?"

"Yes. George woke me up. He's here."

Dylan swore. "Go to the window. Is McCormick outside?"

She hurried down the spiral staircase to the living room on the first floor. She pulled the blinds apart a little and looked out at the courtyard where McCormick usually sat at night. The bench in front of the fountain was empty. "No, he's not there. I don't see him."

He swore again and she heard the ruffle of movement in the background. "Are you sure no one is in your room?"

"I haven't checked under the bed or in the closet or—" Her gaze fell on the downstairs half-bathroom door. It was closed. *Someone could be in there.*

"Alexandra?" Dylan barked, but she dared not say another word.

The doorknob to the bathroom slowly began turning.

George's eyes widened when he followed her gaze. He pointed a finger at her. "Get back!" He puffed out his chest and walked through the bathroom door. Alexandra barely had time to blink

191

before he appeared again. He immediately grabbed the outside door handle and held it firm. "Some man's in there. Got a mask on." He wrinkled his nose. "Stinks to high heaven too. Oh, I think I'm gonna be sick."

Meanwhile, Dylan's voice had risen as he called her name again. "What's happening?"

"He's here, Dylan." She inched backwards. "He's in the bathroom downstairs."

George nodded toward the entryway. "Don't be a cussed fool, girl! Get outta here!"

The door handle rattled ominously in his grip. That was all the encouragement Alexandra needed to bolt barefoot for the room's door, fling it open, and run aimlessly into the courtyard. She ran past the fountain and down the short alley leading to the street. The squeal of brakes as headlights blinded her stopped her in her tracks. She lifted a hand to shield her eyes as the car's door opened.

McCormick's voice called out. "Alexandra, you okay? I got a call to go check an alarm around the corner. I was only gone twenty minutes. What happened?"

She recognized the shape of police lights on top of a patrol car as his silhouette moved forward, hand on his holster.

"Tell me what's happening," he insisted.

She pointed. "Someone's in my room. I think it's the Reaper."

He pressed her behind him, reached for his radio, and called for backup.

Dylan's familiar figure came running between two buildings into the courtyard, and Alexandra realized she still held her phone to her ear while his was nowhere in sight.

"Alexandra, are you hurt?" Grabbing hold of her arm, Dylan's gaze skimmed her from head to foot.

"I'm fine."

She'd almost forgotten how close he lived to her hotel. He

reached inside his jacket and unholstered his gun. "Go sit in McCormick's car. Do it, Alexandra! Lock the doors."

She hated to be bossed around, but she happily did as he said, just this once. Not that she could see much from the alley, but she watched from the passenger seat of McCormick's patrol car as the radio squawked updates from the dispatcher. Blue lights appeared on the street behind her, and a few uniformed officers went running past. One she recognized but didn't know his name rapped on the window.

"Detective Collins told me to wait here with you. Do you need anything?" When she shook her head, he nodded. "Hold tight." The man began pacing around the car. Neither Dylan nor McCormick had reappeared in the courtyard yet.

If the Reaper had been in her hotel room, chances were the old woman demon hadn't been too far. If he'd been after the hex pouch specifically, Barbara was right. The demon was controlling him, and worse, had wanted Alexandra vulnerable.

But why?

She lifted her clasped hands and whispered. "George, where are you? Please be okay."

She almost expected him to chime in with some chirpy greeting from the backseat and scare her half to death, but he didn't respond. Neither did he materialize.

And that scared her almost as much as anything.

Nearly ten minutes later, Dylan came striding toward the car, his gun holstered. His face was sketched in grim lines. He gestured for her to get out of the car.

"Well?"

He shook his head. "There are visible signs of forced entry on the door, but he was gone when we got there."

"How is that possible? Shouldn't I have heard something?"

"I don't know. The downstairs bathroom door looked busted

from the inside out." There was a hint of a question in his comment.

"George was holding the door, giving me time to get away."

He shook his head and ran a hand through his hair. "That sounds crazy, Alexandra." He glanced around and swore. "Is George here now?"

"No. I don't know what happened to him. I think the killer had the pouch, so I'm afraid it did something to George since he stayed to help. Maybe if he's exposed to it for more than a few seconds, it hurts him. I don't know. Maybe he's—"

"I'm sure he's fine. When you see him again, tell him I said thanks." He reached and pulled her into a quick hug. "That was too close. I'm sorry I left."

"It wasn't your fault."

His hold tightened. "I've got to make sure the scene gets checked properly. I'll have McCormick take you someplace safe."

"I don't even have my purse."

"I'll handle it." He loosened his grip and pulled back. He had his cop face on again. His dark gaze brushed over the robe she wore and stopped at her bare feet. He swore and pressed her toward the patrol car. "Text me your clothes size and tell me what you need." He opened the car door and gestured for McCormick.

She slid into the passenger seat and squeezed the lapels of the robe tight together. "I'm scared, Dylan." She hated admitting it, but it was true.

"I know, babe." He bent and pressed a kiss to her forehead. "I won't be long."

Alexandra watched as he met McCormick in front of the car, reached for his wallet, and passed over a credit card. The two men glanced her way and she realized how dependent she suddenly was on each of them.

It wasn't a feeling she liked.

The phone she still held with a death grip in one hand pinged loudly, signaling she had a text message. Confused at who would be sending her a message so early in the morning, she checked the phone and felt her muscles go still.

A picture of her sleeping, eyes closed, her face scrunched, filled the screen above the words *Were you having a bad dream? GR*

She checked the sender's information and saw Dylan's number.

She jerked her gaze up. He was still having a discussion with McCormick and another officer. He hadn't sent this. The killer must have done that thing again where he spoofed Dylan's number.

He'd been that close to her. Close enough to touch her, but he hadn't.

Why?

Chapter Sixteen

Alexandra moved to the window and nudged the curtains aside.

"Hey, I don't think it's a good idea for you to be so close," McCormick said, moving to his feet and hurrying to herd her away.

Pursing her mouth, she gave in and paced the length of her new hotel room, already regretting her decision to invite the overzealous officer into her room so he didn't have to stand in the hallway all morning. "Am I supposed to just stay here all day twiddling my thumbs? What about the stakeout tonight at the brewery?"

She needed to be there. Mostly, she needed to check on George and make sure her ghostly savior was all right. Despite her fear of attracting the old lady, she'd tried reaching out to George last night after Dylan had checked her in, but only managed to entice a dead Confederate soldier wanting to put up his heels and talk about how much he missed his old dog Maxwell. She'd finally booted him out and tried to get some sleep around four o'clock. *Tried* being the operative word. Every time a shadow had moved in the room, she'd jerked wide awake.

"Look. All I know is what Collins told me, and that was to keep you here and safe." Her bodyguard lifted his wrist and checked the time. "I'm sure he'll be here soon to take you to the station."

He'd better be.

A knock on the door startled them both. With uncanny timing, Dylan's voice called out. "McCormick, it's Collins. Let me in."

"See. I told you." Checking the peephole first, the young officer unlatched the door and greeted him. "Everything's clear here. No sign of anything unusual."

Dylan strolled in looking rumpled and sleepy but still kind of hot, even if he did resemble a wreck. It took serious effort not to fling herself at him. She was so glad to see him. He carried a few files, a plastic bag, and her purse. He tossed them all onto one of the double beds. "I brought you some of your things. Forensics still hasn't cleared your room, but they okayed these to go. I thought we could go over some things from here."

"That mean I'm okay to leave?" McCormick asked.

Dylan nodded. "You're switching out with Graham. She's gonna keep watch from the street while I'm here. Go get some sleep."

With a relieved sigh, the officer shuffled out, closing the door behind him.

Alexandra launched herself into Dylan's arms. "I've been so worried about you."

His hands squeezed her in return, but then he pushed her away. "You were worried about *me*?"

She nodded. "Your mother wanted me to come to Charleston because you were in danger. There was a reason she felt that way."

He withdrew completely. "Alexandra, don't start talking about my mom again. Not now. I'm too tired." He sank onto the end of one of the beds and glanced up at her. Rubbing at his eyes, he swore. "Why did she think I was in danger?"

Seriously? The man was asking *that* question after all that had happened? She sat down beside him, her hand covering his knee. "Before this nutcase even knew I was in town, he called the station and wanted to talk to you. Think about it." He moved as if to stand, but her fingers clamped onto his thigh, holding him down, making him listen. "I think he knows you. Maybe he's been following you. I don't know, but I think his original plans involved you somehow. Then I came along and gave him a better target."

"Is this only speculation, or…" He sighed. "Did George or some other ghost tell you this?"

"Call it a hunch."

"All I know is that this maniac is after you now, and that's what I'm focusing on." Lifting a hand, he kneaded his right shoulder and grimaced. Then the corner of his mouth tugged up as his gaze fell to her chest. "Nice shirt."

She glanced down and arched an eyebrow. Around three-thirty in the morning, Dylan had shown up with a bag from Walmart. Cotton underwear, a tacky white T-shirt with a loud flamingo design embroidered with shiny beads, jeans that barely fit, and a pair of green converse knock-offs.

"Thanks. Some guy with really terrible fashion sense got it for me." She expected a wisecrack in return, but all he offered was a tired smile. "Did you get any sleep?"

"Caught a nap at the office." He massaged at his right shoulder again, so she climbed onto the bed behind him, found the hard knot there and let her fingers do their magic. He flinched then moaned. "Ahh, that feels good."

"Massage therapist is just one of the many jobs I've had over the years, thank you very much. Gotta pay the bills somehow." She dug deep into the surrounding muscles. "Did you find anything on that car? The Dodge Avenger?"

"I pulled a list of owners in the state. Some guys are going through it, narrowing it down to locals and people with priors." He moaned softly. "If that lead pans out, you'll have won over the entire department." His voice was starting to slur. "Hope it does."

She scooted back and patted the pillow behind her. "Come on. I think we can squeeze in a little nap, don't you?"

"Shouldn't."

"Do it anyway." Settling on the left side of the bed, she patted the comforter. "Hint to Mr. Clueless: I could use a nap myself but I'm too scared to close my eyes alone."

He crawled to the pillow and collapsed beside her. She lay facing him, grateful for his presence. Poor man was already unconscious.

Sometime later, she opened her eyes and noted the shadows in the room had moved. Dylan grumbled when she shifted out of his arms. Her gaze sought the bedside clock. Two-thirty. They'd slept for a while. Longer than he'd wanted, she was sure.

She slid out of bed and padded toward the bathroom to splash some water on her face. She'd make some coffee and then wake him. It was going to take some serious schmoozing on her part to convince him to let her tag along at tonight's stakeout. Without her help—and God willing, George's—the police would have a heck of a time spotting this bastard.

Tonight was the night they caught this guy. She could feel it.

She opened the bathroom door, rubbing at the ache at the back of her lowered head, still out of it.

A pair of clunky black shoes standing in the doorway startled her. Alexandra looked up and met the menacing gaze of the old woman.

The demon's gravel-rough voice vibrated with an ominous tone. "You will die soon."

Alexandra screamed, stepped back and—

"Alexandra!"

Her shoulder shook beneath someone's grip. Blinking, it took a few seconds for her to realize she'd been dreaming.

"You were asleep." Dylan looked at her over her shoulder. "You're safe."

No.

No, she wasn't. Her vocal cords were paralyzed. Her chest

labored to catch her breath. She wouldn't be safe until she somehow rid herself of the old woman.

"Babe. You're okay." Dylan pulled her back against him. His arms were warm, tight, like a much-needed cocoon. "Promise."

"She was there. In my dream."

"Who?"

"The old woman. The demon."

It took him a few seconds to comprehend her words. Then he muttered a curse and pulled away. Rolling onto her back, she watched as he reached for his cell phone.

"Who are you calling?"

"Reedus."

She propped herself up on her elbows. "What? Why?"

He didn't answer her. Instead he greeted his partner and began a brief conversation about Reedus's amazing recovery from pneumonia.

"Remember that bag Alexandra gave you, the one you said smelled weird?" He paused and glanced over his shoulder at her. "Yeah, it is kinda strange how you got better after she gave it to you. Listen, man, any chance I could borrow it?" He grinned and looked forward again. "What time?"

Alexandra scooted to the end of the bed and grabbed his bicep. "Dylan, I can't take that from him."

He narrowed his eyes in a stern look at her. "Great. I'll send someone over to pick it up before then. Take care, man." Ending the call, he turned to her. "There's a reason this psycho took that pouch from your room last night. Whatever it is, we need to replace it, fast."

"But Reedus—"

"He's fine." He moved to his feet. "They're releasing him from the hospital in a couple of hours. He's going to stay with his son for a few days."

Alexandra glanced at the clock. Two-thirty, just like in her dream.

"Okay." She took a deep breath. She was scared enough to be selfish this once. "Then I also have another favor to ask."

"What?"

Lifting a hand to her neck, she traced down to the area where her cross usually rested. "I'm not arrogant enough to deny I'm in over my head here. I need help. I know you're not a total believer yet, but we're dealing with more than just some guy who gets off on killing people."

He crossed his arms and studied her. "What kind of help?"

"Connor, maybe?"

He said nothing for a long time. "I know a priest." He nodded toward the window. "A cathedral not far from here."

Her shoulders relaxed. "What's wrong with Connor?"

"Don't know him. Neither do you. For all I know, he could be the Reaper."

She had to resist the urge to roll her eyes. Jealousy was cute until a point. "When I couldn't sleep, I looked up the Bellator de Lux on my phone. Dylan, it's real. Some claim it's a shadow agency of the Vatican. Others claim it's a secret part of the government. What everyone agreed on is that they're badass. They deal with demons and scary stuff no one can handle. If you ever meet a member, some serious crap is going down."

He scoffed and spun away from her. "You think that scrawny kid we saw is some kind of demon hunter?"

"He wasn't scrawny."

He spun back toward her. "You were looking?"

"Dylan." She shook her head and reached for her purse.

"No. You can call him." He moved toward the room's phone. "That's it."

"I'd rather talk to him in person."

201

He stopped moving. She slid to her feet and pressed the phone he held back into its cradle. "Alexandra, I'm trying to keep you safe."

"And I'm totally okay with that." She slipped her hand up his arm in a soothing motion. "I also want you to trust me. This is my area of expertise." Well, sorta. Enough that she knew catching this killer might not mean the end to the horror he'd wrought. Extra steps needed to be taken. Steps Dylan didn't understand yet. She wasn't sure she understood them either. That was the problem.

One of his jaw muscles twitched as he met her gaze. "All right. We'll ask him to meet us somewhere. There's a deli not far from here."

"We?"

"You and me. That's how it goes, or not at all. Deal?"

She snorted. As if she would willingly deprive herself of his company. She reached for her purse. "What are you waiting for? An invitation? Let's go, handsome. Times a'wastin'!"

***

What had he gotten himself into?

Dylan hadn't realized he'd been holding his breath as he waited for the scrawny young man he barely knew to respond to Alexandra's outright, in-your-face explanation of the events of the past week. Hearing it paraphrased aloud, the whole thing sounded nuts. He would have never believed it if he hadn't experienced some of it.

Connor's gaze skated over to where Dylan sat, arm stretched around the back of Alexandra's chair. He didn't look skeptical or amused. "This is worse than I thought."

Connor turned his head, his gaze fixed on an empty table to their left. Alexandra looked that way, too. She gasped. "You can see him?" She focused on their companion. "You're a medium too."

A smirk played at the edges of Connor's mouth. "Guilty."

"Have you seen the demon?"

The young man took a sip of his coffee and shook his head. "No, but I've only been here a few weeks, and I didn't know I should be looking for one." He leaned back in his chair. "Since I got here, I've been helping ghosts cross over. It's like as soon as they realized I could see them, they all wanted my help. I've only seen so many ghosts in one place a few times."

"I wondered about that." Alexandra leaned even closer. Dylan got the feeling she'd forgotten he was there. "There are so many here, it's crazy."

"I know." Connor started to lean forward, caught Dylan's narrow-eyed look, and pushed his chair back instead. Good. Dylan didn't like this punk.

Connor cleared his throat. "The Bellator has been monitoring activity in Charleston for at least the past decade. When people show an interest in the paranormal, it creates an energy. That energy can manifest things, gives spirits strength they shouldn't have, attract spirits from other places, and—"

"Create demons," Alexandra finished for him.

Dylan thought he was following. "So all of these ghost tours and things are bad?"

Connor shrugged. "There's an anomaly here now. It's not good."

"It's like I feel drained here," Alexandra said. "Overwhelmed. My defenses are useless. It's—"

"Unhealthy," Connor finished for her, and they both smiled.

Dylan leaned forward, scooted his chair closer to Alexandra. "You didn't tell me that."

She bit at her bottom lip as she looked at him. "I didn't think you'd understand."

No, but good ole Connor did, didn't he?

Dylan aimed a look he usually reserved for interrogation at him.

"If you didn't know about the demon, why did you come here?"

Alexandra's fingers squeezed at his thigh under the table. He clenched his jaw but didn't remove his gaze from Connor's, who smiled and leaned back some more. "Barbara called us, told us she was having visions, and that someone with my skills should probably come check things out. Problem is, I can't see the anomaly. I just sense it's here."

"Is Barbara part of the Bellator?" Alexandra interjected.

Connor nodded. "We work in a network. We have people all over the world. Psychics, like us." His gaze looked Alexandra up and down. "You interested in joining?"

Like hell.

"Tell me, Connor." Dylan's voice was taut. "Do you believe this man, this killer, is possessed or under the influence of evil? Could these not be the actions of someone suffering from a mental illness?"

"Could be. We won't know until you catch him."

A vibration at Dylan's hip alerted him seconds before the ringtone did that he had a call on his mobile. "Excuse me," he told them. Lifting his phone, he sent Alexandra a look he hoped said *Stay put* and stepped into the empty corner. "Collins."

"Man walked in a few minutes ago. Claims he's the Reaper." Capt. Devereux said without greeting. "Get this. He knows the victims all died from chloroform injections."

"I'm on my way."

Dylan pressed END and stepped back toward their table. "Alexandra, we need to go."

She looked up and crossed her arms. "What happened?"

Dylan addressed Connor. "I'm sorry, Connor, but I'm needed at the department. Can we continue this discussion later?"

The other man stood. "Of course."

Nodding for her to follow, Dylan turned and headed for the

door, hoping his luck had taken a turn for the better and they actually had the sonofabitch in custody. Alexandra's sneakered feet squished against the pavement outside as she caught up to him. "Dylan! What's going on?"

He grabbed her arm to hurry her along beside him. He lowered his voice. "Someone's turned himself in. He knows something about the case that hasn't been made public."

"Really?" She sounded confused, wary.

He nodded and kept her moving when her steps slowed.

"Dylan, seriously, do you think this guy would just give up like that?"

"You tell me." She tugged her arm free and stopped, forcing him to turn and ask, "What are you doing?"

"Let me stay and finish talking to Connor. Officer Graham can drive me to the station afterward." She gestured to the uniformed officer who was pacing the sidewalk a few feet away.

Uh-uh. No way.

She took another step back and crossed her arms. "If you've got the killer in custody, what are you worried about? I should be safe." She pointed toward Connor, who'd stepped outside and was watching them with interest. "This guy kills demons for a living, Dylan. I think I'm safe with him."

He had no idea if they'd caught the killer or not, and he didn't intend to chance anything until he did. Leaving her with some punk he barely knew was out of the question. "You're being reckless."

"I promise I won't be long." She shooed him away. "Now go."

Damn stubborn woman. He was debating whether or not to haul her over his shoulder and toss her in the car when she turned and started walking back the way they'd come. "Alexandra!"

He felt Graham's presence before he saw her at his side. "Everything okay?"

He muttered a harsh curse. "Stay with her. Bring her to the

office when you're done here. No stops." Just for good measure, he told her to call in a background check on Connor Manning.

"Sure." Graham hurried to catch the door as it closed behind the woman whose life purpose must have been to drive him crazy. He took a deep breath and slid into the driver's seat of his assigned car. He'd put the lights on to get there faster.

He couldn't get there soon enough.

Chapter Seventeen

Alexandra stepped off the hospital's elevator and took a deep breath.

She'd feel a lot better when she had a new hex bag in her hot little hands, especially now that she had a better idea of what she was up against.

Connor had been eager to go investigate the location of the anomaly after she'd explained where the gray beams seemed to be strongest. He had no idea why she could see them and he couldn't.

"You're a powerful medium." He'd handed her his boss's card. "You really should think about joining us. You wouldn't have to quit your job or move. Just consult with us every now and then. You could learn a lot from the Bellator."

Call her crazy, but she was considering it.

She didn't know what her future with Dylan held, but it was good to know she had one option on the table. That was, if she survived all of this.

Shouting from the floor's waiting room diverted her attention away from her thoughts and onto the two men threatening each other with angry expressions and balled fists.

Beside her, Graham sighed. "Stay here. Let me check on this."

Alexandra nodded. "Reedus's room is right down the hall. Meet you there?"

Graham hesitated and then nodded when noise from the argument grew louder. Alexandra watched through the glass as the officer stepped into the room, put herself between the men, and demanded to know what was happening.

Alexandra heard enough as she passed to speculate the men were brothers who didn't get along. One wanted the other gone.

Some families. Geez.

She had her head tilted, trying to gather whether or not she should go help Graham, when she bumped into someone coming from the opposite direction. "Oh!"

"Miss King. We need to stop running into each other like this."

Alexandra glanced up, slightly startled, and relaxed. It was that medical examiner. What was his name? Watkins, or something like that. The guy who'd seen her faceplant her first day here.

"You aren't kidding." She smiled. "Were you here to see Reedus?"

He nodded. "They're releasing him. Wanted to wish him well before he left." His face scrunched as he lifted a thumb and angled it down the hall. "You knew they moved him to a different room, right?"

"No, I didn't." Truth was, she'd lied to Graham to get the other woman to stop by the hospital. Dylan would have a hissy fit if he knew they'd detoured from his orders. An ache at the back of her head caused her to wince. She got headaches a lot, usually after she'd opened herself up to the other side and chatted with a few ghosts for a while. Sickness was a nasty side effect she often had to deal with.

A wave of nausea accompanied the sharp pain. Great. A migraine was coming on.

She'd been pushing herself too hard.

"Here. I'll show you his room." Watkins placed his hand on her back and directed her around the empty gurney sitting in the hall.

Watkins was suddenly drinking a beer at the Southend Brewery.

208

He was watching someone.

He was watching her and Dylan. He wore a dark cap over his head. The old lady demon was standing right beside him. He pulled something out of his coat pocket and placed it on the bar. The grim reaper drawing on the napkin.

As quickly as the scene flashed through her mind, it was gone.

Alexandra gasped and glanced up at Watkins. He was watching her closely. His eyes behind his glasses were dark. Empty. Dangerous.

This man was the killer.

She opened her mouth to scream but he reacted too fast, grabbing her, lifting a white cloth to her mouth and crowding her against the wall. She inhaled the smell of something sweet. Her body betrayed her, immediately relaxing and going limp against him as she struggled to stay conscious. She tried to push the cloth away, but she was too weak. His hand held it firm against her mouth, forcing her to breathe in the scent.

A few seconds later he maneuvered her onto the gurney, covered her with a sheet, and she sank into the quiet oblivion of sleep.

***

Dylan looked through the window at the man seated alone in the interrogation room.

Curly dark hair. Eyeglasses. Button-down shirt that was soaked from sweat at the underarms. This guy could have been anyone. Average Joe.

His name was Bill Hardman. An accountant. Lived near the Battery.

Their suspect shifted in his seat and kept looking at the watch on his wrist. Every now and then he took a deep breath and blew it out slowly.

Dylan flipped through the pages of the man's original statement that had been hastily typed up by Officer Vinson. The guy sure knew a lot. Method of killing. What types of calling cards had been left at each murder scene. Where the victims had been taken from.

Dylan shook his head. "Something doesn't feel right."

Hands on his hips, Vinson grunted. "Had the same feeling. It's too easy. Guy doesn't strike me as a killer. Something's got him rattled."

"Let's go find out if we're right."

Hardman's eyes widened when Dylan opened the door and stepped into the room, Vinson behind him. "Mr. Hardman. We already have your confession. You understand you can have a lawyer present for questioning?"

The man swallowed, hard. "No lawyer."

Dylan took the seat across from him. "Why 'no lawyer'? Everyone always wants a lawyer."

Hardman blinked rapidly and glanced at his watch. "I don't want one. Can we just get on with this?"

Dylan leaned back, relaxed, in his chair. "You have somewhere you need to be? Hate to tell you, buddy, but you're not going anywhere for a while."

Hardman's right leg was bouncing, causing his entire body to shake. "I confessed. I'm the killer."

Dylan opened the file in front of him and removed two of the crime scene photos. He slid them across the table and watched Hardman closely for a reaction. Eyes widened, the man's face turned at least three shades paler.

"So you did this?" Dylan tapped the last photo. "Even this one?"

"Yeah, I did them all." He tore his gaze away from the second photo, as if he couldn't stand the sight of it.

Dylan glanced over his shoulder and grinned at Vinson. The other cop nodded. "Well, that's funny." He tapped the second photo. It was from a different crime scene, already solved, five years old.

The woman in the picture had a small-caliber bullet wound to the chest. "I don't think you killed anyone. That makes me wonder, how do you know so much? Are you an accomplice?"

The man shot another quick look at his watch. "I told you. I'm the killer! Please, release my name to the press. That's all I ask."

"Why should we release your name?" Dylan shrugged. "I see no reason to charge you."

The man's eyes gleamed with unshed tears and something Dylan could only describe as panic.

"Okay." Dylan leaned forward. "What kind of car did you use when you killed these people?"

Hardman's gaze moved to where Vinson was standing, then back to Dylan. "A van. I used a van." He paused. "I rented it."

"No you didn't."

That was all it took for the accountant's demeanor to crumble. Bursting out with a sob, he begged, "Please, just release my name to the press."

"Why?"

Hardman shook his head. "He'll kill my daughter if you don't."

"Who'll kill your daughter?"

The man could hardly speak through his tears now. "A man… called me this morning. There was a package at my desk. Pictures of my little girl on the playground." He sniffed and struggled for composure. "I'm a single father. My daughter, she's only in first grade. He knew her name. Knew her teachers. Knew what she'd been wearing this morning. He told me what to say. Said he'd kill her if I didn't confess. He wanted me to come in at three o'clock exactly." His chin trembled. "He told me what he'd do to her if I didn't."

Dylan swore. The sick sonofabitch had wanted a diversion. That was all this was. "Mr. Hardman, your daughter is going to be okay." Standing and turning to Vinson, he ordered, "Get some officers to her school. I want his daughter found and in custody. Get someone in here to take this man's statement. His real one this time."

Vinson nodded and hurried out of the room. Dylan wasn't long after him.

He pulled out his phone and dialed Alexandra's number. It went straight to voicemail. Worry clawed at his chest as he called dispatch and asked to be connected with Graham.

She responded promptly.

"Where are you?"

"We're at the hospital. Alexandra said you wanted us to stop and pick up something from Detective Reedus."

"Is she with you?"

There was a pause. "She's just down the hall."

Dylan was already hurrying toward his cruiser. "Dammit! I told you not to let her out of your sight."

"It was just down the hall." There was static for several seconds. "Collins, I don't see her. She's not where she's supposed to be. Reedus hasn't seen her either."

Dylan swore.

"I'm on my way there. Find her."

How could he have been so stupid? This psychopath had already made it clear he enjoyed toying with the police. Dylan should have never left Alexandra at the deli.

He was pushing through the doors to the parking lot when a familiar face headed into the building jolted him back.

What the—?

He hadn't seen his older brother in years, but not much had changed. Zach had filled out, was a little taller, but Dylan would know him anywhere.

He held up a hand as his brother strode toward him with purpose. "I can't deal with you right now."

212

Zach wouldn't let him pass. "Something's happened to Alexandra, hasn't it?"

Dylan hesitated. "What do you know? Did she call you? Where is she?"

"I haven't spoken to her in a couple of days." Zach pushed a hand through his hair and glanced around. "I didn't even know the real reason she was here until this morning."

He did not have time for this. "Look, man, I get it, but I have a bit of an emergency right now. Can we do this later?"

He didn't wait for an answer. He had to find Alexandra.

Zach hurried to match his pace. "Alexandra is in trouble. I'm responsible for this. I'm going with you."

Dylan grunted. "You're accepting responsibility for something? That's a first." He opened the driver's door of his cruiser. "I didn't say my emergency involved Alexandra."

"You didn't have to." Zach opened the passenger side. "I know the woman."

What the hell? Maybe Zach could help him track her down. Right now he wasn't adverse to any help he could get. "Get in."

He didn't wait for his brother to buckle up. He gunned it out of the parking space and put his lights and siren on.

Vinson's voice chirped over the radio, addressing Dylan. He lifted the radio. "What've you got for me?"

"Hardman's daughter is safe. She doesn't remember anything unusual. It was just a distraction."

"Copy that. I'm on my way to the hospital. Call McCormick in. Tell him to meet me there."

Neither he nor Zach said anything for several seconds. It was odd to be sitting in a car with a relative he hadn't seen in, what?, close to fifteen years without fireworks, drama, something happening. The silence grated on his nerves. "Alexandra told me why you left home. That all true?"

Zach's expression gave nothing away. "I don't know what she told you. Never talked to her about it."

Dylan didn't want to have a heart to heart with his brother right now, but he couldn't seem to keep his mouth shut. "Ray never laid a hand on me. I didn't know."

He glanced at his brother. Zach was looking out the window, but Dylan heard the humor in Zach's voice when he said, "Alexandra is good at what she does, isn't she?"

"Yeah, she is."

"Did you ask her to help with this case you're working, or did she volunteer?"

"What do you think?"

Zach rubbed at the bridge of his nose. "I think I'm gonna kill that woman when I see her."

"Why are you here, Zach? How did you know she's in trouble?"

"You wouldn't believe me if I told you."

Not too long ago, that would have been true. "Try me."

"Mom."

"What?"

Zach blew out a deep breath. "Mom told my girlfriend's cat everything. Begged me to get down here to help. She said things were going bad, fast."

"You're kidding."

Zach shook his head. "It's not a con, Dylan. I really am psychic."

"Yeah, sure." Dylan lifted his radio. "Graham, what's your situation?"

A few seconds later, the officer responded, "No sign of Miss King yet. A few patrols came to assist. We're still searching."

Dylan swore and directed the car toward the hospital's main entrance. "Zach, what the hell did your girlfriend's cat tell you. What do you think you know?"

He felt his brother's piercing gaze summing him up. "There's a serial killer. Calls himself the Grim Reaper. Alexandra is meant to be his last victim."

"What do you mean, last victim?"

"There's some evil stuff going down here. This guy isn't making his own decisions. He plans to kill himself. Complete whatever sick plan that's been put in his head. He's being influenced by something…something evil."

"A cat told you all that?"

"Some of it came from the dog."

Dylan shot his brother an incredulous look as he parked the car at the curb. "I think you'd better stop talking now."

"Agreed." Zach pushed out the passenger side, but not before Dylan caught the half smirk on his older brother's face.

Zach had never been much of a practical joker, so what was he playing at? Did he really think he could suddenly talk to cats and dogs?

Man, this whole situation was one for Jerry Springer.

Dylan wiped a hand over his face as he hurried into the building. He spotted the medical examiner carrying a duffle bag, leaving. He stopped the guy.

"Watkins, have you seen the blonde I was here with the other day?" Maybe Alexandra had wanted to ask him some questions. Maybe she'd had a vision or something.

Watkins glanced between him and Zach. His eyes widened a fraction, just enough to be noticeable, but then he focused on Dylan again. "No. Sorry." His keys clanged together as he dangled them from one hand. "I hate to be rude, but I have a body to transfer." He gestured toward the medical examiner's van sitting in the carport. "If I see Miss King, I'll tell her you're looking for her."

Again, Watkins looked at Zach. So the medical examiner knew who Zach was. Interesting. He'd have never figured the man for a reality TV fan.

215

Zach stepped closer, his eyes narrowed as he returned Watkins' inquisitive gaze. Dylan almost shook his head. Watkins was giving off some serious gay vibes right now, and Zach was the object of his fascination. Zach was giving off some weird vibes, too.

"I'll catch you later." Watkins nodded at Dylan and turned away.

Dylan started to move, but Zach grabbed his bicep. He nodded toward the van. "Who was that guy?"

"Medical examiner. Why? You interested?"

Zach reeled back as if offended. "Don't be an ass."

Dylan raised his eyebrows. "So?"

Zach glanced back toward the van and frowned. "I don't know." He scratched his neck. "I don't think he was telling you the truth."

"You can read minds now too?" Dylan shook his head. He really did not have time for this crap. He left Zach standing there as he hurried toward the front desk. He asked the volunteer on duty if she'd seen Alexandra. "Pretty blonde? Fairly tall. She was wearing a loud shirt with a pink flamingo on it. Hard to miss."

"*Alexandra* was?" Zach asked from beside him.

Dylan sent him a scathing look. He wished Zach had waited in the car.

The old woman at the desk shook her head. "I'm sorry. I don't remember seeing her leave. She came in, with a police officer. That's all I remember."

"Thanks." Dylan tapped the desk, acknowledged the young security officer stationed beside it, and moved toward the elevator. He pulled out his mobile radio. "Graham, any sign of Miss King yet?"

"No sign of her. If she's still in this hospital, I have no idea where she'd be."

"She's not here," Zach proclaimed. "Gut feeling."

Dylan jabbed the up button on the elevator anyway. "Does your gut know where she is?"

Zach glanced back toward the entrance. "That guy. Watkins. I think you should question him."

"Why?" The elevator dinged as the doors opened.

"Call it a hunch."

Dylan shook his head as he stepped into the lift. "I work with facts, Zach, not hunches." He held the door open. "You coming or not?"

Zach said something low and menacing beneath his breath, but he stepped into the elevator. "I've been working with Alexandra on developing my senses. She's been teaching how to…pick up on things. That guy is…" He shook his head.

"What?"

"Dark." He swallowed. "Got this sick feeling in the pit of my stomach just looking at him."

Dylan scoffed. "He works with dead bodies for a living. Can't get much darker than that."

"This is different."

Dylan had heard all he could stand. Anger and fear and anxiety bubbled up inside of him so fast, his chest felt like it was imploding. He shoved his brother against the elevator wall. "Why are you here? I haven't seen you in years, and you think you can just come in and make everything all right? Huh?" He shoved at Zack's shoulder again.

So quiet his voice was almost menacing, Zach murmured through clenched teeth, "I don't want to do this now."

The elevator pinged seconds before the door slid open. Zach gave him a humorless look and pushed past him.

He was right. There would be plenty of time for family drama later.

Alexandra was in danger. Dylan felt it in his gut, too. If he had to take a leap of faith and put it all in Zach, he would do it. He would do whatever it took to find her.

Heaven help him, he *would* find her.

Chapter Eighteen

Alexandra had been missing for almost four hours.

The longest four hours of Dylan's life.

He gripped the back of his neck and paced the conference room at the station. He had no clue where to start looking for her now that all of his ideas had been exhausted. Her cell phone wasn't picking up a signal, which meant she either didn't have it or it had been turned off. It was useless as a tracking device. There had been no sign of her at the hospital. Only one witness, an orderly, had seen her talking to a man a few minutes before Graham looked for her.

"I only saw the back of him. Man was in scrubs. I thought it was a doctor," the orderly said. "I didn't think anything about it. They was just talkin'."

Something was gnawing away at Dylan about that statement. None of the doctors who'd been on Reedus's floor that morning had owned up to talking to a woman fitting Alexandra's description. Had the killer stolen scrubs to blend in?

No. The killer was a hospital employee. It made sense. Watkins had indicated the chloroform used in each killing was a low-grade tincture mix, available online, but they'd never been able to find a seller. What if the chloroform wasn't low-grade? What if Watkins had been wrong?

Or what if Zach was right and he was involved?

Dylan took note of his brother seated at the table, being brought up to speed on the case by McCormick. It had been hard convincing the captain to sign Zach on as another consultant. His brother had always been good at charming people and, five minutes after being left alone with the captain, Zach had emerged with a non-disclosure agreement to sign and a cocky smile on his smug face.

Dylan quietly stepped out of the room and used his cell phone to contact Graham. He didn't want this going out over the police scanner.

"You still at the hospital?"

"I was wrapping things up. I don't think we're going to find anything else here tonight. Sorry, Collins."

"Do me a favor. Make some inquiries about Dr. Jeffery Watkins. Find out if anyone there has noticed anything suspicious about him."

"The M.E.?"

"Yeah, the M.E. Find out if any of the supplies there are coming up short. Check his department specifically."

"We already checked. Watkins told us—" She caught herself, seemed to think about what Dylan was implying. "You think he's involved?"

"I didn't say that." He glanced back toward the room. "Maybe."

"Okay." She sounded a little surprised. "I'll let you know if anything throws up a red flag."

He turned to move back into the room, but a young, uniformed woman hurried toward him, her face set in stern lines. "Phone call on line one. The voice is distorted. He asked to speak to Zachary Collins." Her gaze flicked toward the room, and more specifically, his brother. "I think it's the killer, sir."

Dylan hurried to the phone at the center of the table. He hit the speaker feature and then answered line one. "Detective Collins.

Who am I speaking to?"

"Which Collins is this?" The familiar, distorted voice of the killer replied. "I want to speak to The Psychic Detective."

"I'm here." Zach stood, put his hands on the table, and leaned toward the phone. "What have you done to Alexandra King?"

"Nothing, yet." The rasp of breath against the receiver was loud. "I wish you'd joined her sooner. It would have been more fun with both of you here to play my game."

"If you hurt her—" Dylan growled.

"I'm willing to keep her alive a while longer. I want to see if Zachary Collins can find her before I fulfill my plans. I want to see if you're as good as you seemed on TV."

"What do you want from me?" Zach demanded.

"Find her. Stop me."

Dylan watched his brother closely. A twitch in Zach's jaw was his only reaction. "This is Watkins, isn't it?"

A pause. "Who's Watkins?"

"No one else knows I'm here." Dylan met his brother's gaze. Zach was right.

"Wrong!" The response caused the speaker to vibrate. Then, in a much calmer voice, "It's on TV. The news. They're doing a special report about me right now, and you're the new guest star."

Dylan glanced through the open door toward the television mounted on the wall in the other room. Sure enough, a reporter was highlighting footage of him and Zach leaving the hospital. He nodded so Zach would know it was true.

His brother swore beneath his breath.

"I have a question for you, Psychic Detective." Zach said nothing, so the distorted voice continued. "Do you see them too? The ghosts?"

"No. I'm not a psychic medium."

"Shame."

The call disconnected.

Zach pushed away from the table. "Did you trace it?"

McCormick shook his head. "Same trick he used before." He explained to Zach the killer's prior method of escaping a trace.

"We know he has her now." Zach met Dylan's gaze. "Forget these files. Tell me. What leads have you been following to catch this guy?"

Dylan turned to McCormick. "What about the car Alexandra wanted checked out? Where are we on that?"

McCormick shrugged. "Last I heard they were still going through the list. Want me to follow up?"

Dylan nodded and glanced toward his brother when they were alone. Zach was leaning against the wall now, arms crossed, staring at nothing in particular. It was hard for him to admit, but Dylan had to put his pride aside. "I'm all out of ideas here, man. You got something or not?"

Zach turned his dark, intense gaze toward him. "Maybe." He pushed away from the wall. "What kind of car did Alexandra pick up on?"

"Dodge Avenger. Older model. Maybe late nineties."

"Mind if I make a long distance call?" Zach nodded toward the phone.

"Do what you have to do."

Zach punched in a number and asked to talk to "Spider." Dylan blew out an incredulous breath. "You talk to spiders now too?"

Zach's expression gave nothing away. He hit the speaker button and a young female voice said, "What's up, bossman?"

"Spider, I need you to find me information, fast. Alexandra's life might depend on it."

The girl's voice sounded worried. "What's happened to Alexandra?"

"Short version: We think she's been kidnapped."

The sound of typing was loud and fast in the speaker. "I'm on it. What do ya need?"

"I'm looking for the owner of a Dodge Avenger, nineties model, Charleston, South Carolina area. I want you to dig into a guy named Watkins. He's a medical examiner at the Medical University of South Carolina. Tell me if he owns that model of car."

"Got it." She was tapping the keyboard fast and furious. "Watkins. Jeffrey. Age 36. That the dude?"

Dylan placed his hands on the table and leaned forward. "That's him." How had she found it so fast?

"Um, he doesn't have a Dodge Avenger registered with the DMV."

Dylan pushed away from the table. They shouldn't be wasting time on this.

"However." The girl drew out the word's syllables. "There's a blue '97 Dodge Avenger registered to a Martha Watkins, and guess what? They're related. The dude used to have the same address, so I'm guessing maybe she's his mom or something. I dunno." She kept typing. "Seriously, this guy is weird."

Dylan turned around and met his brother's gaze. Zach asked, "What do you mean?"

"I just hacked into his IP address. He's looked at our agency's website about a hundred times in the past week. I mean, who does that?" There were more clacking sounds. Hell. They didn't have a warrant to be obtaining this kind of information, so Dylan moved and shut the door as the girl continued talking. "He's done a lot of internet searching for Alexandra's name. There's some websites about ghosts in Charleston that this guy is keeping in business. I mean, seriously, the paranormal to porn ratio here is scary. Oh, get this. He's a frequent visitor to CallerIDSpoof.org. Why would he be spoofing phone numbers?"

Zach stood straight, put his hands on his hips, and blew out a frustrated sigh. "He's gotta be our guy. Is there any way to track his cell phone or something to find out his current location?"

Spider huffed. "Depends on what kind of phone he has and if it's turned on. Hold on. That one might take a few minutes."

Opening the door, Dylan stepped into the doorway and gestured to Vinson. When the older officer came over, he said, "Jeffrey Watkins, the medical examiner. Get me his address, phone number, everything you can find. Get his photo from the hospital or DMV. Send it around to the tour guides we've already questioned and see if any of them recognize him."

When Dylan stepped back into the room and shut the door behind him, the girl was saying, "His mobile isn't pinging off any towers right now."

"Where was the last place it pinged?" Dylan asked her.

There was a brief hesitation. "Looks like the hospital there. Hold on. Let me check something." Damn she was killing that keyboard. "Yep. His cell phone and Alexandra's cell phone both pinged off the same tower at 3:22 p.m. Both lost their signals around the same time."

"Who the devil is this person?" Dylan nodded toward the phone. "She's impressive."

Zach half smiled. "Dylan, meet Spider. She's my cyber security specialist."

"Dylan, as in Collins? As in your brother?" The girl sounded delighted. The soft slap of skin on skin indicated she was clapping. "Cool. Kickass. Knew we'd find him." More typing. "What else you need?"

Zach turned and paced the length of the room. "Spider, how fast can you book a private jet and get Hannah and her animals here?"

"Dunno. Could probably find someone and have them there in a few hours. Why?"

Dylan would love to know that too.

Zach sighed. "I'm thinking my mother can help us. Problem is, I need animals to communicate with her. You don't have a pet, do you?" He directed the comment to Dylan.

"No, but there's a shelter not far from here. I think McCormick has a dog."

"We can try, but my hunch is that she's hanging around my animals." Zach shook his head. "Abbott's the smart one. I need him here, but Hannah's not going to leave the dogs at home."

The girl scoffed. "Well, duh. Ever heard of Skype? Video chat. Way easier and less expensive. Just sayin'."

Zach seemed interested. "How fast can we do it?"

"Where's Hannah?"

"Home."

"I can be there in maybe fifteen minutes."

"Do it."

"You gonna be able to get hooked up there without me, bossman?" Spider's voice sounded doubtful. The sound of shuffling indicated she was already moving. She was fast at everything.

"Just call me on my cell when you're ready." Zach ended the call and sent Dylan a pointed look. "I'm gonna need a laptop."

Dylan moved to the doorway and yelled McCormick's name across the precinct. The younger cop ended his phone call and hurried over. Dylan placed a hand on his shoulder. "Get me a laptop in here. Fast. You know anything about Skype?"

"Sure. I use it to talk to my nephew."

"We've got fifteen minutes to get it up and running. Go."

Always eager, McCormick turned and sprinted toward their IT department. He was back in under five minutes carrying the equipment. He sat it on the table and booted the machine. "It's an easy program to use." He glanced up at Dylan. "What are we doing again?"

Dylan almost laughed. He wasn't about to admit his estranged brother was gonna use the thing to try to communicate with their dead mother through a cat.

"A consultation."

"A private consultation," Zach added, crossing his arms.

McCormick frowned but got the program running. "I can stay and help if you want."

Zach pulled out the chair in front of the laptop and moved to take a seat. "I appreciate your offer, but I need to do this alone. Please shut the door behind you and make sure we aren't disturbed."

Looking at Dylan for approval, McCormick reluctantly did as requested, leaving Dylan alone with his brother again. Zach pulled the laptop closer and glanced at where Dylan stood. "I might have more success doing this alone."

"No way. I'm staying." He already hated the fact he'd relied on Zach so much until this point. It was as if his brother had walked in and taken over the entire investigation. Dylan felt useless. He was still reeling from the revelation Watkins seemed to be the Grim Reaper. He'd stood right there and let the man leave the hospital. Had Alexandra been in the van? Clenching his teeth at the thought, he moved to the conference room blinds and closed the ones that were open, giving them more privacy. "You really think this is gonna work?"

"Hell if I know. Right now, it's the only thing I can think to try." Zack was testing the computer, getting familiar with the program.

Dylan sank into the chair beside him. "Alexandra told me Mom had pestered her to come find me. Didn't believe her at first."

Zach glanced toward him. "Yeah, she tried to convince me to look for you myself."

"Why didn't you?"

"Figured it would be a wasted effort. Doubted you would even talk to me."

He'd been right. It had taken Alexandra storming into his life and kicking down his walls to open his mind to reconciliation. That beautiful, gutsy woman. "She'd better be safe when we find her. Otherwise, I'm gonna kill the sonofabitch."

Zach's eyes narrowed on him again. "You two have gotten close."

"I care about her."

"*I* care about her," Zach countered. "She's a pain in the ass and if you tell her I said this, I'll kick yours, but she's like family. Something tells me you don't feel the same way I do." Zach looked toward the computer. "You're in love with her."

Dylan reeled back. "I barely know her."

A slight smile tugged at his brother's mouth. "It happens that way sometimes."

Did he love Alexandra? Hell. Maybe. He'd never felt this jumbled mix of emotion for any other woman, not like this. His chest tightened. "Let's just find her." He'd deal with his feelings for her then.

Zach's phone rang, and he answered. Spider must have been guiding him through ways to connect with her because he kept grunting "Uh huh" as he tinkered with the computer. "Got it. I see you." He put his cell phone on the table.

A young woman with shocking blue hair and wearing blue lipstick stared back at them on the computer screen. "Wicked awesome." She seemed to look right at Dylan. "Whoa, mama! Double hottie alert." She waved. "Hi there. You must be bossman's brother."

He waved in reply. "Dylan."

"Spider. Wassup, gorgeous?"

Despite the circumstances, he couldn't help but smile. She seemed like an interesting character.

Zach asked impatiently, "Is Hannah there?"

"Yep." The screen moved and a very pretty woman with long dark hair smiled back at them. "Hi." She bit her lip and focused on Zach. "I've got the boys right here. Which one do you want?"

For the first time since he'd seen Zach again, his brother seemed to relax. "Which one do you think?"

"Be right back." She stood, and Dylan asked, "That's Hannah?" Zach nodded. "Alexandra told me about her."

The computer screen angled back toward Spider. "Your darn dog is humping my leg right now, boss. I deserve a raise for this." She angled the computer to show a dog standing on stubby legs gripping her thigh and panting heavily.

Dylan squinted at the screen. Looked like a Golden retriever, but different. Maybe a corgi or something. "What the devil kind of dog is that?"

"Mutt. Dumb as a brick." Zach focused on the animal. "Costello, quit humping Spider."

The dog looked at the screen, tilted its head, and damn if it didn't give a toothy grin. The screen moved back into position, but then Spider squawked as another dog seemed to come out of nowhere and jump in her lap, almost knocking her and the computer both over.

Zach cursed. "Charlie, get off Spider! Down, buddy."

The dog—far too large to be a lap dog—immediately obeyed. Spider blew her long hair out of her face and rolled her eyes. "Seriously, we need to talk about that raise when you get back."

"Done." Zach pulled the laptop closer. "Where's Abbott?"

"Here," Hannah said and came into view again holding a black and white cat. "Sorry. He was hiding."

Zach arched an eyebrow. "Of course he was." He blew out a breath and rubbed his hands together. "Okay, Abbott. We need your help. I'll bring you a fresh tuna right out of the ocean if you make this easy. Is my mother still there?"

Dylan shifted his attention between the cat and the man sitting beside him. Zach's brow furrowed even as his shoulders straightened again. "What?" Dylan demanded.

"She's not there."

Dylan swore.

"She's here, with you and me."

The hairs on the back of his neck rose. He glanced around, even though he knew they were alone in the room. The cat's eyes seemed to be watching something off to the right.

Zach swallowed hard and turned his head that way. "Mom, we need your help. We need to know how to find Alexandra. Do you know where she is?"

The cat stared so intently into the camera it started to give Dylan the creeps.

"Some kind of theater. Lots of red. Does that mean anything to you?" Zach asked Dylan.

Dylan's entire body tensed. "Alexandra had a dream about the Dock Street Theater. We checked it out, but couldn't find anything."

"Is she still alive?" Zach asked loudly. Seconds passed as he and the cat looked at one another. "She's alive. He's drugged her." Zach's eyes narrowed on the screen as if he was listening. "How do we stop it?" After a beat, he turned to Dylan. "Alexandra visited someone from the Bellator. We're gonna need his help."

How did his brother know that?

"Thanks, Mom." Zach pushed the computer away. "Hannah, we gotta go."

"Please find her," Hannah said, lowering the cat. "Please be careful."

"I'll let you know what happens."

Dylan stood, feeling a sense of urgency. He hesitated, leaned down toward the screen before Zach could close it. "Hey, Spider?"

She appeared. "Yeah?"

"What's your real name?"

She frowned and seemed reluctant to answer. "Emma."

"Emma, I could kiss you right now. Thank you."

She turned red. "Just bring Alexandra home, okay?"

"Count on it."

Chapter Nineteen

The faint touch of a hand against her shoulder helped pull Alexandra back toward consciousness.

"Alexandra? Wake up. For the love of Pete, wake up."

Her eyelids felt glued together. She struggled to pry them apart. Dim light flooded her vision once she did, but as dim as it was, it still hurt her eyes. She lifted a hand to block the light, and George's familiar features blurred into focus.

"W-what?" She moved to push herself up. A sharp pain in her head wrenched a groan from her chest.

Migraine.

"We don't have much time. He'll be back." George was leaning over her, his expression dire. The glimpse of red material at her arm tore her attention away from him.

"George, why am I wearing a red dress?" She hadn't been wearing this before. She felt down her body. It was a clingy fabric that seemed to flare at her waist.

"He put it on ya while ya were half seas over."

"Half seas what?"

"Ya know." He frowned. "Knocked out."

His words made her skin crawl, imagining a stranger's hands touching her while she was both unaware and helpless to resist. George glanced toward her again, no trace of humor in his expression. "He's made ya up to favor Nettie."

"Who?"

"She died here, long time ago."

Alexandra's senses were beginning to clear. She looked around. "Where is she now?"

"Hidin' from yer ole woman. They all are." He stood and moved to the door. "I'm the only one fool enough to be here."

She pushed herself to her feet. The room she was in was familiar. White-trimmed windows stood out amongst the dark red walls. At least the carpet at her bare feet was mostly gray.

So much freaking red everywhere.

"I dreamt about this place." She took an unsteady step forward, and George hurried to catch her when she lost her balance. Instead of finding support in his arms, she fell through him, collapsing onto her knees on the carpet.

"Sorry, love. That stink done somethin' to me. I'm not as strong as I usually am. If I were, I'd unlock that door."

She lifted her gaze to the windows. They were shaded, but dark.

How long had she been here?

She swallowed the foul taste in her mouth. "Tell me about Nettie. How did she die?"

The killer was keen to recreate ghosts' deaths. She rubbed the palm of her hand against her right eye, where the pain was strongest. Maybe knowing what he, what Dr. Watkins, had planned would give her an advantage. She gave herself a minute, tried to will the migraine away, before moving to stand again.

"Nettie?" she reminded when George said nothing.

"Well, now, she was…ya know." George gestured at her dress and then tugged at his collar.

"No, I don't know." She looked at him. Then something clicked in her brain. "Wait. She was a prostitute?"

"If the scuttlebutt's to be believed." He moved around the room,

231

glancing up and down as if he were searching for something. "A bit of a sad story really. This used to be a hotel back in the day. One night, poor Nettie was out on the balcony during a storm. Got struck by lightning. Killed her instantly."

Think, Alexandra.

The killer had been murdering his victims by injecting them with chloroform, but he liked to stage their bodies afterward to reflect someone else's death scene. If Nettie had been electrocuted on the balcony, that must be where he planned to take Alexandra.

But Watkins hadn't yet killed Alexandra, and he could have easily done so.

Her death was meant to be different somehow.

"Do you know where he is now, what he's doing?" Alexandra asked as she checked the first window she saw. Tree limbs blocked her view of everything.

Maybe she could climb out if she could get the stupid window open. The windows were tall, old. She tried to lift up on the bottom but was too weak to budge it.

Dammit.

"He's downstairs," George grunted. "Puttin' somethin' together under the stage."

"The stage?" That didn't seem right. He should have been setting up something on the balcony. She tried to think harder and squinted against the pain in her head. "What are you looking for?" She moved to the only other window in the room and lifted the shade. There was only an empty alley.

George reached his hand toward her. "Com'ere." He was standing in front of a desk in the corner of the room. She hurried to join him. He pointed at a paperclip lying on the surface. "Grab that. We can use it to pick the door's lock."

She snatched the paperclip and rushed to the door. It was an old door with a large keyhole. "I don't know how to pick a lock."

"I'll tell ya what to do. Hurry."

Kneeling, she followed George's instructions. The first try, nothing happened. The second time, a slight metallic click was heard.

Alexandra turned the knob and the door creaked open.

"Run to your left. He's coming up the stairs." George hurried in front of her, using hand gestures to guide her along the dark hallway. He pointed to another door. "Quick. Hide in here."

It was a closet! Alexandra pushed against the clothes hanging inside, tugging the door shut behind her as quietly as possible. She stilled and tried to calm her breathing. She couldn't see anything. The closet was too dark.

The creak of footsteps nearby echoed eerily in the small space. They stopped suddenly.

"Alexandra?" A man's voice bellowed her name from somewhere nearby. In a softer tone, she heard him say, "You smart girl." Louder, he called in a sing-song voice, "Alex-an-dra? Come out, come out, wherever you are."

The floor creaked again, and again, coming closer.

Sweat coated her palms, and the doorknob began to slip from her grasp. She pulled on it, keeping it shut. He wasn't getting into this closet without a fight. She'd rather die than let him touch her again.

"I'm impressed!" The man yelled, alerting her that he was standing on the other side of the door. Another creak in the floorboard. "I thought Collins might come and try to rescue you, but I was getting impatient. I never counted on you freeing yourself!"

All movement on the other side of the door stopped. Alexandra swallowed, struggling not to move, not to breathe. Then, a loud thump in the distance was followed by the man's muttered, "Dammit!" She could tell by his heavy footfall that he was running back the way he'd come. She closed her eyes and listened. The

233

thump of his feet seemed to be going down.

"Someone's come to help." George's voice whispered in the dark. "Hurry."

Breathing a sigh of relief, she released the doorknob and pushed it open. George stood on the other side, but he wasn't alone.

Rebecca Collins stood beside him.

Alexandra freed a sigh of relief and stepped toward Dylan's mother. She must have made the noise downstairs to distract Watkins. Bless her heart.

George tilted his hat toward Rebecca in greeting. "Nice thinkin', ma'am."

"I'm so sorry, Alexandra." The other woman shook her head. "Dylan and Zachary know you're here. They're on the way, but we have to get you safe."

Alexandra started to move but stalled at the unexpected information. "Zach is here?"

"Come on now, ya need to light a shuck this way. We're not safe yet." George ushered them both back down the hall, opposite of the way Watkins had run. With very little light to guide her, Alexandra held onto Rebecca's hand and ran through a doorway, then another, trusting George completely. Light began to pour into the hallway, and Alexandra instinctively ran toward it.

The theater's interior was lit with stage lights. She was standing in the balcony section above the stage.

Oh no. The stage.

Something had been drawn on the stage. A circle. She was too far away, it was too dark, to see it clearly.

Rebecca tugged at her hand. "We shouldn't be here."

George nodded, his expression panicked.

Boom.

Alexandra spun around at the sound of a door being slammed behind her. She rushed to try the doorknob. It wouldn't budge.

She couldn't go back the way she'd came.

"George?"

But George was no longer there. Neither was Rebecca.

Boom.

Another door slammed on the other side of the room.

Down. I need to go down.

The red glow of an EXIT sign above a door beside the stage beckoned to her. Alexandra hurried along the wall, behind the seats, ignoring the slamming doors, one after another, in front, behind and below her, in every direction. She finally found a doorway that led to a set of stairs.

Alexandra nearly tripped over the skirt of her dress as she rushed down the steps, clinging to the brass handrail for balance in her bare feet. At the bottom, she could see large, open windows leading to the street. That way. She needed to go that way.

A man's shadow fell on the wall.

She couldn't go that way. That had to be Watkins approaching.

She turned and ran through a dark hall that led her into the well-lit orchestra section of the theater. Casting anxious looks over her shoulder, she moved toward the illuminated EXIT sign.

"Not safe. The stage. Hide under the stage."

The whispered words in her ear sounded familiar. Feminine. Rebecca? Dylan's mother was still trying to help.

Alexandra glanced toward the emergency exit, hesitating. It made the most sense. She started that way again.

"That way isn't safe. Hide under the stage."

The door began rattling, as if someone on the other side were trying to enter. Alexandra turned and clambered for the stage. Watkins might not expect her to hide there. Maybe she could find a spot behind something, somewhere. Just long enough for the police to get here.

Her feet had just touched the stage when the overheard lights shut off, pitching her into darkness again.

The flicker of candlelight lit part of the stage, casting shadows that danced eerily on the curtains and across mannequins draped with costumes.

It was the only source of light, so Alexandra's feet slowly moved in that direction.

As she grew closer to it, she could see it was a pentagram drawn in white on the stage's floor. Seeing that was all it took for her to turn and get out of there.

It hadn't been Rebecca's whisper she'd heard. It had been the demon, manipulating her.

Click-clack. Click-clack.

Alexandra spun around at the sound of hard-heeled shoes walking behind her.

Click-clack.

The sound stopped.

The old woman stood a few feet away, her eyes as dark as night. A menacing smirk curved her mouth upward.

"We've been waiting for you, Alexandra."

Alexandra took a step back as her fingers curled into fists at her side. All she could seem to think was *Crap! What am I supposed to do now?*

***

Dylan looked over to make sure Zach's flak jacket was on right as he secured his own. They'd set up a barricade a block away from the theater. Patrol cars and officers obstructed it on all sides. The FBI had been called in, but the two agents seemed happy to let Dylan keep the lead on this operation.

"Ready for this?" Dylan asked his brother.

A SWAT team was in position to move, awaiting Dylan's order.

He planned to be with them, and Zach had made it clear he was going, with or without the police's consent. It had taken the threat of handcuffs and the reminder that Dylan's reputation was on the line to convince him to fall back.

Dylan nodded toward the barricade where Connor Manning stood, watching. "Zach, you're waiting here until I give you the clear to come in with him. Got it?"

Zach's expression was stoic. "I'll give you five minutes after you enter the building. If I haven't heard from you then, I'm coming in. Just so you know."

Shaking his head, Dylan lifted his radio and gave the command to move forward, discreetly. Last thing they wanted was to alert Watkins they had the building surrounded.

Graham had discovered that the medical examiner had been volunteering at the theater for almost six months. That meant he probably knew his way around and hadn't raised suspicion going in and out at all hours. He'd probably stolen or copied someone's key and would know well enough that there were no auditions or rehearsals tonight.

Dylan had never been inside, but he'd familiarized himself with the blueprints while his team had been getting into position. He and Zach had agreed Alexandra was probably being held in one of the private upstairs rooms, or one of the dressing rooms behind the stage. Those places were his priority to search first.

He followed a man in full SWAT gear across the street, ducking behind trashcans and clinging to the side of the building, praying Watkins wasn't keeping an eye on the street. Dylan gestured to the first SWAT officer, and the large man entered the building.

The lobby was substantial, with elegant spiral staircases leading up to the balcony on two sides. His men branched off, and Dylan motioned to McCormick to follow him up the service stairs. They'd start there first.

Gun drawn, Dylan entered one room, then another.

In the second room, McCormick pointed toward a chair. Alexandra's clothes were draped across the furniture. Dylan's shoulder muscles tightened.

She'd been here, but she wasn't now.

Advancing back into the hallway, he nodded to his left. They would access the balcony, move down and check the dressing rooms behind the stage.

The balcony seemed extremely dark as he stepped into the area. There was some light, very dim, coming from the stage.

Alexandra stood, tall and straight in a red dress, staring intently at something in front of her. Dylan saw no one on the stage with her.

The door behind him suddenly slammed shut.

He spun and saw Watkins dart from the shadows toward a row of seats further down. The man rounded the section as Dylan gave chase, weaving in and out of rows of seats.

"Dylan!" Alexandra yelled his name, but he didn't take his eyes off Watkins.

Where the hell had McCormick gone?

Watkins was headed toward a doorway. Dylan sprang over the row of seats, pushed his foot off the back of a chair, and launched himself at the man from a sideways angle.

His teeth rattled in his head as their bodies impacted at the shoulders. His hands grabbed Watkins' upper limbs and threw him onto his back. He landed a hard punch to the man's jaw.

"Grrrrrrr!" Watkins' groan was close to an unearthly growl, his features twisted into something ugly.

His left hand pushed against Dylan's chest. He quickly lifted his right hand. Dylan glimpsed the hypodermic needle before it sank into his skin. Groaning, Dylan punched his knee forward, connecting with Watkins' groin. Watkins lost his grip on the needle and doubled over in pain.

Too soon he clambered to his feet again.

Dylan had just pulled the needle out of his arm and flung it across the aisle's carpet when Watkins roared and launched toward Dylan again. Light glinted off a knife clutched in his right hand.

The boom of a gun echoed loudly in the theater.

Watkins's body fell forward onto Dylan before sagging limply to the floor.

"Collins, you okay?" McCormick called.

Pushing away from the lifeless body beside him, Dylan scrambled on his knees toward the needle. The plunger handle was still up, the vial still full of liquid. He rubbed at the slight sting in his arm. Close call. Too close. His chest sank in relief.

A SWAT team member was perched on the balcony on the other side of the room, his rifle aimed at where Watkins had fallen. Some of the SWAT team had also entered the orchestra area below.

"I'm fine," he called back, drawing attention to where he stood. He squinted toward the stage. "Alexandra?"

No response.

Dylan found the stairs, hurried into the lower section, and approached the stage.

She was still standing there, staring straight ahead, looking out to where the audience would sit, not moving. Probably in shock.

"Alexandra, are you okay?"

She turned her head and looked at him. The force of that malicious stare startled him.

What the—?

Unnatural black eyes watched him.

Eyes that did not belong to the woman he knew.

Chapter Twenty

Get. Out. Of. Me.
Alexandra directed all of her energy toward pushing the old woman as far away as she could manage. Pain ripped through her head, and she flattened her ears with both hands and squeezed, trying to release some of the tension. A scream of agony spilled from her mouth as tiny claws tore at the insides of her body.

The pain. It was too much. She doubled over, falling to her knees.

Alexandra struggled to stay conscious. There had only been two times when entities had tried to enter her body. She recognized the familiar tingling, the intense pressure. The old woman, the demon, whatever it was, was trying to overtake her.

No!

As the pain lapsed, she realized with surprise that she was standing again. Forcing herself to focus on her surroundings, she saw Dylan watching her, approaching carefully as if she were a rabid animal he wanted to corner. McCormick and some other officers in black stood not far away, staring at her, eyes widened. No one reacted to her cries for help. No one rushed forward when she sank to the stage in agony.

Hadn't they heard her scream? Seen her pain?

"Alexandra?" Dylan held out his hand, palm toward her. "Can you hear me?"

Yes.

The word formed in her mind, but she was unable to push it past her lips.

Oh, heaven, please help me. She was under attack, mind and body, and not winning.

This shouldn't be happening. She had stopped this in the past. Her grandmother had taught her how to protect herself from possession.

Oh, no. Of course.

Alexandra had been drugged, weak. She hadn't awoken and closed herself off from contact the way she normally did. She hadn't placed any veils of protection or said any prayers. She'd been afraid, panicked, not thinking clearly. That had left her vulnerable, and that's exactly what this entity had wanted.

Her arm lifted without her permission. Her finger pointed at Dylan.

"I don't want you here." Her voice. She'd spoken the words, but they weren't hers.

"Hey, Alexandra, you okay?" McCormick asked as he shuffled forward.

The young officer hadn't moved more than six feet before he jerked backwards unnaturally. Alexandra watched, open-mouthed and helpless, as his body was flung away from the stage. He fell unconscious in the aisle.

A SWAT officer to her left lifted his gun, but it was flung from his hands. He, too, was tossed back by an unseen force.

The other men in the theater retreated then, hiding behind seats or heading for the exits, calling, "No one enter the theater. Draw back." Dylan held his ground. His eyes were round with a mixture of wonder, disbelief, and fear as he stared at where McCormick lay unmoving.

Please, Dylan, leave!

She did not want him getting hurt. This entity was more powerful than she'd dared imagine, made more so by Alexandra's abilities. It had the power to manipulate its environment. It had the power to harm.

Get. Out. Of. Me!

Alexandra summoned all of her strength and pushed. She could feel the demon struggling to maintain its hold over her.

She stumbled sideways and saw the old woman crouched on the stage, her black eyes gleaming with malicious intent as she growled at Alexandra.

Alexandra swallowed. She didn't take her eyes off the creature, but she said, "Dylan, please."

She heard her voice murmur the plea. She was temporarily in control.

The old woman lunged for her, and Alexandra braced herself for the attack. They both tumbled to the stage, hands and claws ripping and pulling at each other.

Pain lanced through her abdomen. Alexandra screamed. She didn't know if she could hold the entity off for much longer.

***

Dylan couldn't find the will to move.

Alexandra fell to the stage as if she'd been hit head-on by a linebacker. He saw no one on top of her, but she seemed to be fighting someone.

What the devil was going on?

Zach. Connor. He needed their help. This was beyond his comprehension.

Forcing himself to run up the aisle rather than jump to the stage and help her, he stopped at the first officer he saw. The man was peeking over a seat, watching the stage. Dylan grabbed him by the shoulder. "Use your radio. Tell them to let Zach Collins and Connor Manning into this theater. Do it! Now!"

The officer's voice trembled as he rattled off the information.

Dylan rushed back toward the stage. Another ear-piercing scream tore from Alexandra's body.

"Alexandra!" He leapt onto the raised floor and carefully moved toward her writhing form. "What can I do?"

"I can't!" she yelled in response. "Oh! I can't win this."

The bang of wood striking wood as a door slammed against the wall drew his attention toward one of the side entrances. Zach jogged forward, Connor not far behind him. One of the FBI agents entered more carefully, his gun drawn at the ready.

"What's happening?" Zach demanded.

"Get up here!" Dylan called to them. "She's being...possessed or something."

Zach took the stage steps two at a time until he was beside Dylan. They both stared at the woman rolling around. Her right hand lifted to her neck and a trail of blood appeared as she scraped at her own skin.

Dylan sprang forward and wrenched Alexandra's arms behind her back. "Grab her legs." Zach quickly knelt and pushed her flailing legs to the floor. "We need to secure her."

Zach looked sideways and swore. "What's *that*? A pentagram?" He muttered a curse.

Damn, but Alexandra was strong. It took all of Dylan's effort to keep her from wiggling from his hold. "Connor, what do we need to do?"

Connor's face was pale as he took in the gravity of the scene before him. He dropped a bag to the stage at his feet and retrieved a leather-bound book. "Keep holding her down. Whatever you do, don't let her go." He opened the book and began reading. Dylan didn't understand the words. They sounded foreign.

Alexandra roared with agony.

***

Oh, it hurt.

"Shhhh," Dylan whispered in her ear. "Fight it, Alexandra. You're strong. You've got this."

She felt his warmth surround and comfort her. The pain subsided and every cell in her being went numb.

She felt oddly disconnected from the situation now. It was as if she were a casual observer, watching the scene unfold.

She saw Dylan and his brother holding the old woman—not an old woman at all, but a long-limbed grotesque creature. Its skin was black, and its face was contorted like a gargoyle's.

"He's right, ya know?" She turned her head and saw George standing beside her spirit form. "Yer strong enough to defeat that thing. We're all here to help ya do it. If ya don't—"

Rebecca stood beside him, her expression terrified, but resigned. "I'm so sorry, Alexandra. This is all my fault."

Alexandra shook her head. "No, it's not."

"It is." Rebecca nodded. "That…thing manipulated me to get closer to you. When it saw you—"

"Wait. The demon was attached to you?"

"I first saw it before you arrived. It somehow knew I was the mother of a sensitive, so it attached to me. It waited for an opportunity to get near Zach, but—"

"I was the medium, so it preferred me."

"Every time I tried to warn you, it stopped me. It could control every word I said. It made me feel sick, as if I were alive again and still dying. I've felt so…helpless."

Two other people Alexandra recognized stood around the stage. Ghosts she'd encountered since she'd come to Charleston. The

244

Reaper's victim, Candice Christopher. The confederate soldier who'd visited her hotel room. There was also a gray-pallored woman dressed in a red dress. That must be Nettie, the woman who haunted this theater.

"If I don't fight it, then what?"

"You'll be joining us, love." George reached for his collar and tugged. "Worse, that thing will still be running amuck. Who knows what'll happen then."

"Aren't you all still afraid of it?" Alexandra asked. She was. She was terrified. Perhaps remaining with George and Rebecca, trapped here on the other side, was the easier alternative.

"We're afraid for *you*," Rebecca answered.

"Besides, we've got help now," George agreed, tipping his hat back and nodding toward the living people a few feet away. "That scrawny fella is weakening it. Don't ya see?"

Connor's voice echoed around the theater as it grew louder with each phrase he uttered in Latin. "I command you to leave this dimension. I command you not to harm this woman. Be gone!" He flung water from the bottle in his hand toward Alexandra's torso.

The evil being screeched in protest and shook its head the way a wet dog would do if sprayed.

Alexandra's earthly body writhed against Dylan and Zach's hold, releasing a similar pained sound.

"You're temporarily freed from its grip, Alexandra." Rebecca slid her hand in hers. "But if you go back over there, and you fight it, you can force it out into the open. You can make it vulnerable again."

"I'm not strong enough." Grief swamped her at the sad realization.

Rebecca's hands gently framed her face. "Oh, Alexandra, that's just not true." She pushed the hair away from Alexandra's forehead. "Think about it. What are the things that evil thrives on? Hate.

Fear. Anger. Indifference." Rebecca's lop-sided smile was at odds with the situation, but comforting nonetheless. "Use the opposite to defeat it. Courage. Love."

Her attention strayed to Dylan. He had one arm wrapped around the creature's torso, the other curved under its arm holding its face still, determined not to let go. Even so, he murmured soothing words in its ear. She strained to hear them.

"I've got you. We'll get through this. Fight it, Alexandra. Do it for me, baby. Come on."

Love.

Rebecca was right. She did have love for Dylan, but enough to do this?

Yes.

She wasn't alone. She didn't have to fight this monster on her own, but it all hinged on her. She knew that, just as she knew she had to go back inside her body and fight, no matter how painful it was.

"Once it's outta ya, we can grab hold of it and let the scrawny kid do the rest." George forced a crooked smile. "Whadaya say, love?"

She straightened her shoulders and turned to her dead friends. "Each of you, I need you to all repeat what Connor is saying. We'll magnify its message, weaken this thing even more." She moved to step forward, but the long skirt of her dress tangled around her calves. She bent and ripped at the material until it tore in a line above the knee. She tossed the extra red material at George. "Can you use that to restrain it in this realm? Will it work?"

His grin kicked up a notch. "Atta girl. Guess we'll find out." He turned to the others. "Ready?"

Rebecca's voice led them as they each began repeating the words Connor now chanted.

"We drive you from us, whoever you may be, unclean spirits, all infernal invaders, all wicked legions, assemblies and sects…"

The evil being shrieked and began struggling harder. Its right leg jutted out and connected with Zach's chin, but he didn't let go, stubborn as ever. Alexandra closed her eyes and said a silent prayer. *God, please give me the strength to do this.* Then she took a running leap and hurled herself onto the demon's body.

Suddenly, she was on her back being held by Dylan again. The beast's claws tore at her neck and the pain threatened to drag Alexandra into darkness. The demon's teeth gnashed at her face as she struggled to hold it away. It shifted its focus to Dylan and Alexandra watched, helpless, as her own fingers dug into the skin at his arm, drawing blood. He yelled in pain, but didn't budge.

That was it. This thing had messed with the wrong woman. *Get. Out!*

Concentrating all of her mental powers into her hands, Alexandra shoved at the being's chest, sending it sprawling backward onto the stage.

George sprang into action, looping the red cloth around its neck from behind and sliding the material down until its arms were pinned to its side. Its body was becoming transparent. It was weak. It struggled against George's hold, but he held fast.

The demon tilted its head back and howled in rage.

***

A strangled gasp emerged from Alexandra's mouth that didn't sound like any of the other sounds she'd been making since this ordeal began, and Dylan feared he was hurting her. He refused to loosen his grip, even when she turned her eyes up toward him and he saw her clear, familiar blue gaze staring back at him.

"Alexandra?"

"Dylan," she managed, but her voice was husky and weak.

"Oh, sweetheart." He pressed a kiss to her forehead. "I knew

247

you could do it."

"Not…over…yet." She barely managed to get the words out. Gasping for breath, she seemed to get a second wind. More clearly, she whispered, "You need to let me go. I need to get up."

Was this a trick?

"It's me, Dylan. Promise."

Reluctantly, he loosened his arms. He exchanged a pointed look with Zach, who also let go of her legs. Connor paused his speech and took a step closer.

Turning onto her side, Alexandra struggled to her knees. "Keep going, Connor."

The younger man's features became taut as he started chanting again. Alexandra's voice joined his, repeating the words. She pushed to her feet and stared at an unseen presence to the right of where Zach now stood.

"Be gone, evil spirit!" She yelled the words and then flinched before falling to her knees again. Dylan rushed to her side.

"Alexandra?"

"It's gone." Her chest rose and fell on deep breaths. "It's gone." He tugged her into his arms and squeezed. She lifted her head, looked around, and her face brightened with a smile. "They're all safe. We all made it."

With a groan, her body went limp against him.

"Alexandra?" He lowered her to the floor, felt for a pulse. It was weak, but there.

"Is she alright?" Zach hovered over his shoulder.

"Someone call an ambulance!" Dylan shouted to no one in particular.

The FBI agent who'd been hanging back and watching lifted his radio and ordered medical assistance. The gray-haired man stepped around the pentagram drawn on the stage but couldn't seem to take his gaze away from it. "Detective Collins, what in the hell just happened?"

He shook his head. This beautiful, wonderful woman had just survived a demonic possession straight out of a horror film, *that's* what happened. "You saw it. You tell me."

The man took a deep breath. "How am I supposed to put this in a report?"

Dylan could care less.

"Owww!" McCormick groaned as he touched the back of his head. The young officer stumbled toward the stage. "Collins, is Alexandra okay? What happened?"

Dylan's chest tightened as he watched her stomach rise and fall with shallow breaths. Where was that ambulance?

Zach's hand squeezed his shoulder. "She'll be okay, man. Don't worry."

The confident words helped calm his fears, and for the first time in a long time, Dylan was glad to have his brother with him again.

Chapter Twenty One

"So are you staying here in Charleston or coming back to Atlanta?" Zach's voice gave nothing away as to what he preferred. Frustrating man.

Alexandra feigned a shudder. "Atlanta, definitely. I mean, the firm would fall to pieces if I quit."

His mouth quirked up in a smile. "Probably." Then the smile faded. "I thought you and my brother had something going on between you."

She stopped in front of the water fountain and gazed out at the ocean beyond the trees. She'd convinced him and Dylan to meet her in the park near the Battery—neutral ground. There was something they all needed to do, and soon. She would have done it sooner, but she had been left exhausted from the whole possessed-by-a-demon thing and had spent most of the last twenty-four hours sleeping it off. She still felt weak, but she could do this. She focused on Zach's question. Was it so obvious to him that she had fallen for his brother?

She took a deep breath. "I have feelings for him. Strong feelings. Can't deny that."

He shrugged. "Doesn't bother me. All I want is for my brother to be happy. If that means you need to stay in Charleston, I'll deal with it. I want you to be happy too. I mean that."

"I know, but…" She shook her head. "This city drains me. There's too much history here. Too many dead people. For my own sake, I'd rather not make it my home."

If she stayed, it would be a constant battle against her inherent need to help every ghost she met and the sickness that often followed when she did. Connor had performed a ritual that had weakened the anomaly, but it was still there. He hoped it could be eliminated in time, but he didn't know.

Zach frowned. "Atlanta's an old city, too."

"It is, but it's really not as bad as this one. Trust me." She'd have to explain it all to him sometime.

Speaking of Connor and the Bellator…

"Zach, are you interested in hiring other psychics for the agency?"

He sighed. "We've picked up a lot of business from it. I might. Someday. Why?"

She was still considering the offer to join the Bellator. Connor had even suggested following her to Atlanta to work with her on learning more about the organization.

"I met someone who might be interested. He could probably use the work."

"What about Dylan?"

She'd opened her mouth to respond when another voice asked, "What *about* Dylan?"

Speak of the devil.

"Sorry I'm late. Got snagged by a reporter on my way out the door." Leaning over, he gently kissed Alexandra on the lips. His arm slid around her back, pulling her into his side. "How do you feel?"

She forced a smile. "Like I got knocked on my ass by a demon. But tons better than I did."

He reached his other hand out to Zach as he greeted his brother. "How's it going?"

"Can't complain." Zach arched a brow as he looked at her. "We were just discussing when Alexandra was coming back to work."

"Really?" Dylan glanced down at her. "And?"

She slid her hand into his back pocket and squeezed. "I thought I'd stay in Charleston a few more days, give myself time to recover."

"Good." His smile reflected boyish glee. Pervert. She knew exactly how he wanted to spend the next few days. Disappointment threatened to sour her mood. She'd hoped he would show more regret that she was leaving. Make an offer to leave with her. Try to talk her into staying. That he'd show some emotion—any emotion besides lust—toward her.

Zach fake cleared his throat. "Should we get on with this? I've got a plane to catch tonight."

Alexandra bit her lip, not happy with that news. She'd hoped he'd stay a few days and get to know Dylan again.

He reached and pulled a small jeweler's box out of his coat pocket. "I got this for Hannah this morning. After everything I saw yesterday, I decided life's too short to keep putting off the big decisions. I'm kind of eager to get home." He opened the box and showed them a modest but gorgeous diamond ring she knew Hannah would flip over. "What do you think?"

Alexandra smiled. "I think I'd better be a bridesmaid or I'm kicking both your asses for all you've put me through."

Zach smiled before shifting his attention to Dylan. "She, uh, hasn't said yes yet, but if she does, I could use a best man. You interested?"

Alexandra held her breath, waiting for the answer. This was a big gesture on Zach's part. Risky. She'd slap the crap out of Dylan if he didn't accept.

Holding his hand out again, he grinned as Zach's hand clasped his. "Why not? Congratulations, Zach. I'm happy for you."

Emotion glazed Zach's eyes, and she looked away, feeling

intrusive. "Thanks, Dylan. She hasn't said yes yet."

"She will." Dylan nodded. "Call it a hunch."

Alexandra smiled up at him. She really, really wanted to kiss him right now. She knew the brothers still needed work—she could tell by the physical distance Dylan kept putting between himself and Zach—but at least it was a start.

"So…?" Zach murmured. "We gonna do this or what?"

Right. Alexandra blinked and focused on the task at hand. She gestured to their left. "There's a nice spot over there."

She sat in the middle of the park bench and motioned for the men to join her on each side. She sucked in a deep breath and closed her eyes, silently dropping the mental wall she'd put in place to keep spirits away. After her ordeal with the demon, she'd been wary of letting it down, even if it had meant blocking out George and Rebecca for the past twenty-four hours.

Okay, Rebecca. You're welcome to communicate with me now. Where are you, lady?

She opened her eyes, and Rebecca stood directly in front of them.

A sigh of relief escaped her lips. "She's here." Alexandra reached out her left hand to grasp Dylan's. She held her right hand out for Zach. He hesitated only for a few seconds before sliding his fingers into hers. They were all connected now, not because they needed to be to communicate with Rebecca, but because Alexandra sensed it would please their mother.

"Thank you." Rebecca clasped her hands together beneath her breasts. A tear fell from her right eye. "Oh, my boys. My beautiful boys, together again."

Alexandra swallowed. "She's happy you're together."

Rebecca covered her mouth. She sniffled before speaking again. "Tell them I want them to work on their relationship. I want Dylan to forgive Zach, and I want Zach to insist on being a part of his

253

life, even if Dylan tries to push him away. Tell them that. Go on."

Alexandra did, repeating the wish carefully and clearly, trying to keep emotion from clouding her tone.

Rebecca reached a hand forward and cupped Zach's cheek. He flinched, as if he felt the gesture. "What was that?" he asked, glancing around.

"She touched your face."

He swallowed hard but said nothing.

Rebecca reached out and did the same to Dylan, cupping his face with both hands. "Oh, my sweet baby."

"Is she touching me now?" Dylan asked softly.

"Yes."

He nodded. "I think I can feel it." His eyes gleamed with unshed tears. "She's really here."

"I told you she was." Alexandra pushed back the lump that was swelling in her throat. She leaned forward. "Rebecca, your sons are together again. They're safe." She swallowed hard, finding it hard to say the next words. "Do you want to move on? I can help you cross over if you're ready."

"I don't know if I can go." The older woman sucked in a deep breath. "What if they need me? What if they start fighting again?"

Alexandra shook her head. "You have to think of yourself." She'd explained to both Rebecca and George that the longer they remained, the greater the risk of becoming demons. Both had expressed disbelief before horror and acceptance.

"What's she saying?" Zach demanded.

"She doesn't want to leave either of you. She thinks you might need her to stay."

"You're our mother," Zach whispered. "We'll always need you, but—" He shook his head. "We want you to be at peace. I *need* you to be at peace."

Dylan's fingers tightened their hold on Alexandra's hand. "We've got each other now. We can take care of each other, me and Zach. He's right, Mom. You should go. This chance might not come again, and we don't want you stuck here."

Rebecca nodded. "I suppose they're right. I don't want to become like that thing. I don't ever want to be controlled by one again either." Nodding, she looked at Zach. "I'm so proud of the man you've become. I approve of your young woman. She's good for you. She loves you, and no one deserves to be loved more."

Alexandra struggled to repeat the words without getting emotional. A tear escaped Zach's control, and he wiped it away. "Thanks, Mom."

"And you," Rebecca said, focusing on Dylan. "You're the best thing I ever accomplished. You're so honorable and courageous. I'm so proud of both of you." She looked at Alexandra. "I'm so happy to know that you love my son, and that he loves you. I never had a daughter...until I met you, Alexandra. Take care of him. Promise me."

She thinks he loves you.

Alexandra nodded and shifted uncomfortably. She wasn't so sure. She repeated the words to Dylan, leaving off that last bit. The last thing the poor man needed was to hear a declaration of love right now, or to feel pressured into one of his own. It would probably send him running for the water.

Rebecca shook her head knowingly at her when she remained tight-lipped about it. "You're not ready yet, but you will be. I have faith in the two of you. Please have faith in it, too."

Alexandra nodded.

"What's she saying now?" Dylan asked.

Rebecca knelt in front of them and placed her hands on Alexandra's knees. "When Dylan was four, he got out of the house without me knowing and climbed up a neighbor's tree. He fell and broke his arm. Zach heard him screaming and found him. He was only eight, but he carried his little brother three blocks and rode with him in the back seat to the hospital, cuddling Dylan and reassuring him everything would be okay. Dylan took strength in his big brother that day. Remind them both of that. Tell them never to forget that bond they used to share. It never goes away, no matter what else happens. They're family."

Alexandra repeated the story. Dylan chuckled. "It's one of my first memories. I was so scared and then you came and picked me up. I knew everything would be okay."

"You screamed like you were being murdered." Zach snorted at the memory. "I was so scared you were really hurt."

Rebecca laughed with them and stood. "I think I'm ready now." She leaned down to Dylan, kissed his cheek, and whispered something in his ear. His face paled as he seemed to stop breathing for a few seconds. She repeated the action with Zach before straightening. "What do I do, Alexandra?"

"You cross over by going into the circle. We have to ask for it to appear. If you're ready, it will."

With a nod, Rebecca closed her eyes.

"Here we go," Alexandra whispered, exchanging glances with both Dylan and Zach before closing her eyes and praying for Rebecca to find peace. She opened her eyes as a whitened hole seemed to swallow the scenery in front of them. Rebecca turned and gasped, "Oh, it's so beautiful. So peaceful. Do you feel it?"

She stepped forward until the light engulfed her.

Then she was gone.

Alexandra blinked rapidly as the scenery returned to normal.

"She's gone. She's crossed over." She looked between Zach and Dylan. "Your mother is finally at peace."

Both men remained quiet. Neither attempted to remove their hands from hers, which spoke volumes. This was a familiar scene, one she'd performed before with other people helping loved ones cross over. But it had never felt this personal for Alexandra.

Goodbye, my friend. I'll miss you.

Zach was the first to stand. "Thank you, Alexandra."

She rose too and was surprised when he pulled her into an awkward hug. "You're welcome, boss."

Pulling back, he smiled wryly at that. He looked past her shoulder, growing more serious. "I know you're my brother and all, but she's practically my family, too. You hurt her and I'll kick your ass."

"I'd like to see you try." But the comment was good-natured.

They spent the rest of the afternoon in that tone, and Alexandra was relieved to see that the two brothers were getting along— finally. She and Dylan accompanied Zach to the airport, wished him luck with his proposal, and then watched as his plane left the ground.

Dylan was quiet on the drive back to his place. She'd already agreed to stay with him for the remainder of her time here. She had no idea what the future held for them, or if he even wanted a future with her, but she planned to make the best of the next few days with him.

When they got out of the car, he slid his hand in hers and tugged her along after him. "I remember someone telling me she wanted to take a carriage ride before she left."

"Yeah, but *now*?"

"It'll give us a chance to talk. I don't trust myself to do that if we're not in public." He leaned down and whispered, "I want to take you to bed so bad."

"Why don't you?"

"We need to talk."

"Talking is overrated."

He chuckled and led her to a nearby carriage stop. He forked over a wad of cash and then gestured for her to climb into the carriage. He settled next to her, tucking her into the curve of his arm.

This city really was quite beautiful at night. Very romantic.

"I was wondering what your plans are when you leave." Alexandra's ear was pressed to his chest, and Dylan's heartbeat seemed to gallop into overdrive when he spoke the words. She lifted her head to look at him.

"My life is in Atlanta now. I have a job that I actually love, and friends." She took a leap of faith. "But I'm not opposed to visiting Charleston every now and then."

He seemed pleased by that. "Good, cause I understand why you wouldn't want to live here. Quite frankly, I don't blame you." He glanced around. "Not sure I'll ever look at the place the same."

"It's still a beautiful city, Dylan."

"Yes, it is." He smirked down at her. "But I have a feeling it's about to lose a lot of its appeal for me."

"What do you mean?"

He shrugged and pointed out a large water fountain lit and framed against the ocean. The moon, so large and half full, cast a dreamy glow on the water. They rounded a corner and the Southend Brewery came into view. A familiar face was leaning against the side of the building, a mug of beer in one hand. Smiling, George tipped his hat to her and held his mug up in salute.

She smiled and waved back at him. Dylan leaned forward and followed her gaze. "Let me guess. Our dear friend, George."

"Yep."

"Are you going to help him cross over before you leave?"

She'd given the idea a lot of thought. "Yes, but only when he's ready. He's happy here. He doesn't want to cross over, so he shouldn't be forced to." Besides, she planned to have a discussion with the friendly ghost before she left. She was going to invite him to attach to her, which meant he could accompany her to Atlanta if he wanted. She suspected he would choose to stay here, but the line of communication would always be open between them. She'd check in every now and then, and if she ever saw any signs he was unstable or transforming, she'd force the issue.

"I put in for a transfer this morning." Dylan's words startled her.

"You did what?"

He nodded and grinned, looking somewhat nervous at the same time. "Figured my brother's in Atlanta. My girl's in Atlanta. Why not?"

His...girl?

She leaned back and stared at him. "You would move to Atlanta to be near Zach?"

"If it were only Zach, probably not. I think I mentioned my girl was there, too." He rubbed at his chin. "She is, isn't she?"

She bit her bottom lip, delighted beyond belief. "Does this *girl* have a name? Do I know her or—" She squealed when he jerked her back down to him.

"Are you my girl or not?"

She laughed. "That's such a high school term."

He mock growled and kissed her. "You know what I'm asking."

She cleared her throat and tried to look seriously offended. "I'm *not* your girl." His eyes widened and deepened with disappointment, so she was quick to add, "I'm your *woman*."

His features relaxed. "Whew. I was starting to think my mother was yanking my chain earlier."

"Huh?"

"Maybe I was hearing things, but—" He shrugged one shoulder. "I heard someone who sounded like her whisper something pretty interesting in my ear."

She grabbed hold of his shirt. "What'd she say?"

"Only that we would make beautiful children together and I'd better make an honest woman out of you since you are so crazy

259

about me." He grinned.

Alexandra gasped. "She didn't!" She narrowed her eyes on him. Zach might have heard Rebecca talking, but no way Dylan could have. She settled back against him, dumbfounded by his words. She whistled. "Your mom approves of me. That puts a lot of pressure on you, doesn't it? I mean, I admittedly give new definition to the term psycho girlfriend being that I was recently possessed by a demon and all. I suppose some would say I'm quite the handful."

His voice was laced with amusement. "I think I can handle it." He pressed her close to his side. "Look. I know we barely know each other, but this thing between us is pretty damn exciting. I'm not ready to give it up."

She held her breath, waiting for him to elaborate. It took all of her willpower not to fling herself at him and murmur words of undying love. That was so…out of character for her. She'd never been this out of her head gaga over a man before. It was both exciting and terrifying.

But before she made a complete fool of herself, she needed to know he felt the same.

He took a deep breath. "You have to know I'm crazy about you."

It wasn't *I love you*, but it was close enough. The poor man had been through a lot today. It probably wasn't a good idea to encourage him to overdo it.

His eyes simmered with the same mixture of hope and anxiety she'd been experiencing. She lifted a hand and caressed his face. "I'm glad the feeling is mutual." She pressed a kiss to his mouth, then cuddled close to him. "You're actually moving to Atlanta?"

"Takes a while for transfers to go through. I've also got to sell my house. Should make a good buck off it." He kissed the top of her head. "I'd like to meet my future sister-in-law and there's this crazy girl who calls herself Spider I need to take out for coffee. Thought I'd visit you and my brother in Atlanta, and you can come down every now and then. I figure we can handle a five-hour drive between us for a while."

"It's a five-hour drive?"

"I looked up directions."

He had it all figured out. Her chest swelled. "Hmm." Perhaps she should point out he was about to have a very wealthy sister-in-law who would probably pitch in for airline fees if it meant he spent time with his brother.

Dylan tilted her chin up. "I'm not rushing you, am I?"

Hardly. She pressed a kiss to his cheek. "I admit it. I was wrong."

"'Bout what?"

"Talking." She kissed his puckered chin. "Don't get used to it though. I'm usually right."

His hearty laughter carried through the night. He lifted her face to capture her mouth in a not-so-gentle kiss.

Alexandra couldn't see what the future held, but his kiss felt like more than just a promise.

BONUS MATERIAL

And here's an exclusive sneak peek of book three...

Chapter One

Oh yeah. She was sooo gonna kill that mutt when she got her hands on him. And the cat too, just because.

Emma "Spider" Fisher rattled the locked doorknob one more time and glared at the animals watching her from the other side of the front window. Costello, the dog, panted happily as his stubby legs grasped the windowsill, which barely lifted his head over the ledge, to give her a tongue-lolling, open-mouthed grin. Abbott, the cat, stood in the bay window beside him, watching her with disinterested, narrowed eyes as if she were the stupidest human he'd ever met.

Which was a distinct possibility.

"Ugh!" She rattled the front doorknob again and slapped the doorframe. Yeah, as if that would make it open.

It was the morning after her first night of house-sitting for Zach and Hannah, and she'd already locked herself out. Correction. One of the dogs had escaped the fence, she'd given chase in her PJs, and when she'd ran back to call for help after not being able to catch Charlie, Costello had bumped and shut the door she'd left cracked open.

Locking her out. Without a key. Without a phone.

Without a hope of not being killed by her boss when he returned from his honeymoon.

His beloved blind dog had disappeared after she'd chased him into some trees on the other side of the street. No telling where Charlie was now. God forbid, he could be lying dead on the highway. Might have fallen down a well somewhere. Joined a gang. Who knew?

In fact, who knew a blind dog could run so darn fast to begin with? She'd bet that dog had some Cheetah in his genes.

Heaving a half laugh, half sob, she turned and slid down the door until her bottom met the cold concrete of the front doorstep. A quick scan of the other houses and manicured lawns lining the quiet subdivision was no comfort. Well, maybe it was. No one seemed to peek out of curtains or be aware of her humiliating predicament, although she would have to start pounding on doors soon to see if someone would let her use his or her phone.

Who would she call? One of the so-hot-they-could-melt-the-panties-off-her guys she worked with? She groaned.

This could *not* be happening to her.

A flash of brown movement to her left caught Spider's attention and sent her heart thumping wildly against her ribcage again.

Charlie was sniffing the grass and following an invisible trail beside the sidewalk in front of the house. *Near the freaking road!* Uttering a squeak, Spider sprang to her bare feet and hurried down the driveway, muttering "owww" and "ouch" every time she stepped on a rock or something sharp in the grass.

She had a hard and fast policy against swearing, but she was seriously reconsidering that rule this morning.

"Charlie!" Her voice carried down the street. She clicked her tongue. "Com'ere boy!"

The dog lifted his head but kept prancing forward as a car came around the curve toward him. Panic seized her chest, releasing its grip only when the vehicle slowed and turned down a side street. The too-smart-for-his-own-good canine perked his ears up and looked in that direction. *Ohmygosh, he's blind and following sounds.* She had to catch him. She *had* to. If he got out of the subdivision and found a main road—

She whistled and jumped up and down, hoping her feet would smack the pavement and divert his attention. "Charlie!" He turned and took three slow steps toward her.

Good boy! She whistled again and patted the front of her thighs. The long-legged retriever mix lowered his head, wiggled his raised butt, barked, and darted in the opposite direction.

"No, no, no!" Spider immediately gave chase, hollering his name as often as her winded lungs could manage.

He thought they were playing a game. Oh, for the love of—!

At least the dog was running in circles, not straying outside the neighborhood. She had no idea how long they ran up and down the suburban street lined with a mixture of classic Georgian, English cottage and modern-styled houses. It was mid-morning, and no one had come outside to see what she was blabbering on about. Geez. She didn't know if that was a good thing or a bad thing. What kind of neighbors were these?

Honestly, she would have been thrilled if someone had called the cops on her. Maybe then she could at least get help.

"Char...Char...Charlie!" Winded, she had to slow down until she was barely moving at all. Hands on her thighs, leaning over, she watched helpless as Charlie plowed headfirst into a neighbor's bushes. Startled, he hunched low and took slow, careful steps around the hedge. His tongue dangled out of his mouth, but otherwise, he looked ready to resume his marathon sprint. What the heck did Hannah feed that dog? Crack cocaine?

One step. Two steps. Spider inched closer. Charlie turned, and she used all of her reserves to leap toward him.

Yes! Their bodies collided, and she rolled with him onto the grass, the forty-pound dog using her as his personal cushion, not that she cared. Not as long as she had a tight grip on him.

She laughed in triumph and then groaned when a wet tongue found her mouth. Ewww. Disgusting. Doggy slobber. So gross.

It took a few more minutes of her wrangling him on the neighbor's lawn to get into a position where she actually could pick him up. New rule. The dogs were going to wear their leashes twenty-four seven while they were under her watch.

She'd once thought she might like to have a dog, but uh uh. Not anymore. Cats were sooo much easier than dogs.

The two of them lumbered back to the house and collapsed together inside the fenced yard. *Oh, thank heaven.* Now she just had to figure out how to get back inside the locked home she was supposed to be protecting.

Chest heaving, she lie sprawled in the grass for a few minutes, thinking about it.

Man, she had to pee.

Pushing herself up on her elbows, she considered each of the windows. She'd already checked most of them except for a few. Her gaze fell on one. The bathroom. Had she locked it back after cracking it open last night when someone whose name rhymed with Costello had pooped mushy stuff in the floor?

Remind her to never give him part of her burrito again. Ever.

Struggling to her feet, she glared at Charlie as she made her way to that side of the house. He was happily prancing about the yard again as if the past hour had never happened. Insane dog.

Spider nearly burst into tears when she saw through the pane that the window wasn't latched. Yes! She pushed it up as far as she could, lifted herself up, and...

Holy blazes!

A pulsating siren startled her so much she squealed and fell backwards, landing flat on her butt in the grass.

"Oh, no, no, no." The house's high-tech smart alarm system

was programmed to automatically arm itself after fifteen minutes if the doors and windows remained inactive. Zach had warned of that at least a dozen times. It was a new system he was testing for clients of his private security firm.

It took Spider a few tries to pull herself up so her waist was aligned with the windowsill. A pair of almond-shaped eyes were there waiting for her when she did. Perched on the sink, Abbott's black and white feline body was drawn back and ready to spring as he stared at the opening in the window.

"No!" Spider yelled at him as she grappled to lift her left leg up. "Don't even think about it, mister."

With a growl, the cat took a leap in the opposite direction and darted through the bathroom doorway as she managed to get her leg over the windowsill. She was half in and half out. Basically. Almost. Her foot was inside the bathroom anyway. That was progress.

"Hello?" a man's deep voice called from not too far away. "Everything okay back there?"

Oh, for the love of Pete.

Straddling the window, Spider wiggled, trying to swing her other leg over and into the bathroom. Much harder to do than she'd expected. Her left side was pressed to the pane of glass on the outside of the house. No matter how hard she pushed, she couldn't get the window to raise high enough to let her maneuver inside.

The house phone began ringing, and seconds later, the alarm stopped. Well, that was something at least.

Furry legs grabbed onto Spider's calf inside the house.

"Hello?" the man called again.

"Uh, yeah! We're okay." Still trying to shove the window up, she glanced down and saw Costello humping away at her leg.

You've got to be kidding me.

She tried to jostle the dog off, which only managed to get her stuck in a more awkward position. Uh. She was wedged in there pretty good now.

The back fence moved inward. Spider reached a hand out and screamed, "Don't let the dog out!"

A man she didn't recognize grabbed Charlie's collar just as the dog ran toward the gate. That dog must have some superpower for detecting openings he couldn't see. She'd swear her life on it. Her body sagged against the window frame on a loud sigh of relief that he hadn't escaped again.

The stranger snapped the gate shut behind him and gave Charlie a generous rub on both ears. Spider snorted when the dog lapped the man's face with his tongue. Some guard dogs these two were.

"Are you sure you don't need help?"

Seriously? He wanted to help her *now*?

The guy lifted his delicious chocolate gaze, which widened when it found her. He swore. "Are you stuck in the window?"

She stifled a groan. He would have to be a total hottie, wouldn't he?

Please, someone shoot me now.

Noah West rubbed the playful dog behind its ears and considered the sight before him.

Young woman, scantily dressed. Half in, half out of the window at a house where he knew she didn't live.

He probably should have called the cops like he'd almost done when he'd looked out the window and seen the unfamiliar redhead chasing the dog up and down the street. He'd been sleeping when he'd heard someone yelling "Chaaarrrlie!" over and over outside his bedroom window. By the time he'd fumbled into his jeans and found a shirt, his neighbor's alarm had been shrieking out the formula for a migraine.

He lifted a hand and scratched at the heavy stubble on his cheek.

He'd had a late night—something that was becoming more and more common lately—or else he wouldn't have been home right now. He *wished* he hadn't been home right now.

For one, his house gave him the creeps, and he wasn't even convinced the sounds he'd been hearing, the objects he'd seen moving, meant he was roommates with Casper the not-so-friendly ghost. There was always a logical explanation for that stuff, but until he figured out what it was, he preferred to avoid the place. For another, he needed to be working right now, not playing hero to a young damsel in distress.

He cleared his throat and approached cautiously. She'd probably locked herself out, but you never knew.

"Name's Noah. I live across the street."

Her body was shaking unnaturally, as if she were having spasms or doing something really, really naughty with that windowsill. He was afraid to ask.

"Spider."

He jerked back. "Where? What kind?"

"No, my name is Spider. I'm a friend of Zach and Hannah's. I'm house-sitting, and I got locked out."

He hurried over and shoved the window further up, giving her some extra space to move. Through the opening, he spotted a furry blond mutt humping her other leg.

A startled bark of laughter escaped his control. The girl—Spider—narrowed her eyes at him before maneuvering the rest of her body through the widened opening. She tumbled onto the floor with a thump and a squeal.

"You okay?"

She lifted a hand and waved back at him dismissively as she found her feet and scurried out of the room. A few seconds later, the ringing telephone stopped. He could hear her talking, but he couldn't make out what she said.

269

The blond mutt's head popped up in front of him before he could lower the window again. Weird-looking dog, but she sure was cute. He reached a hand up to pet her, but the creature growled and showed a long snout full of some serious-looking teeth.

Whoa. The window slid down with a hiss as Noah jerked his hand back and let it fall. The dog's barking grew muffled as the animal disappeared into the house.

The back door ripped open, and the ginger-haired girl poked her head out. "I'm fine. Everything's fine. Thanks for your, um, help."

He nodded and tried not to stare at her shapely legs when she stepped onto the back deck. She was only wearing skimpy shorts and a tank top that left little to the imagination. Perky breasts pressed against the light green shirt that read "Gamers do it all night." He focused on her feet. Blue toenails. That was kinda hot.

"Excuse me, sir," a gruff voice called out. "Do you live here?"

Noah turned and saw a uniformed officer pushing his way through the fence. He reached and constrained the other dog before it had a chance to get out again.

The gray-haired cop's face was set in grim, stern lines as he approached, one hand hovering over the gun holster at his hip.

"Eeek!"

Both men turned toward the woman who'd made the sound.

"Emma?" the officer asked.

She was doing her best to cover her front with one arm while her other hand tugged the hem of her shorts down. "Hi Jack. How's it going?" She fidgeted from one foot to the other.

Emma? He thought she'd said her name was Spider.

The officer returned his confused look to Noah. He unsnapped his holster. "This guy bothering you?"

Noah released the dog and stepped back. Last thing he wanted was to give the officer more cause for concern.

"No!" The girl risked a step forward. "He's a neighbor. He came over to help." She heaved a sigh. "I got myself locked out and the alarm went off when I was crawling through the window and—"

The officer hiked a thumb in Noah's direction. "This his house? Does your daddy know you're here?"

"What?" She shifted a look between the two men. "No. I'm house-sitting for my boss. He just got married and is on his honeymoon." She gestured toward Noah and spoke her words slowly. "This man is their neighbor. He came over to help. I already told you that."

Officer Jack settled both hands on his hips, his lips twitching as his gaze looked her up and down. "Got yourself locked out, huh?"

"*Please* don't tell my dad."

"I gotta call this in, kiddo. You know that."

"Yeah, but do you have to mention my name?"

Noah hooked his thumbs on his belt loops and hung back. If he hadn't thought the situation interesting before, he was fascinated now.

The officer shook his head, but smiled. "All right. Verify the homeowner's information for me, and I'll *try* to keep your name out of it."

She rattled off a few details about Hannah Dawson—now Hannah Collins—while the officer scribbled them down. Wasn't anything Noah didn't already know. Hannah was a pretty nurse who'd lived here for about a year. Her then boyfriend—husband now—had moved in a couple of months ago.

The cop glanced up and returned his attention to Noah. "I'm gonna need to see your identification, son."

Clenching his jaw muscles, Noah pulled out his wallet and handed over his driver's license. He'd had the ID updated a few weeks ago. He matched the dark-haired picture of himself perfectly. While the officer jotted down his information, Noah glanced toward the enticing girl. He tried to guess her age. Late teens, he thought. Cute. Had great legs. Probably jailbait, his luck.

He realized in a fleeting moment of self consciousness that he was behaving like a true male member of the West family, trying to judge how easy it would be to take a woman who'd caught his eye to bed. Well, so what? She had to be at least eighteen if she was staying here alone. This was a woman who stirred his blood, and there was no fighting heredity. Noah intended to find out more about her.

The officer grunted and handed the ID back. "Thanks for coming to help, Mr. West. Why don't I walk you back to your house now?"

Not that he needed the escort. Didn't take a genius to read this situation.

Noah tipped his head toward the young woman anyway. "I live in the two-story stone house if you need anything while you're here. See you around, Spider."

She flashed him an awkward wave. "Seriously. Thanks for your help!"

Officer Jack followed him to the edge of the yard before saying, "You lived around here long, Mr. West?"

Noah sighed and turned to face the man. Last thing he needed was to capture the attention of a snooping cop. "No. I'm renting the house across the street. Moved in a couple of months ago."

The cop squinted against the early afternoon sun. "Tell you what. That young woman in there is special. Make sure you don't get any ideas while she's here. Got that?"

"Sure." He held back the smile that would have betrayed the fact it was too late.

"Good."

The officer started to move away, but Noah couldn't resist asking, "Her dad is a cop, right?" It was the only thing that made sense. It would be a helluva reason to keep his distance, but then

272

again, he loved a good challenge.

Jack nodded, but a smile played at his mouth as he opened his car door and looked back at Noah. "Not just any cop. Chief of police. You have a good day now, you hear?"

Printed by RR Donnelley at Glasgow, UK